ORDER

by

DOMINE T

Published by **CHIMERA**
ISBN 9781780807492

CHAPTER ONE

INTROITUS

Kneeling, naked on her floor, back to the door, Louise glanced around her room. Her toys were laid out neatly on the table, and a look at her clock told her it was five minutes to; time for her to put on the blindfold.

As she knelt there, with nothing to see, her mind drifted off, back to when she first encountered him. She was happy enough in her job, with its good salary and the responsibilities, but she felt there was something missing in her life. Feeling the need for some excitement, something a little different, she began to explore some of the more interesting and unusual online forums, and came across a few of his posts. Intrigued, she contacted him, and so a new adventure in her life began.

They'd chatted at first, and she confided in him about how she found her job was getting more and more mundane; she expressed her deepest, darkest desires, things she dared not tell anyone else, but felt safe enough to confide in him. Then he challenged her. He'd said she should spice up her time at work. He suggested she go into work with a short skirt, and no underwear. She reddened when she read his comment, but after a couple of days she plucked up the courage; mid-afternoon found her in the ladies relieving herself of the excitement that'd built up during the course of the day.

That evening, feeling a little liberated, she'd told him all about the day, and how it had made her feel. So he challenged her to more and more daring things; a flash of flesh in the supermarket, using a concealed vibrator on the tube, and he got her to go into a bar to pick up two guys at the same time. However, his rules dictated that she shouldn't do anything more with them; she should leave the bar alone.

That was challenging for her. She thought back to her student days, and of her friend who was always flirting and playing around; what did she wear to attract attention? Almost anything low cut, but she had the cleavage, whereas Louise did not. She decided upon a short dress and stockings, giving ample opportunity for her hem to ride up, revealing her stocking tops.

In the bar she spotted a couple of guys who were likely candidates. When she was sure they were watching she'd cross or uncross her legs, or more to give them more of a glimpse. Sure enough, they came over and chatted with her. She spent half an hour flirting with the two guys, and got them both raring to go; the bulges in their trousers showed just how interested they were. She was unsure how she would be able to lose them though. She'd slipped off to the ladies to contemplate her escape. Unable to think of anything, she decided just to walk out, and hope they didn't notice. On her way out she glanced over to see the two guys distracted by three women, who were all over them. She felt a little peeved that they had moved on so quickly, but also relieved that there would be no awkward scenes.

They then moved onto webcams, or rather, she did. She neither heard his voice nor saw him on camera, which made it more exciting; some faceless fellow directing her actions, as she played with herself for their mutual pleasure. He bought her clothes to wear and toys to use, which she would pick up at the shops he specified.

Curiosity eventually got the better of her, and she asked if they could meet. But he had rules, which she'd been steadily learning. She would have to earn his presence by following his requests, and if she pleased him things could progress, whatever that meant. So she continued to perform for him, dutifully following his requests, before the day came that he would come to see her.

She'd followed his instructions, and hoped it was enough to please him. She sat, waiting.

She wasn't sure whether fifteen or twenty minutes had passed, but she began to have doubts. What predicament had she put herself in? Here she was, making herself totally vulnerable for a man she'd never met, opening up her home for him, sitting there, naked, an open invitation for all kinds of abuse.

A few moments later she calmed herself. She must have been sat there twenty minutes, and he hadn't turned up. She felt foolish, and relieved. She shifted to get up.

'Keep still!' said an eerie, synthesised voice. Her mind reeled; was he disabled? Is this why she never saw him on camera? A mixture of pity and discomfort came over her, until she heard a quiet footstep and felt his hand gently stroking her back, making its way from the base of her spine, swirling its way up around her erogenous zones, between her shoulder blades, before caressing her neck. She shuddered slightly as a tingle shot up her spine.

She began to speak, only to be interrupted.

'Keep quiet.'

Had he lost his voice?

He ran his fingers slowly through her hair, before the electronic voice spoke again.

'Stand.'

She carefully stood. He gently pulled her up by her hair with one hand, the other holding her arm in support. He stroked her cheeks, before slowly brushing her neck again. She tilted her head towards his hand, only to have both hands gently place her head upright again. She understood what was wanted of her, and stood as still as she could, upright. His hands brushed across her shoulders, down her arms a little way, before crossing to her breasts. Cupping both, he gently squeezed them before moving to pinch her nipples between his fingers. He pulled at them gently, pulling her off balance slightly. She shifted her weight to regain balance, before he let go. She rocked back slightly and waited for his next move.

She tried to listen out for him; his breath, footsteps, something to give her some clue as to where he was, and what he might do next. But she could hear nothing. Had he gone?

After a while she felt hands cupping her buttocks, slowly following their shape, gently squeezing. Then suddenly he slapped her; she kept as still as she could. Her buttocks tingled slightly, warming her. Then the voice spoke again.

'Lean forward.'

She started to bend and felt a hand guiding her, placing her palms on the table and pushing her down. She felt a nudge on her inner thighs and splayed her legs, her thigh muscles pulling taut, bringing her torso level with her outstretched arms, holding the table for support.

He caressed her back, starting at her neck, working his way down her back. She gasped as she felt a tingle rise up her spine again. He continued stroking gently over her buttocks, down her thigh and calf. She felt his breath on her back as he reached around to pinch her nipples again, tweaking them for a few moments.

She could feel them getting larger. He stopped abruptly and moved away; again she tried to listen to what he was doing, but there was nothing. She then felt something being clipped onto her nipples, pulling them down slightly. Weights, perhaps? She began to arch her back before realising she was stuck, held down by the clamps on her nipples.

She heard the sound of latex gloves being stretched and put on. With a mixture of trepidation and anticipation she wondered what might be in store for her next.

It seemed like an age before she felt his breath on her back, giving her goose bumps. She shuddered slightly, her whole body now tingling. She felt his hand on the inside of her thighs, slowly making its way up, stroking gently. When his finger reached her hard clit she quivered, beginning to feel slightly moist. He stroked slowly around it at first. She tried willing him to move in, to stop teasing, but he seemed to resist her will, teasing her until she felt she couldn't take any more. As if he knew he started to rub her clit, and she felt like she'd jumped out of her skin in reaction.

As he continued to caress she felt as though she was flooding juices, and imagined that if her torment continued for much longer, she'd be dribbling down her thighs. Her torment continued for a few more minutes. She gritted her teeth and screwed her eyes, holding her breath.

She felt his finger move tentatively inside, and she gasped, moving slightly, which rewarded her with a slap to her bottom, a reminder to keep still. She resolved to keep steady. His finger resumed its movement inside her, and she resisted the urge to tighten her muscles around him. Its removal came as a shock to her, and then she felt his finger softly pushing at her lips, encouraging her to taste her own juices. She allowed him into her mouth, licking his finger. This wasn't the first time she'd tasted herself, as he'd encouraged her to do this before. But this time the added latex smell and feel made it different, seemingly more exciting; naughtier.

He moved his hand away, and then she heard the familiar sound of her lube bottle being squeezed just before she felt the cool gel landing on her buttocks. He pushed them apart and massaged around her arsehole; it felt good to her. She let out an involuntary groan and expected another smack, which didn't happen. Instead, he started to push into her. She tried to relax her rectal muscles to allow him freer access. His finger massaged inside her gently, a pleasant sensation; and when he removed his finger she let out a small sigh.

She felt his finger back at her lips; conscious of where it had just been she tried to pull away, but she was pulling against the nipple clamps, causing her pain. She relented, and instead of the expected unpleasantness she was instead treated to the taste of sweet cherry. It took her a few moments to work out he'd switched fingers; he'd been testing her obedience.

She heard the sound of latex gloves being removed, and then being put in her bin. She listened out for him, trying to gauge what may happen next. She felt the clamps being unclipped from her nipples; her breasts suddenly free again, throbbed a little.

'You may kneel.'

She carefully got into the kneeling position, just as she'd started off. Again she felt his breath against her skin, and her whole body seemed sensitive.

'Are you feeling frustrated? Do you need to relieve yourself?'

Louise felt as randy as hell, quietly answering, 'Yes,' pausing before finishing with, 'Sir.'

'Then let me see you pleasure yourself.'

Louise's hand slipped down between her thighs, which she opened to allow access, and started to massage her swollen clitoris. Starting off slowly, her hand movements increased in speed until she was frantically rubbing herself. She found herself bucking against her own hand, the intensity of the experience heightened by the thought of her spectator. Her whole body seemed to go into spasm, her breath quickening as she reached her orgasm, where she let out a groan louder than she expected. She fell to the floor gasping from the sudden shock of her explosion.

It took her a while to recover. She heard a mobile bleep. It wasn't a familiar sound, so it must've been his. It bleeped again after a few moments.

'Do you need to get that?' she asked, tentatively.

There was no reply. She waited for a few moments, listening, but heard nothing.

Still tingling, she removed her blindfold and looked around. Her visitor had gone. Had he left his phone by mistake? Perhaps she could find out a little more about the mystery man from it.

The phone bleeped again; it was her phone. She picked it up, and noticed a new application had been installed: 'YMV'. She stared at the screen. Questions filled her mind. Why did he use that voice? Why didn't he let her see him? At what point during her masturbation did he leave?

She looked at the YMV application; she could only receive messages. She wondered if she would get any from him. After three days she got her answer to that question, at least.

Helen had called Louise to say she had some news. They arranged to meet one lunchtime in one of the quieter pubs near to where Louise worked.

Louise walked in and looked around. A group of young guys in suits boasting amongst themselves were around a table at one side, two smartly dressed women at the bar chatting away, and at the other side of the room in a booth sat Helen, two glasses of white wine on the table. Helen waved, and as Louise walked over she turned her hand to show off the rather ostentatious ring on her finger. Louise felt a pang of jealousy.

They'd been roommates at Uni, and went around almost everywhere together. Helen was the one who was very outgoing, very popular, and getting into trouble; Louise was the one that made sure they both got home safely afterwards. But they did have fun together, despite a few close calls. Back then Louise sometimes wondered if she'd wanted a different kind of relationship with her, but was afraid; maybe afraid of rejection, or maybe she was afraid of what others would think.

And now Helen was telling her 'best mate from Uni' about her impending nuptials. Louise didn't have a man in her life, mainly because of her career. But then, there was Him. She didn't know where that was going, and it seemed a little wrong. Maybe that's why she enjoyed it so much, having always done the *right* thing, to be given permission to try something different.

Louise heard the bleep she'd heard at their meeting. She scrabbled in her handbag for her phone, but it wasn't hers. Helen hadn't stopped talking, showing pictures of her and her fiancé, playing with the new ring on her finger; would she ever take a breath?

They finished their drinks, and Helen nipped off to the loo. Louise had just picked up her handbag to leave when the barman placed a small glass of ruby liquid on the table.

'You have an admirer,' he said with a smile, before turning and returning behind the bar.

Louise shrugged and took a sip, and froze. The taste of the sweet cherry liqueur brought back the memory of His visit, and when she heard a phone bleep she knew this time it was hers. She took it out of her bag, and read the message.

Enjoy your drink.

She finished the drink and dashed over to the barman; she could find out who her mystery master was at last!

'Who sent the drink over?'

The barman pointed to the door, just closing after someone had left. She ran out to see which of the suits he was. She got out of the door in time to see the two women getting into a cab. One of them looked at her, smiled, giving a slight wave and a nod, before ducking in and closing the door. The cab drove away as Louise watched, stunned.

Helen came out.

'Is everything all right, pet?'

Louise was a little flustered. 'Yea, yea, I'm OK.'

They arranged to call to arrange the hen night before going their separate ways. Helen walked off, leaving Louise to her thoughts. Her mind was awash with confusion and questions; who was the woman? Why did she send over the drink? Could it be that her mysterious master was a mistress?

Chapter Two

Supplicium

Since installing the YMV app on her phone she'd not had any other communication with her mystery acquaintance. She'd tried the old forums they'd met on, and even the email and messenger accounts they'd used, but she'd had no response. After the incident in the pub she'd emailed, trying to discover if the woman in the taxi was indeed the person pushing her to do these things, but she received no response.

The following afternoon Louise received a new YMV message. She was to be outside the door of an apartment at seven-thirty that evening, prompt. The address was in an expensive area in London. Were they to meet 'officially' at last? Curiously, it asked her to make sure she had her Bluetooth headset with her.

Helen called later, asking to meet up that evening to start planning her hen night. Louise suggested they meet Friday evening instead, so they could make more of a night of it.

The rest of the afternoon was a blur; meetings seemed to merge into one, but little time seemed to have passed before she was outside the address she'd been given. She could hear music, classical music, coming from the apartment. She clipped her earpiece onto her ear and waited, hoping no one would see her and wonder why she was hanging around the corridor. At the appointed time her earpiece crackled into life, with the same voice she'd heard in their previous encounter.

'The door is open. Make sure you put the catch back on once you're inside.'

She pushed gently at the door, and sure enough it swung open. She took the snib off the lock as she quietly closed the door.

'Go into the room on your left.'

She could hear the music coming from in there, opened the door, and saw a naked woman in the room. She had dark hair, put into a ponytail, and wore leather wrist and ankle bands, along with a blindfold. Louise also noticed she had a butt plug inserted into her arse. Louise looked around the room, seeing various pieces of equipment laid out neatly, just as she had laid out her toys for her visit. She also noticed the computer, where the music was coming from, and five web cameras positioned about the room; somebody wanted a good view from every angle.

The earpiece crackled again.

'Quietly walk around her to her front, keeping your distance.'

Louise obeyed, and as she moved around, recognised the woman in the taxi from the previous day. In her ear the voice spoke again.

'Nod if you recognise her.'

Louise nodded.

'Yesterday she broke one of our rules. Today you will see what happens when you break the rules. You may sit.'

Louise saw a chair in the corner and sat, facing the woman. She heard the voice again, this time from the computer.

'You broke the rules. You know this has consequences.'

The woman replied. 'I do, my Master.'

'Are you prepared to accept the consequences of your actions?'

She licked her lips before responding.

'I am, my Master.'

Louise's earpiece sounded. 'Take off your shoes and stand behind her, not too close.'

Louise slipped her shoes off; she had come straight from work, so was still in her business suit and stilettos. When she stood behind the woman the voice came from the computer speaker.

'Put your hands together, in front of you.'

As the woman did so Louise heard in her ear, 'Fasten her wrists.'

Louise noticed the bands on her wrists had clips on them, obviously to facilitate this very thing. She clipped them together.

The computer spoke. 'Anna. Why did you break the rules?'

The woman, Anna, replied. 'She looked sweet.'

Louise wondered who she was talking about, and looked straight into her face.

After a pause the computer spoke again.

'You would like her as a playmate?'

'That could be fun,' she replied.

Again, a pause. 'What would you do if she were here?'

Louise noticed Anna smile, and was a little surprised when Anna turned her head in her direction. Louise held her breath.

'I'd see how she tasted.'

The voice came from Louise's earpiece.

'It seems you have an admirer.'

Louise blushed.

'Do you like her?'

Louise's eyes widened as she felt a little anxious. She'd told him all about her adventures with Helen at Uni In fact she'd found herself telling him all kinds of things; she just seemed to open up to him completely.

That is, of course, assuming he was indeed a 'he'. She'd thought before it could've been this Anna, but now realised it wasn't. For all she knew *he* could be yet another woman.

But what if it was? Louise had felt more satisfied, more alive, in the past few months.

The sound from the computer broke her reverie.

'On your knees.'

Anna paused, before carefully getting down on her hands and knees.

Louise's earpiece gave her the next instruction.

'Pull her head up by her hair, and slap her face on both sides.'

Louise pulled Anna by her ponytail and slapped her left cheek hard, before swapping hands and slapping her right cheek.

'Again.'

Louise did the same again.

'Keep doing it until I tell you to stop.'

Louise slapped Anna's face five more times on each cheek before she was told to stop. Anna's cheeks had reddened.

'Pick up the riding crop from the table.'

She walked to the table and looked over the assortment of dildos, beads and whips. She picked up the crop.

'Give her six of your best.'

Louise paused.

'Across her rump.'

Louise moved to Anna's side, hitting her buttocks with the whip, with some trepidation.

'Harder.'

She tried again, a little harder.

'Harder.'

Louise took a deep breath and swung the crop around, landing it on the top of Anna's thighs with a noticeable crack, causing Anna to wince.

'Three more like that.'

Louise hit Anna three more times on his instruction, leaving Anna with four red lines across her cheeks.

The computer spoke.

'Stand up.'

Anna carefully rose.

'Feet a little further apart.'

Anna smiled, opening her legs.

Louise's next instruction came.

'Pull on her nipples. Both at the same time.'

Holding the crop in her hand she pinched Anna's nipples and pulled. Louise recalled her earlier experience.

'Slap them with the crop.'

Louise released the nipples, before gently hitting each one in turn. She giggled to herself as she then hit one rapidly, repeatedly.

'That's good. Now do the other one.'

As she did she noticed Anna's nipples growing and hardening. Anna lifted her head slightly, her breathing slowing and getting deeper.

'Now a couple of hard whacks across her breasts.'

Louise stepped to one side, hitting Anna's breasts with the crop; her breasts wobbled a little with each strike.

'Now use the crop on her clitoris, just as you did on her nipples.'

Louise moved to face Anna and repeatedly hit her between the legs, and Anna opened her legs slightly further to accommodate, her breathing quickening.

'Keep going.'

Louise continued, hoping she didn't get cramp in her hand before she had to stop. Anna's breathing became irregular, as Louise realised she was enjoying the punishment.

And though uncertain of herself Louise found herself enjoying inflicting pain, and pleasure, on this woman.

As Louise patted Anna's clit, Anna began to groan quietly. Louise wondered what their Master would do. Would he stop and punish Anna, or would he make Louise continue, to see how far she would go?

Anna's groans became louder; she lifted her hands to her breasts, pulling and rubbing them. She rolled her head back, her breathing getting more pronounced. Louise expected him to say something, but he stayed quiet.

Anna began to thrust her pelvis a little and pulled her breasts harder, rolling her head around. Louise seemed to feed off her excitement and made a grab for Anna's breast with her free hand, continuing the tapping with the crop. Anna let out a grunt in response.

Louise began to wonder if the link had gone down; she thought she'd better stop, but also wanted to carry on. Unconsciously, the rate of her repetition slowed slightly.

'Keep up the rate,' she heard in her ear.

He was still watching and listening. Louise tried to pick up the pace again. Anna began bucking a little against the crop, groaning louder still; it was obvious to Louise that Anna was approaching orgasm.

'Stop.'

Louise stopped. Anna screamed and grabbed Louise, pulling her close. Anna passionately kissed her, thrusting her tongue into her mouth. Louise froze, while Anna ground her pelvis against her, desperate to finish. The computer interrupted.

'Stop.'

Louise tried to pull back but Anna held on, moving toward her.

'Stop.'

Anna paused, and then stepped back, shaking a little. Louise was still reeling a little from the shock.

'Get down on the floor.'
Anna curled up before Louise. Louise heard the voice through her earpiece.
'Put on the latex gloves.'
Louise found the gloves on the table, recalling the familiar sound from her first meeting.
'Finish her off.'
Louise stopped for a moment, before bending behind Anna. Resting one hand on the small of Anna's back she reached between her thighs and started to rub, gently at first, increasing speed. Anna started moaning again, gyrating her pelvis, pushing against Louise's fingers.
'Push a finger inside her.'
Louise moved her hand slightly, and carefully pushed a finger inside Anna's pussy; it slid in easily. She massaged Anna slowly, and Anna bore down on her finger in response.
'You should taste her.'
Louise's mouth went dry. She pulled her hand away and licked her finger. Anna tasted sweet, though different to her own taste.
'Push two fingers into her.'
Louise did so, thrusting in and out a little harder. Anna responded by pushing back against her hand again, groaning and twisting.
'Make Anna taste her pussy.'
Louise removed her fingers, pushing them into Anna's mouth. Anna sucked, eagerly licking off her juices.
'Ever wondered what it's like to have another woman lick you?'
In anticipation Louise removed her skirt, and as she began to pull down her knickers her earpiece spoke again.
'I didn't say you should do that.'
Louise paused, a little embarrassed.
'You should remove your knickers.'
Louise took her knickers off. When she dropped them on the floor the computer spoke.
'Anna, stick out your tongue.'
Louise's earpiece took over again.
'Use her ponytail to guide her face to your pussy.'
Louise grabbed Anna's hair, pulling her head up level with her pussy. She was moist already. She gasped as Anna's tongue started to lap against her clitoris.
It was Louise's turn to start bucking, pulling Anna in tighter as she approached her orgasm. She was surprised how quickly it came about. Anna continued to push her tongue between Louise's legs, sometimes thrusting, sometimes lapping, and occasionally humming, which seemed to intensify the feeling. Louise became breathless, her body tingling. As her orgasm subsided Anna slowed her licking, and Louise released Anna's head. Anna giggled to herself as Louise stood, waiting to catch her breath.

After a few moments she was given her next instruction.

'Now remove her butt plug, and push that into her mouth.'

Louise blushed, before moving around behind Anna. She pulled the butt plug slowly out; she felt Anna tighten her anus, resisting the removal. Louise continued to pull it out. Anna sighed. Louise brushed the plug against her lips. Louise was a little surprised when Anna moved forward, sucking it into her mouth. Louise let go.

She watched in amazement as Anna seemed to be rolling it around her tongue, savouring the taste. She couldn't imagine herself doing that; though she felt liberated of late, there were still some taboos she felt uneasy about.

Louise stood back, watching. Music came over the computer speakers again, before the earpiece spoke.

'I think you've done enough for one night. Get dressed and take your leave. I'll be in touch soon.'

Dismissed, Louise put her knickers, skirt and shoes back on, and quietly left. After closing the door she remembered she'd left Anna's wrists tied. She heard the music stop, and considered knocking on the door to make sure everything was OK. When she heard Anna moaning again she realised she was getting close to her own climax, and decided to leave her to it.

When she got home she went to the computer. She started typing a mail to him. After several attempts, where she considered what she should ask, she eventually typed one question: who came around to her apartment?

The reply came rather quickly; it was he who came to her, in person. And in anticipation of her next question, he also added that they would meet again, and she wouldn't be blindfolded next time.

She sent a message back asking when, but there was no reply.

CHAPTER THREE

SALVATA

Friday evening, Louise walked into the pub. Helen was sat at a table, bottle of wine open in front of her, two glasses already poured, and two men stood talking to her. As Helen waved at Louise they looked over at her with a leer Louise didn't particularly like, before moving to the bar. Louise walked over and Helen stood; they kissed each other on the cheeks, and sat. Helen downed the glass quickly. Louise sipped hers; she didn't like the taste, so she left it, and got herself a soft drink from the bar instead.

Helen was bubbling over with excitement of her wedding, and the possibilities for her hen night. But she also wanted a special evening out, just for her and Louise, and she had an idea of what they should do.

Louise listened. Helen had heard about a fetish club, though she didn't know where it met, and who organised it. Louise laughed, and asked how they could get into such a club, not knowing where it was, or anyone who went. Helen had been asking in some 'dubious' forums on the internet. She named a few, and Louise looked away when one particular forum was mentioned - the forum where she'd met him - and spotted a familiar face at the bar.

Anna looked around from her drink and noticing Louise, gave a discreet smile. Louise smiled back, before they both quickly looked away. Helen was too engrossed in her own monologue to notice.

After a couple more drinks Helen seemed to be struggling to stay coherent. Louise suggested they go back to her place, as it was only around the corner. They got up and Helen teetered, so Louise supported her and suggested they go back to her place.

They left the bar, and a little way down the street Louise heard the bar doors open again. She glanced over Helen's shoulder to see the two men leaving. She had a bad feeling, so tried to hurry Helen up a bit. She heard the men following, and hoped her fears were unfounded.

Helen was getting more giggly and heavier, and Louise was getting more nervous. She heard a car racing down the street, and almost screamed when it pulled up beside them. The driver's window opened, revealing Anna.

'Louise! Get in, quick!'

Louise looked back, and seeing the men looking at each other a little bewildered, opened the back door, pushing Helen in, and jumped in after her. She'd only just slammed the door when Anna sped off. She looked out of the back window. The men had started running, but Anna was increasing the distance between them rapidly.

Louise managed to get a floppy Helen upright and belted in, before she strapped herself in.

'I'm not far away from here,' she said.

'It's too close, I wouldn't trust them. I'll take you to my place. You can both stay the night.'

All Louise could say in response was a meek, 'OK.'

Helen was unconscious.

'They drugged your wine,' Anna said.

'I didn't think Helen had drunk that much,' Louise said. Helen was usually used to excessive drinking.

'I'm just glad you didn't drink it.' Louise was a little surprised by Anna's admission. They stayed quiet for the rest of the journey.

Ten minutes later they were pulling into the basement car park of Anna's apartment building. Between them, Anna and Louise got Helen out of the car and up to Anna's apartment. Louise remembered it from a few days earlier, and glanced at the door to *that* room as they entered.

'Let's put her in the other bedroom,' Anna said, as though to reassure her that Helen wouldn't see anything she shouldn't. They got Helen onto the bed, and Anna left to get a drink while Louise undressed her. Helen came round a little.

'Hey, Louie, what're you doing to me?' Helen giggled.

'I'm trying to get you into bed,' Louise answered, concerned.

Helen grinned and put her arms around her. 'Come to bed with me! I've always wanted to!'

Louise's head seemed to ring. Helen had felt the same way she had, unless this was the drink or drug talking.

She stripped Helen down to her bra and knickers and tucked her in. Helen groped her breasts.

'You've got lovely titties. I wish mine were like yours.'

Louise laughed to herself; she'd always been envious of Helen's larger breasts.

Anna came in with a drink.

'Our hero!' Helen proclaimed.

'Drink this,' she said abruptly.

Helen took it and started to drink.

'This is my best friend from Uni She always looks after me.' She leaned in closer to Louise.

'You should be glad she was there for you tonight.'

Helen put the drink down and lifted herself up in the bed. 'I'm sorry, I'm Helen, Louise's friend. Who are you?'

'Anna.'

Helen turned to Louise. 'Where are we?'

'Anna's place. We thought it'd be safer here.'

Helen snuggled into Louise. 'I'm always safe with you around.' She closed her eyes, and was asleep within minutes. Louise gently moved her back under the sheets, before she and Anna left the room, closing the door quietly behind them. They went into the kitchen.

'Will you get into trouble?' Louise asked, and Anna looked quizzically at her. 'Like last time?'

Realisation dawned on Anna's face, and she shook her head. 'No. He knows you're here. He suggested I pick you both up.'

'Was he there? Was he one of those guys?'

Anna smiled. 'No. I let him know you were in trouble and he suggested I make sure you were all right. Coffee?'

Louise nodded, and Anna set about making two cups.

'How long have you known him?'

'A few years.'

'What's he like?'

Anna just looked at Louise, and smiled.

'Have you ever seen him?'

Anna laughed.

'What's with the electronic voice thing?'

'You'll find out soon enough. Now, no more talk of him. Tell me about Helen.'

Anna handed Louise her drink and walked through into her lounge. Louise followed. Anna sat on a leather sofa and patted the seat next to her. Louise sat down, carefully placing her drink on the coffee table in front of them.

'I've known her since Uni'

'Tell me something I don't know. You were with her the other day when I sent the drink over.'

Memories of the cherry drink returned, but Louise didn't mention it.

'Yes. She's getting married and wanted to organise a hen party.' Louise paused, before adding, 'Or two.'

'Two?' Anna laughed.

'She wants one for just her and me. She's heard of some parties she wants to go to. But she doesn't know who runs them, or who goes to them.'

Anna sat back. 'That could be tricky. How did she hear about them?'

Louise shrugged, before sitting back herself. The sofa was very comfortable, and she felt herself relaxing, and yawning. She covered her mouth with her hand and apologised.

'She's been trawling the forums that...' Louise paused before continuing, 'where I met you-know-who.'

Anna snorted. 'I think I can imagine what kind of party she was looking for.' Louise shot Anna a glance, before Anna continued. 'Your friend wants a walk on the wild side before she gets married.'

Louise felt Anna's arm squeeze around her shoulder.

'So...' Anna gazed into her eyes, 'here we are. The two of us. I'm not tied up this time. What should we do?'

Louise's eyes widened and she blushed. Anna laughed at her reaction.

'N-no, I'm sorry,' Louise stammered. Anna started to remove her arm but Louise grabbed it. Anna looked slightly bemused. 'I've never...'

'Not even with Helen?'

Louise shook her head. 'No. I didn't think she would.'

'How did you feel about what she said earlier then?'

Louise took a deep breath. 'Surprised, I suppose.'

Anna gently caressed Louise's cheek, and Louise looked into her eyes.

'So if that *surprised* you,' she said, 'what about this?' She moved closer and kissed Louise softly on the lips. Louise breathed in as the kiss lingered. She closed her eyes, enjoying Anna's scent, taste, and the sensation. She felt lightheaded, a little anxious, but very excited and turned on. She moved her hand to stroke Anna's neck, and felt Anna gently squeezing her thigh. She groaned, moving closer. Anna slipped astride Louise's lap, gently pushing her tongue into her mouth, exploring. Anna's tongue was soft and warm, and Louise's parried with it. Louise moved her hands to Anna's sides, caressing, moving around her back and gently holding her.

Anna pulled away suddenly, grabbing Louise's arms, and pinned her down. She looked into Louise's eyes, before moving in for a more passionate kiss. Louise felt an adrenaline surge, her heart racing; she really did get a kick out of submission, and was more than happy for Anna to take control in this new situation.

As suddenly as Anna had moved in, she pulled away.

'You like to be submissive.' It was a statement, not a question.

'Yes,' she answered quietly.

'Would you like to spend some time in the other room?' Anna looked at her suggestively. 'I could play with you.'

She got up, kicked her shoes off, and held out a hand for Louise. Louise stood too, took her hand, and followed her.

Anna's attitude changed as soon as she walked into the playroom, becoming stern. She closed the door behind them and stood Louise in the middle of the floor. Louise took her cue from Anna, bowing her head slightly, showing her subservience. Anna walked around, looking her up and down, before stopping behind her. She unzipped Louise's dress, and let it fall to the floor. Anna gently stroked Louise's skin; Louise tingled at the contact. Anna unclasped Louise's brassiere, and again allowed it to fall to the floor.

She moved around to the front, admiring, and gently feeling Louise's breasts. Louise could feel herself getting moist in anticipation. Anna's hands stroked down Louise's sides, and she moved down level with them until they met Louise's knickers. She paused, inhaling female scent, before continuing her downward journey, pulling Louise's knickers down.

Anna stood, and again walked behind Louise. There were a few moments before Louise felt fingernails drawing slowly up her thigh, over her buttocks. She drew herself up in reaction. She looked around as she heard Anna walking away from her. Anna smiled as she untied a rope on the wall, and Louise looked up to see a pair of leather manacles being lowered. Tying the rope off Anna fastened Louise's wrists in the cuffs. She then returned to pull the rope, raising Louise's hands a little above her head.

Anna took her time as she sauntered the short distance back, building up Louise's anticipation. She stood behind Louise, reaching round to hold her breasts, squeezing them a little before pinching her nipples. She pulled, gently stretching them. Louise leaned back slightly. With a tug Anna released the nipples and Louise bucked slightly. Anna's hands returned to Louise's breasts, this time massaging around the nipples.

'You have very nice tits,' she whispered.

All Louise could manage in reply was a weak, 'Thank you.'

Anna's hands wandered slowly over Louise's stomach, stroking her skin softly. Louise closed her eyes, enjoying the feeling. The hands moved down to her thighs, gently squeezing and stroking, before returning upwards, caressing her belly, ending up back at her breasts.

'Now I have you I can't decide what to do first.'

Louise lifted a foot, felt around for Anna's leg, stroking it. Anna took a step back and Louise turned to look at her.

'Will I have to restrain your legs as well?' Anna said sternly.

Louise looked down coyly, and shook her head.

Anna lifted Louise's chin, looking her in the eye. She moved in to kiss her. Louise closed her eyes and felt herself melting, her body relaxing, allowing the manacles and rope to take some of her weight. Anna pulled away and gently pushed Louise's chin back up, then put her arms around her and kissed her again. While Anna's tongue began to explore her mouth again Louise lifted her legs, one at a time, and wrapped them around Anna's waist, pulling her yet closer. The kissing became more passionate and animated, Anna's hands moving down to Louise's buttocks, squeezing them and pulling her tight. Breathlessly Anna pulled away again, her hands moving along Louise's thighs, pulling them from behind her. Louise, panting, placed her feet back on the floor. They stared at each other for a few moments. Louise hadn't felt such intensity from a kiss in a long time.

Anna went over to a cupboard.

'I guess I will have to restrain your legs too,' she said, as she pulled out a pole with ankle straps on each end.

She fastened Louise's ankles, spreading her feet about two feet apart. Louise offered no resistance. If anything she was curious as to what might happen next. Anna stroked the insides of Louise's legs, slowly moving up, caressing, admiring the shape of her calves, thighs, and just as Louise anticipated Anna's hands between her legs, Anna moved them outside Louise's thighs, moving upwards over her hips, waist, back to her breasts, massaging around her nipples with her thumbs.

Anna bent down a little, licked around Louise's left nipple, and then blew gently across it. The cooling of the nipple caused it to harden. Louise groaned softly. Anna repeated the same on the other nipple, getting the same reaction before teasing it with her tongue. She looked up at Louise's face, whose eyes were half closed. She bit gently, Louise jerked back. She pulled Louise's nipple out, before giving it a quick slap. Louise just smiled, her eyes half closed.

Anna reached around and grabbed Louise's buttocks in each hand, squeezing hard before slapping one. Louise moved a little towards Anna at the sting. Again Anna grabbed her buttocks and shook them. Louise swayed giddily with the motion. Anna again slapped her, and then started to gently rub her buttocks. Louise's flesh still tingled from the slaps, but she enjoyed the feel of Anna's hands stroking her.

Anna kissed her again, teasing with her tongue again. Louise moaned, enjoying the taste of Anna's tongue. She felt a hand stroking her neck, then fingers moving through her hair. Anna started to move down, planting sensual kisses on Louise's neck, shoulder, and breasts. She lingered around her nipples, flicking them with her tongue, before moving down again, sliding her hands down Louise's sides, poking her tongue into her navel, pausing when she reached silky pubic hair. She breathed in, as though savouring the aroma of a fine wine, then kissed around, leading to her thigh. Her hands moved down to Louise's thighs, stroking slowly up and down.

Louise gazed dreamily down. Artful fingers moved, stroking her inner thigh, moving up to trace around her clit. Anna moved in to give a few licks with her tongue. Suddenly aware she was groaning, Louise tried to restrain herself, very aware that her best friend was sleeping in the room next door.

Anna didn't let up, greedily licking and sucking. Louise felt the intensity build and couldn't help starting to buck her hips, Anna holding her tight, trying to keep her still. Her orgasm seemed to go on and on, and Anna was unrelenting with her oral skills.

When her orgasm eventually subsided Anna's grip lessened, her tongue movements became more languid. Anna stood and forced her tongue into Louise's mouth. Louise could taste her own sweet juices, making her feel more excited still.

She was a little disappointed when Anna walked away; she hoped this wasn't the end of the session, and wasn't disappointed when Anna returned from her cupboard with a collar and lead. She placed it around Louise's neck before unstrapping her ankles and arms from the shackles. She then moved to an easy chair, pulling Louise along behind her, and sat facing Louise. She lifted her skirt and removed her knickers, and began rubbing herself.

'Have you ever been down on a woman?' she asked. Louise shook her head. 'I hope you're a fast learner.'

Anna pulled down on the lead, forcing Louise onto her hands and knees, and opened her legs wide enough to allow Louise access to her. Louise placed her palms on Anna's thighs for support, and leaned closer to Anna's shaven pussy. She started with a thumb, gently massaging Anna's clitoris, before trying a few tentative licks while Anna stroked her head.

Louise pushed Anna's thighs slightly wider apart so she could get better access. She uncovered Anna's clit with her fingers, and went for direct stimulation with her tongue.

'Mmmmm, that's nice,' Anna purred.

Louise continued working on Anna's clit for a while longer, before focussing on her pussy, at first licking around it, then pushing her tongue inside her. Anna gave a short deep giggle, continuing to stroke Louise's head affectionately. As Louise started thrusting her tongue into Anna, harder and deeper, she began to caress Anna's clitoris with her thumb again, circling and teasing. Anna responded with a sigh, pushing Louise a little. Louise knelt back, waiting to see what Anna wanted next.

Keeping hold of the lead, trailing between her legs, Anna turned over and thrust her arse towards Louise, whilst pulling one of her buttocks with her free hand.

'You can lick my arse now,' she said, pulling on the lead. Louise bent down, her nose between Anna's buttocks, and began to lick, her tongue soft and flat riding up Anna's crack, making her nice and wet, and then hardening her tongue to push its way into Anna's arsehole.

'Oh, you are a good girl, aren't you?' Anna murmured. Louise continued, switching between licking and thrusting. Then she felt Anna pull again on the lead, and moved back to lick her pussy and clit. Anna groaned happily, loosening her grip on the lead. Louise carried on regardless, enjoying pleasing her new mistress.

Anna reached out to a drawer, opened it, and withdrew a gag with a dildo attached. She rolled over onto her back and pulled Louise forward. She held Louise's head as she kissed her aggressively, her tongue thrusting into Louise's mouth again, then pulled away suddenly. She pushed Louise back down onto her knees, and then strapped the gag on her. She then took the whole cock into her mouth and Louise heard her slurping, wetting, lubricating it. Anna maintained eye contact with her all the while, making Louise feel warm. After a few slides up and down the shaft she pulled back and pushed Louise's face down to her pussy. She guided the dildo into herself, and Louise started thrusting with her head, slowly at first, gradually building speed. She adjusted her position to make herself more comfortable, and watched Anna rub her own clitoris as Louise fucked her. She could smell Anna's aroma getting stronger as she forced the dildo in and out of her. Anna's hand moved faster as began to moan with pleasure. Louise's neck began to ache a little, but she kept the momentum going, in and out, in and out, pounding Anna's pussy with the plastic prick.

Anna began to shake. Louise put her hands on Anna's thighs to keep them still, allowing her to maintain the momentum. This was payback for Anna's unrelenting torment earlier. Anna's hips were shaking, her hand a blur as Louise focused on her task.

With a squeal Anna's fingers slowed, then stopped. Louise took the cue and slowed to a stop too, the dildo fully inserted, her flushed face tight in Anna's groin. She enjoyed Anna's scent, taking a few deep breaths through her nose.

Anna gently pushed Louise's head back, taking the dildo out of her pussy. She removed the gag and fed the dildo into her mouth, savouring her own juices. Louise felt a little envious, and when Anna pulled it out she licked up the shaft and then pushed her tongue into Anna's mouth, hoping to get some of the taste. Between them they licked and sucked the cock until there was no trace of Anna's juices left on it.

Anna removed the collar from Louise's neck, kissing her softly on the lips.

'If I had a cock I'd love to have those lips around them,' she said.

Louise blushed, not knowing what to say. Seemingly from nowhere a yawn overcame her. Anna laughed.

'I suppose it has been an eventful day. I'll make you up a bed while you have a shower.'

Anna showed her to the bathroom, found her a towel and a robe, and left her to it. When she emerged she found Anna had not only made up the sofa bed, but also made another drink for them both and had changed into black and purple silk pyjamas.

'Those are nice,' she said, feeling the material.

'They were a gift,' Anna replied.

Louise removed the robe and got into the bed in her underwear. Anna handed her the drink, and got in beside her.

'Hope you don't mind us sharing. My other bedroom isn't really for sleeping in.'

Louise laughed. 'No, I suppose it isn't.' She thought for a moment. 'Were the cameras on?'

Anna laughed this time. 'No. I only put them out when required, and tonight they were all packed safely away. No prying eyes.'

Louise smiled. She'd enjoyed her session with Anna, but was wondering if she was expecting some kind of commitment. Anna broke her train of thought.

'I checked in on your friend. She's still out for the count.'

'Thanks.' Louise felt guilty; she hadn't given Helen a thought.

'I hope I haven't overstepped any boundaries.'

Louise looked at Anna. 'No, why?'

'You're a little quiet.'

Not wanting to let Anna know her thoughts, she changed tack. 'What do you suppose he would make of tonight?'

Anna turned serious for a moment. 'He mustn't know.'

Louise looked quizzically at her.

'He's our Master, and we didn't have his consent.'

Louise continued to stare.

'It's all about control. He's got to be in control. And if we disobey, we get punished.'

'Like when you were punished the other day. But wasn't that fun?'

Anna lightened a little and paused, maybe recalling the events. 'It was fun, and I do like to misbehave because I do like the consequences. But this is different. I've encroached on his territory. He is the Master, so this has to stay our secret, OK?'

Louise nodded. 'I hope we can do it again though.'

Anna beamed. 'Good. We will. But not for a little while.'

Louise grinned, and leaned over to Anna. 'How soon?'

Anna laughed and shook her head.

A puzzled Louise asked, 'What's wrong?'

'I just realised, I was about to say something he would say.'

'Which was?'

Anna paused before answering.

'Patience.'

The next morning Louise woke to find Anna already up and dressed. She sat up, and Anna handed her a hot cup of tea.

'Is Helen up yet?' she asked.

'I haven't heard her, but it might be an idea if you go in and check on her.'

Louise got up and headed to the bedroom. Anna passed her a drink for Helen, which Louise took in with her own. She opened the door and saw Helen stirring. She put the drinks on a bedside cabinet.

'How are you feeling?'

Helen groaned. 'How much did we drink last night?' She rubbed her head.

'You had a bottle of wine.'

'That all? It feels much worse! No shots?'

'A couple of guys dropped something into the wine.'

Helen sat bolt upright, getting agitated. 'What?'

'It's OK. Nothing happened. Anna picked us up and brought us to her place.'

Helen stared blankly for a few moments.

'Uh, I can remember bits.' She paused. 'Anna? Dark hair? Driving the car?'

'That's right.'

'Shit!'

Louise handed Helen her drink. 'It's OK. You're fine.'

Helen looked sheepishly at Louise. 'I didn't, er, embarrass myself last night, did I?'

Louise shook her head. 'No. You were drugged. You weren't in control.'

'I didn't say anything... odd?'

Louise twigged what Helen was referring to, and let her off easily.

'Not that I recall.'

Helen looked into her eyes for a moment. Louise shifted her gaze around the room. Anna picked the ideal time to enter.

'Breakfast, ladies?'

Helen looked at her and blushed. 'I'm sorry about last night; thanks for helping us out.'

'That's fine,' she sang. 'Us girls should stick together. Shouldn't we, Lou?' She put her arm around Louise and squeezed.

'Of course,' said Louise.

Anna looked at Helen and spoke seriously. 'After last night you really should have something to eat.'

Helen relented. 'OK. What have you got?'

Anna grinned. 'Nothing. But there's a great place just up the street that does a fantastic Eggs Benedict Royale. My treat.'

Helen and Louise protested, but Anna was adamant.

'I'll leave you to get straight, and then we'll go and eat. There are spare towels in the bathroom.'

Helen watched Anna leave the room, and then turned to Louise. 'Is there anything going on between you two?'

Taken aback, Louise replied, 'What do you mean?'

Helen faltered. 'Well, you haven't had a man in some time, so have you decided to, er...?'

Louise felt herself blush, but interrupted her. 'No, nothing like that at all.'

Was she too emphatic? Helen just looked at her, before getting out of bed, finding her clothes and going into the bathroom. Louise went through to the lounge and retrieved her dress and shoes. Anna looked over and winked; Louise just smiled and shook her head. When Helen emerged freshly showered and looking much better, Louise went and had a wash.

When she returned she was a little unnerved to find Helen and Anna giggling about something. She gave Anna a look, who mouthed, 'It's OK,' out of Helen's sight. They left the apartment together and enjoyed their breakfasts in each other's company.

Later on that day Louise's phone beeped. She read the YMV message.

Are you and your friend OK?

The YMV app had a dialogue field for her to reply.

'Yes, thanks to Anna's intervention.'

She can be relied upon in a crisis.

Louise smiled to herself, and started to write another message. She rewrote it a few times before sending.

'When can I have another session?'

Direct and to the point seemed to be the best way.

There was no immediate answer, so she put the phone away. A few minutes later it buzzed again.

Tuesday evening. 8pm. Web cam.

There was no chance of reply this time, so that was it. She just had to wait until Tuesday. The anticipation began to build straight away.

It was also Tuesday when she got a call whilst at work from Helen. She was excited as her research had paid off; there was a party the following Saturday, and she'd been sent tickets. Louise was busy, so they arranged to meet that evening at her place. It was late afternoon before Louise realised Helen was coming around, and she was due to have the session with her Master. She'd have to wait until she got home before she could mail him, though she also knew she'd be home only just before Helen was due to arrive. She wondered what punishment would be in store for missing a session.

Helen arrived that evening with a bottle of wine just as Louise got home. They entered Louise's apartment and Helen opened the bottle, poured two glasses, and passed one to Louise. Louise's phone buzzed. She looked at the time: it was five to eight.

Feeling tense she excused herself for a moment and checked the message.

Something has cropped up requiring my full attention, so cannot make our appointment. I will reschedule.

Louise felt both relieved and disappointed. She wondered what would keep him away; business perhaps, though she didn't know what he did. Her thoughts returned to Helen in the other room.

When she went through the tickets were on the table. They were matt-black postcard size, with a purple motif and gold lettering and borders.

The members of the Purple Court cordially invite you to our bi-monthly soiree for likeminded adults. Please dress discretely for your arrival.

Overleaf was the address, date and time.

Louise downed her glass, putting it back on the table. 'What are you getting us into?'

Helen smiled. 'We'll find out Saturday.' She sipped her drink nonchalantly.

'Anything could happen.'

'That's part of the excitement. Just like at Uni But as long as we stick together, we'll be fine.'

Louise had reservations. Only the previous Friday they'd had a close call, and Anna had rescued them. She thought about seeing if Anna could come along, to make sure they'd be fine, but there were only two tickets. She also wondered if that would have been breaking the rules.

They finished off the wine, and Helen returned home. Louise had half-expected her to come on to her again after a few drinks; relieved when she hadn't. But she still really wasn't sure about Saturday night.

CHAPTER FOUR

BACCHANALIA

They met in a bar for drinks beforehand, both dressed in the infamous LBDs. Helen's was low cut, showing off her ample cleavage, and that combined with the frequent flash of stocking tops, was getting a lot of glances from the men around. Louise wasn't too happy; she'd had enough of unwanted attention.

They caught a cab outside and gave the cabbie the address. The cabbie shrugged, and started driving.

Fifteen minutes, the cab pulled up in a car park of a warehouse building. It would have looked fairly innocuous had it not been for the CCTV cameras all around, and the collection of expensive cars parked outside.

They paid the fare, and Louise asked the cabbie to wait until they were inside. Helen marched on towards a door, the only apparent entrance. She paused, waiting for Louise to catch up, and then she pulled on the bell rope. A panel opened and a pair of eyes looked out.

'Hi,' Helen said brightly. 'We have invitations.' She flashed the invites.

The eyes looked for a moment before the panel closed. The two of them stood there, waiting for a few minutes. Louise looked back to see the cabbie was still there; she wasn't sure how long he'd wait for, but she hoped they wouldn't get stranded there.

The door opened, and the two of them walked inside. It was dimly lit with a red light, and as the door closed behind them Louise noticed two stocky men wearing suits, top hats with a purple band around them, and masks across the eyes. She was a little reassured when the both tipped their brims to them; they were polite at least. A female voice spoke.

'Would you like to come this way?'

They turned to where the voice had come from. The woman was tall and wore an eye mask, a dark purple choker, a black leather corset with broad purple stitching and lacing, opaque black tights and calf-length lace up boots with two inch heels. Louise was wondering whether, rather than the wild party Helen had envisaged, they'd instead gate-crashed a Victorian themed masque ball. But then she noticed the bullwhip coiled, hanging by her side.

As Louise and Helen turned to follow her she nodded to the two men.

'Ianitoris,' she said.

'Arbitra,' they replied together, each with a Court bow.

They walked down a short corridor and into a room. Around the room were rails of clothes, some racks with regular clothes, others with various costumes.

Arbitra closed the door behind them. 'First timers?'

Louise wasn't sure whether she was asking or telling.

'Yes,' Helen replied.

'OK. You can get changed here. Would you like me to find you something suitable?'

Louise and Helen looked at each other.

'OK,' said Helen.

Arbitra walked to one of the rails and selected two costumes.

'I'm sure these will be to your satisfaction,' she said as she handed a black cat suit, complete with full face mask with whiskers and ears, to Helen. Louise got a pair of black PVC hot pants, bra, eye mask and an Alice band with small mouse ears.

Helen stripped down to her underwear and started to slip into the suit.

'You'd find it better if you take your bra off,' their dresser advised.

Helen paused, looking at her breasts.

'I'm sure you'll have enough support in the suit.'

Helen complied, and was helped to zip up the suit. It was skin-tight and fitted perfectly, even supporting her ample bosom. She played with the tail, making a few whipping motions.

'I see you've discovered what the tail's for,' Arbitra said with a wink. 'You'll make a fine dom for the evening.'

She passed Helen a pair of lace up high-heeled shoes, which Helen put on, then started strutting around in them, mewing and purring.

Louise watched Helen's antics with some amusement. She was certainly getting into character.

'I'm glad you like it.'

'Yes, it's lurrrvely,' Helen purred.

Arbitra laughed. 'Can you keep that up all night?'

'I'll try,' replied Helen.

'Then you just need to put on the mask.'

She helped Helen with it, tying her hair back into a ponytail. The mask seemed to emphasise Helen's full lips.

Meanwhile Louise had disrobed completely and donned her costume, mask and ears.

'We just need one more thing for this particular cat and mouse,' Arbitra said, as she produced a collar and a lead. She fastened the collar around Louise's neck, and passed the lead to Helen.

'Here's your pet mouse, to play with as you please.'

Helen laughed, and started rubbing herself against Louise.

'Did you hear that, mouse?' she purred. Louise felt a little embarrassed.

Arbitra hung up their clothes and walked to a second door in the room. 'I'll give you a quick tour, give you the house rules, and then you can go off and enjoy yourselves.' She opened the door, allowing Helen and Louise to go through before she followed them.

The tour of the place started on some very practical notes; what to do if there's a fire, where to find first aid, and so on. Then there was a run though of etiquette; slaves could only speak when spoken to, doms were responsible for ensuring a slave's boundaries weren't crossed - they even had safe words and safe signs for when someone wasn't comfortable. Helen strutted by the side of Arbitra, her emphatically sexy walk causing her tail to swing from side to side, and Louise followed, at the end of the lead.

There were lots of people milling around; talking, drinking, all in various costumes, a relative few in Victorian attire. There was none of the action Louise or Helen expected. Helen listened attentively to their guide, while Louise looked around.

Arbitra led them into a room where the scene was quite different. There were chains hanging from the ceiling, a table with manacles attached, cabinets with an array of whips, cuffs, medical instruments, and a small sink.

There were also two people in there. Standing was a woman in high heeled thigh length boots, a short PVC skirt, PVC waistcoat and PVC eye mask. Lying on the table was a man in a full head mask. He had even been blindfolded; the only sight of his flesh was his lips, clamped by a gag tied around his head.

The woman nodded at Arbitra as they entered, who nodded in return.

'May I introduce Madam Belle?'

Madame Belle gave a bow to Helen. 'And you are?'

Helen faltered, so Arbitra interjected. 'Mistress Felis.'

Helen paused, then bowed in return. 'Yes, Mistress Felis,' she purred.

'And this must be your subbie, Mus,' Belle said, circling Louise, eyeing her up, making her feel more than a little self-conscious.

'I shall leave our guests in your company, Madame.' Arbitra bowed to Belle and Helen before leaving the room.

'Would you like to assist me to punish my very disobedient slave?' Belle strutted over to the man, and ran a hand up his body from foot to chest.

'What's he done?' purred Helen.

Belle laughed. 'Does it really matter? Let's just say, he's disappointed his Mistress terribly. And that is reason enough.'

Helen stood at the side of the man, looking up and down his body. 'Who's a bad boy?'

Belle looked over at Louise. 'I don't even think he's worthy of being punished by his Mistress. How about getting your mus to do the work for us?'

Helen looked at Louise quizzically. 'Yes, why not?'

The two ladies moved away from the man, and Belle beckoned Louise over. She obeyed, standing by the table.

'I think we'll start with some topiary,' said Belle. 'I do like a nicely turned out bush.' She pulled down his trousers enough to reveal his bushy pubic hair and cock. 'How about a nice heart shape, to show his love for his Mistress?'

Belle passed an electric trimmer to Louise, who started trimming the length of the hair, before shaping it into a heart. Louise felt herself shaking a little, but tried to be as steady as she could. When she had finished with the trimmer Belle put a bowl of hot water on his chest, with a razor soaking in it. She produced a can of shaving foam and sprayed it around his hair. Louise then picked up the razor and tidied up the trimming, making sure he was smooth where the hair had been cut away.

When finished she washed away the last of the foam and dried him. She stepped back to let the two ladies inspect, dropping her head.

Belle ran a hand around the newly shaved area. 'Very good. You have an attentive slave.'

'Thank you,' Helen replied, still in her feline voice.

'It's a shame he wasn't that attentive.' Belle grabbed his face and squeezed his cheeks tightly. 'He does so enjoy pleasing his Mistress...' She paused between each word, slapping his face each time she spoke. 'In... any... and... every... possible... way!'

Belle looked at Helen. 'Would you like him to please you?' she asked. 'He's very good with his mouth.'

Helen shook her head. Belle looked at Louise.

'Or would you like him to play with your mus?'

Louise glared at Helen.

Helen thought on her feet for once, to Louise's relief. 'I don't think I'd want her sullied with a bad boy.'

'Very well,' said Belle. 'But I think he deserves a good caning.'

She walked over to one of the cabinets and withdrew a cane. She handed it to Louise, and then flipped him over, his bare bottom facing upwards. She looked at Louise expectantly.

Louise hit him gently across the backside. Belle snorted.

'My, you are a timid little mouse, aren't you?'

She took the cane back from Louise and beat him hard.

'Would you like to try?' she said to Helen. Helen was a little hesitant.

'He can really take a good thrashing,' Belle encouraged.

Helen took the cane and gave him six of her very best, leaving several red marks across his buttocks.

Belle laughed. 'Excellent! You have a gift, my dear. You've made me wet just watching that. I'm going to have to relieve myself.'

She pulled him off the table, making him lie on the floor. She replaced the gag with a dildo gag. Then she squatted over him. He was unaware, still being blindfolded. Louise went to stand by Helen, who was watching in fascination.

As he lay on his back, dildo pointing straight upwards, she lifted her skirt and slowly lowered herself onto the dildo. She took it slowly all the way in, and then paused. She groaned, and then started to work her way up and down its length. She steadied herself with her hands on his chest as she began to move faster and faster, her breathing getting heavier. Then she stopped. Louise realised she had relieved herself, as liquid dribbled down the shaft and over his face.

Belle shook herself a little, before lifting herself off. She then walked between his legs and separated them with her feet, wide enough for her to stand between.

'That's the only way you're fucking with me,' she spat at him, before she gave him a hard kick in the testicles. He doubled up, hands over his balls, his moans gagged. She dragged him to the side of the room and tied him up.

Louise thought this was a little too realistic for role play, but said nothing, feeling for the guy.

Belle dusted herself off and walked over to Helen and Louise. 'So, how about I show you around some of the other areas?' she asked, as though nothing had happened.

'Sounds delightful,' replied Helen, waving her tail eagerly.

They strolled around the main hall, Belle and Helen together, with Louise led by the lead.

'So, what kind of fetishes do you enjoy? We cater for all kinds of tastes.'

'Such as?' Helen asked curiously.

'As well as the usual bondage and role play, there are those with medical fetishes, water sports, hard sports... as long as it's not illegal and everyone's consenting, it's fine.'

Another lady in a black and purple corset and whip hanging at her side approached them. Belle greeted her with a nod.

'Arbitra.'

Louise and Helen were confused; though dressed similarly, this was not the lady who let them in.

'Madame Belle. Allow me to take your guest's slave for a while, to allow you to show your guest around unhindered.

Belle seemed reluctant, returning this arbitra's gaze with a suspicious look. Helen, however, thought it might be a good idea. Louise gave her a glare, but Helen was too distracted to notice.

Louise was led into a similar room to the one they'd just left. In this one there were three sets of chains hanging from the ceiling, and three boxes. Two were open, but the other was padlocked and Louise thought she saw someone inside peering from behind the grille in the door.

'Let's make you comfortable,' the arbitra said, fastening first her wrists and then her ankles, and then hoisting the chains and lifting Louise's arms above her head. As she gagged Louise she continued. 'And let's not have any distracting noises from you.'

Louise heard a bang come from the closed box. The arbitra ignored it.

'Well aren't you a pretty little thing?' she said, squeezing Louise's cheeks. 'Nice butt, too,' she said as she gave Louise's buttocks a slap. 'But now it's time for payment for infraction of our rules,' she said, taking the whip from her side.

Louise tried to protest. This must be mistaken identity; she'd not broken any rules, none she was aware of, anyway. But the gag muffled her protestations. She struggled, but her feet were fixed to the floor and her arms were held high; she had to endure the woman's punishment.

The first crack hit her across her back, and it stung. There was more banging from the box. Louise tried to look round to see, but she was promptly turned back.

'It's much easier for you if you face that way, otherwise it'll just hurt more,' the woman said with a sneer. 'Poor little mouse.'

Louise braced herself when the second crack was on its way, but it still stung. There was more banging from behind her. The whipping continued a third, fourth, fifth and sixth time.

'Now I'll let you see the consequences of your actions!'

Louise didn't know what she was talking about, and was confused when the woman walked to the box and unfastened its padlock. The door burst open, knocking her back, and out sprang another woman whose mouth and wrists were taped up. Louise watched as the arbitra woman was head-butted on the nose, causing it to bleed.

'You little bitch!' the woman screamed, and the two of them struggled to the floor. As Louise was watching the women fighting she didn't notice the door open and three women, with different versions of the black and purple corsets, came in and separated them.

'Tie the improba up, and I'll teach her a lesson,' screamed the arbitra. Two of the women started to comply, when another female voice called for them to stop. Louise looked around to the door, and saw a man and a woman standing there. She was wearing a PVC corset with purple ribbons; he was dressed in a black suit, purple shirt and tie under a waistcoat, a black cloak with purple lining, a porcelain style mask covering his face, and a broad-brimmed hat with a purple feather.

He walked over to Louise, turned her, and stroked her back gently. Louise winced as he ran a finger over where the whip had caught her. He turned to the other ladies and gave a signal. They released the bound woman and took the arbitra, binding her in the chains next to Louise.

'We agreed the improba had to be punished. This was the best way for her to learn her lesson.' The arbitra's complaints were silenced when he gagged her. He then turned to Louise, who felt nervous, not knowing what to expect. She didn't want any more pain - she didn't even want to be here.

He signalled his assistant, who started to undo her restrains as he removed his cloak. Louise feared the worst, but once free he wrapped his cloak around her. Louise turned around to find the other ladies had removed the tape from the bound woman from the box. It was Anna. She stared at her for a moment, and was about to ask what was going on when she signalled to be quiet.

The man led Louise to Anna, who put a comforting arm around her. He then picked up the whip the arbitra had been using and ran it through his hands, studying the strands. He walked over to her and unlaced her corset, dropping it to the floor. After taking a couple of steps back he faced the arbitra, and whipped her six times. Unlike Louise she seemed to enjoy her treatment, but Louise was horrified to see welts appearing where the whip had hit. She felt around her back, the skin tender and stinging.

After the whipping the woman seemed to be laughing maniacally; she'd loved her punishment. The masked man took out a knife, Louise gasped, and Anna held her a little tighter. He walked to the arbitra and put the knife to her throat, and Louise watched stunned as he cut the purple choker from her and dropped it to the floor. The woman's expression changed and she started to struggle, her protestations muffled by the gag. He walked to Louise and gently picked her up in his arms. She put an arm around his shoulder to brace herself. He nodded to two of his assistants and they opened the door.

As they walked through the hall people turned to look, parting to allow the party through. They walked over to another room, and when two of the ladies entered she heard a stern female voice telling them off for barging in. When he walked into the room the chastisement stopped. Louise looked around. It was an office, with solid oak furniture. Sat on the desk was a woman in a smart business suit, and between her legs was the head of an older man. He looked around and she pushed him away, before straightening her skirt.

'Mr Jenkins, wait outside for a moment,' she said in a strict tone.

'Of course, Miss Jones.'

He stood, wiped his beard, nodded to the man in the mask and left the room, quietly closing the door behind him.

Miss Jones eased off the desk and the masked man laid Louise upon it, opening his cloak. He pushed her onto her front, and she felt fingers gently exploring her back.

Miss Jones spoke in a softer voice. 'I think it'll heal with no scarring.' She looked up at the assistants by the door. 'Could you ask Mr Jenkins to return for a moment?' The masked man looked at Miss Jones. 'He's head of dermatology at my hospital; he'll know what's best.'

Mr Jenkins was led in and walked to the desk. Louise felt his hands on her back.

'There'll be no scarring, but I have a cream that will help with the healing,' he said. 'There's some in my car.'

'Shall I go get it for you, Robert?'

He handed a set of keys to Miss Jones, who left the room. 'What happened?' There was concern in his voice.

One of the assistants responded. 'An arbitra used unsanctioned equipment.' Her voice was distinctly Eastern European.

'Well you'll be right in time for the next Purple Court meeting, my dear.' After seeing the man between a woman's legs, Louise thought it funny how he could sound again like a condescending old consultant.

'She's not in the Order,' the Eastern European said.

Mr Jenkins was aghast. 'Then where's the arbitra responsible?'

'Tied up, and disgraced.'

The door opened and Miss Jones entered. She handed the pot of cream to Mr Jenkins, who passed it to the masked man. He nodded, and gestured for him and Miss Jones to leave.

'Thank you, Dominus,' Miss Jones nodded as they left.

He beckoned Anna over to the desk. He passed her the pot of cream, and Louise felt Anna's hands gently massaging the cool cream into her back. Louise flattened herself on the desk and felt another pair of hands massaging her back - his.

One of his assistants was sent out for a towel, which he and Anna used to wipe their hands. He whispered something to the Eastern European lady, before leaving the room. The lady then spoke.

'Our Master will arrange for a driver to take you and your friend home. Anna, he would like you to look after Louise while he attends to some of his duties.'

Anna replied, 'Thank you, Vox Domino,' bowing her head slightly. Vox Domino left the room.

Louise sat up, drawing the cloak around herself again.

'Are you OK?' Anna asked, her voice filled with concern.

'Yes. My back's a bit tender, but yes. Look, can you tell me what's going on?'

Anna sat on the desk beside her. 'I'm sorry, but it's my fault. I sent the invites to Helen. All invitees are supposed to be vetted. Helen wasn't.'

'So I have been?' Louise asked, puzzled.

'Yes.'

Questions filled her mind. 'Why? When? Who vetted me? You?'

Anna looked into her eyes. 'He arranged it. Our Master.'

Louise shook her head. 'What's he got to do with anything?'

Anna paused before answering. 'This is his party.'

Louise's mouth dropped. 'That was him? The guy in the mask?'

Anna nodded.

Vox Domino returned with Louise's clothes. 'You should put these on. Your friend will be through shortly.'

Vox Domino left the room again and Louise changed into her clothes, with Anna helping to put on her dress, being careful with her back.

There was a knock at the door. One of the Master's assistants entered. 'Your friend is waiting in the entrance hall.'

Anna thanked her, and turned to Louise.

'Why did he have me whipped?'

'He didn't.' Anna sighed. 'I was the one being punished. The arbitra decided that to get to me she should hurt you.'

Anna drew Louise close and hugged her. She whispered in Louise's ear. 'I'll come see you tomorrow. If that's OK.'

Louise nodded and hugged her back.

Helen was waiting outside. A limousine drew up, driven by one of the ianitoris. They got in the back. Helen was excited, and told Louise about some of the sights she saw; the examination room with the stirrups, the roman orgy room, and the room where a girl slave had her mouth held open by a dominatrix while male slaves wanked into it. Then she stopped and looked at Louise.

'Lou, are you all right?'

'Yeah, I'm just tired. Did you have a good night?'

Helen smiled. 'Yes, I think I did. My last wild night before I settle down.'

Louise looked at her. 'Did you do anything?'

Helen shrugged. 'No! I wouldn't. I just watched.'

Louise smiled back weakly. 'OK.'

Louise closed her eyes, tired, and woke when the car pulled up at her apartment block. Helen waved as the car drove off.

Louise got into her apartment, stripped off, and climbed into bed. After tonight she wasn't sure whether she wanted to continue with him. But she didn't have time to dwell on those thoughts, as she was asleep within minutes.

Louise awoke next morning to the sound of her doorbell ringing. She sat up, groggily grabbed a robe and put it on, and shuffled her way to the door. She opened it to find Anna standing there.

'Mind if I come in?' she asked.

'Sure.' They wandered through to the kitchen.

'Drink?' Louise yawned.

Anna steered her to a seat and sat her down. 'I'll make the drinks.'

Louise sat down, half dazed, and watched Anna as she set about making coffees. Anna put them on the table and sat down opposite.

'How are you feeling this morning?'

'Tired.' Louise yawned again.

'How's your back?'

Louise managed to gather her thoughts enough to recall the events of the night before. 'It's OK, I think,' she replied.

'Let me see.'

Louise stood and allowed the robe to drop from her shoulders, although she didn't intend it to fall to the floor.

'Are you trying to tempt me?' Anna said with a smile. Louise blushed.

Anna held her still while she examined her back.

'There's a little marking still, but that'll go soon enough.' She then started to kiss Louise's shoulders. Her lips felt nice and soft against her back, and Louise let out a sigh. Anna stroked Louise's arms as her kisses moved to her neck. Then she stopped.

'Have you had any breakfast?'

Louise, confused, wondering if this was some kind of euphemism, gave Anna a puzzled look.

Anna giggled. 'Food!'

Louise closed her eyes and smiled, a little embarrassed.

Anna picked up the robe and wrapped it around her. 'Go and get dressed, and I'll find something to eat.'

Louise went through to the bathroom, switched on the shower and stepped into the hot stream. She closed her eyes for a few moments, enjoying the warmth of the liquid running down her body. She stretched before reaching for the shower gel, poured some into her hands, and started to rub the soap slowly and sensuously over her shoulders, down her arms, and then her breasts. She rubbed them a little, causing her nipples to harden. Applying more shower gel she circled her nipples; they ached for attention so she started to play with them, while her other hand slid down her belly, between her legs. She put her head back, the water streaming over her face, beginning to feel warmth both outside and inside her body.

'Would you like a hand with that?'

Louise opened her eyes suddenly, and looking through the shower door she could see Anna peeling off her clothes. Anna opened the shower door, letting herself in. She squeezed some gel onto her hands, and then started by gently massaging Louise's shoulders.

'I thought you were making breakfast.'

'I couldn't find anything in the kitchen I fancied. Your bathroom, however, is a different matter,' she added suggestively.

Louise turned and they kissed, the water streaming over them both. The kiss was gentle, soft, warming. Louise closed her eyes and put a hand around Anna's head, running her fingers through her wet hair. She felt Anna's hand stroking her neck, her skin tingling in response to the light touch.

Anna turned Louise around, pushing her forward slightly. Louise put her hands against the wall for stability. Anna slowly and carefully washed Louise's back.

'I'll apply some cream again when we get out.'

She ran her hands around Louise's ribcage to her breasts, pulling Louise back against her.

'Mmm, I find your tits incredibly addictive,' she whispered in Louise's ear, as she squeezed her nipples between fingers and thumbs.

'I always thought they were too small,' Louise replied honestly.

'I think they're perfect,' Anna countered. One of her hands moved down to Louise's hip and pulled her tightly back. 'And your arse feels great too.'

Louise gyrated against Anna playfully. 'You feel good against me too,' she said. Her hand moved up and reached around for Anna's head, as Anna kissed her shoulders and neck.

'You're so delicious, I could eat you up.'

Louise pushed Anna back before turning to face her. 'Go on then,' she challenged with a grin.

Anna got down on her knees. Louise opened her legs, squatting slightly she leaned back in the corner while Anna moved in, holding her thighs, massaging them with her thumbs. Louise breathed deeply as Anna's tongue hit her clit. Fingers moved up her thigh to help expose Louise's clitoris more, giving better access for Anna's tongue. Louise sighed and closed her eyes as Anna's tongue massaged her, teasing with gentle flicks. Louise absent-mindedly started to squeeze her own breasts, pulling at her nipples.

Anna eased her tongue into Louise's pussy, her nose nudging Louise's clit each time she pushed her head forward a little. Anna's hands tightened around Louise's thighs, pulling her in so her tongue could penetrate deeper still. Louise found herself pulling and squeezing her breasts harder as her breathing became quicker. She felt a warmth filling her body and began to tremble. Anna squeezed her thighs tightly as she tried to get deeper still, and Louise's hand moved to Anna's head, pulling her closer, making sure she wasn't going to pull away until the impending orgasm had taken full effect. Anna continued to tongue her pussy, bringing one of her hands to Louise's arse, massaging her anus with her thumb.

Eventually Louise came; Anna gripped her, her tongue pushing in as deep as she could. The orgasm was a massive relief, leaving Louise panting. Anna gently withdrew and moved up to kiss her, licking her lips and allowing Louise to taste her own juices. It was one of the sexiest kisses Louise had ever experienced.

She gazed deeply into Anna's eyes and they stood like that for a little while, until Anna broke the spell.

'I suppose I'd better fix you that breakfast now.'

'I thought that's what we were having.'

Anna gave Louise a peck on the lips. 'You need to eat food.'

'Do I not get to eat you?'

Anna laughed. 'Maybe later,' she said with a wink. She got out of the shower and Louise watched as she dried herself, wrapped a towel around her hair and got dressed. She picked up another towel and holding it up, beckoned to Louise. She wrapped her in the large towel, and started to dry her too.

'I could get used to this,' Louise said. 'Personal service.'

Anna slapped her bum. 'I'm not your slave, you know.'

Once dry she pushed Louise into her bedroom, telling her to get dressed.

'I want to stay like this all day,' Louise said, trying to pull Anna to her.

'No. You need to get dressed. Who knows, you might have a visitor today.'

'Really? Who?'

'Who knows? Now go and get dressed.' Anna gave her a playful smack, and went off to the kitchen.

Louise thought back, and wondered if her Master might be visiting. He had said previously that they'd meet soon... but then again, they'd met the previous night. He probably had more 'duties' to attend to, whatever that meant, so wouldn't bother with her.

She dressed and returned to the kitchen where Anna was poaching some eggs.

'How are you feeling now?' she asked.

Louise moved behind her and wrapped her arms around her. 'Much better, thank you.' She felt Anna tense a little.

'You sit down and I'll serve in a minute,' she said, as she removed Louise's arms from her.

Louise wondered if she'd imagined Anna's rejection. She sat down, and a minute or two later Anna served her with poached egg on toast. Louise cut a piece of toast, dipped it in the yolk and put it in her mouth. She felt some of the yolk dribble from her lips, and Anna's finger wiped it and slipped it into her own mouth, closing her eyes has she sucked seductively.

Louise was a little confused. She heard her phone buzz.

'That'll be him,' said Anna, matter-of-factly.

'How do you know?' Louise asked, just as she remembered the distinctive sound of the YMV app.

'He's just buzzed me, asking if I could visit you.'

Louise looked at Anna.

'I didn't reply. As I was already here I didn't see the point.'

'Won't you get into trouble again?'

Anna laughed. 'Rules are there to be broken, and I enjoy breaking them and taking the consequences. That's my role.'

Louise paused. 'What if I get punished instead?' she asked.

Anna looked her in the eye. 'That should not have happened, and will not happen again. She is no longer an arbitra for the Court. She won't be punishing anybody for Court breaches for a long time. That's if she's allowed to stay in the Court.'

'Tell me about the Court.'

Anna paused.

'Go and see what our Master wants. I'll tell you later.'

Louise waited for a moment before picking up her phone. She read the message.

Are you all right?

Louise answered, *Yes.*

I would have had Anna check on you, but I'm unable to contact her.

She's with me.

Good. Can you meet me some time this week?

Louise reread the message. He had never asked before. He had suggested, or told; never asked.

Anna saw the look on Louise's face. 'What's wrong?' Louise showed her the message.

'I've never known our Master ask for anything.' She paused before adding, 'It must be important.'

Louise replied to the YMV. *When?*

The reply came within seconds. *Tuesday evening.*

OK.

I'll send a car.

The YMV closed, not allowing her to ask anything more. What should she wear? Should she bring any toys? She began to feel excited about the prospect of meeting him again.

Anna's phone buzzed, and Anna checked at it.

'What does yours say?'

'He wants to see me.'

'He's asked you too?'

'No. He's told me.'

Anna laughed at Louise's expression. 'Unlike you, I'm bound to do as I'm told.'

'But you like breaking the rules.'

'There are rules, and there are rules. He is my Master, and this I must do.'

'Why did he ask me then?'

Anna took a breath. 'We're not supposed to talk about Court business outside the Order. But as you've already been exposed to Court business, I can tell you something of it.'

Anna refreshed her drink and sat again.

'Our Master is also the Master of the Purple Court. The Purple Court is just one Court in what's collectively known as the Order, though I can't tell you the real name of the Order. There are different Courts that are run differently, and attract different people with different, er, interests; kinks, fetishes and suchlike.'

'So the Purple Court is the BDSM Court?' asked Louise.

'There are other BDSM Courts, each with a different modus operandi. The Purple Court is more about the control and domination. Other Courts specialise in other things, like bondage, torture, fetish wear. Though our Master does have a thing about steampunk, so there tends to be some Victorian costumes, with some odd mechanical gadgets. There's a Victorian vibrator doing the rounds.'

'What's it like?'

'I don't know. I haven't seen it yet. Clockwork, I would imagine.'

'Did the Victorians have vibrators?'

'They invented them.'

Louise laughed. Anna nodded, affirming the fact.

'So what's your role? To be punished?'

'Improba.'

'That's what that woman called you, isn't it?'

'Yes. It means I'm the naughty one and I take the punishments for the Court's wrongdoings, symbolically. It also means I can be disobedient and get the punishment a naughty girl like me deserves.' Anna smiled a cheeky smile.

'But there are rules you don't break?'

'Standing rules of the Court. There are rules all of the aula - that's what the members of the Court are called collectively - must abide by. Even the Master himself is subject to rules.'

'It sounds very complicated.'

'Not really, not when you get into it. Basically, the whole system of the Order and the Courts were started to protect those of us who enjoy, ah, different pursuits. The structure gives us some protection, and we know we can trust other members of the Court. If anyone breaks the rules of the Court, or the Order, the consequences can be severe. Those rules I would not break. And though I'd disobey our Master, I would not disobey our Master when he's acting as the Dominus Aulae, the Master of our Court.'

'Why all the Latin?'

'It takes it out of the ordinary, makes it a bit special. It also helps to spot other Order members.'

Anna drained her cup and stood up. 'Well I think that's enough of that for now. How about we go out and do something?'

'I thought we could stay in,' Louise replied suggestively.

Anna laughed. 'My, aren't you eager!' She straddled Louise's lap and took her head gently between her hands. 'Let's build up the anticipation, and try a little retail therapy. Maybe we should get some nice lingerie... or some toys.'

Louise took a deep intake of breath, and sighed. 'That sounds... nice.'

They took the tube to the West End and wandered around the shops. Anna led Louise off Oxford Street, into an Agent Provocateur boutique. She tried to talk Louise into buying some bondage style underwear, apparently inspired by the Traitors' Gate, but after looking at some lingerie sets with black lace over red tulle linings, Louise instead chose a purple and black corset. Anna tried to put her off, but Louise persisted, and was surprised when Anna put it on her account, despite her apparent disapproval.

Anna then took her to another more specialised store, and together they perused the various devices, debating the relative merits and pitfalls of each one. Then Anna spotted a forfeit game; they both read the instructions on the back of the box, and decided they would try it out later. Anna also bought a few extra treats to use later, but wouldn't show Louise what they were.

They shared tapas for a late lunch, and after a stroll along Regents Street, made their way back to Louise's place. A guy on the tube tried to strike up a conversation with them about their lingerie purchases, but they just huddled together and giggled. He tried again to intervene, but they didn't take any of it, just laughing it off. He left the train at the next stop, suitably embarrassed.

They arrived back late afternoon, and Louise noticed her phone flashing on the table. She hadn't realised she'd gone out without it, and hurriedly read the message. It was from Helen; she was on her way over, wanting to stay a few nights. Louise rolled her eyes; just when she thought things were going to get interesting with Anna Helen was coming to stay.

CHAPTER FIVE

LUDUNT

Louise told Anna that Helen was on her way, and Anna offered to stay, to 'lend moral support'. Louise wondered what she meant by that. But then again, she had expected Louise to have a visitor; what did she know? Or had she really expected their Master to come?

Louise busied herself preparing her spare room for Helen's arrival, and Anna offered to go out to get some groceries. Anna returned with a case of wine.

'You were short on stock, so I topped you up,' she said. Louise wasn't entirely happy with the mixture of Helen and wine in her apartment; it tended to end in trouble. Or tears. Or both.

Helen arrived about an hour later with her overnight bag and a bottle of wine, looking serious. She greeted Louise with a kiss on the cheek, and then saw Anna.

'Oh, I didn't realise you had company,' she said.

'Don't mind me,' said Anna. 'We've just got back from a shopping spree.'

'Oh.' Helen looked a little uncomfortable.

'Louise, why don't you put Helen's bag in her room, and I'll get her a drink.' Anna bustled Helen into the lounge, leaving Louise wondering what was going on. It seemed she didn't have any control over the situation. Louise put the bag in the spare room, and went into the lounge to find them both with a glass of wine in hand. Anna stood when she came in, and passed Louise another glass of wine.

'I'll just go make some snacks,' she said, before whispering in Louise's ear. 'I think she needs to talk about something.'

Louise watched Anna walk into the kitchen, and then sat down by Helen.

'I thought there was nothing going on between you two,' Helen said.

Louise shuffled. 'There isn't. She's just a friend.'

Helen looked unsure, but before she tried to continue with the conversation Louise asked her what was wrong. Helen sat back, and Louise could see she was almost in tears. 'Wedding's off.'

Louise stared at her. 'What?'

'The bastard's been cheating on me,' she said coldly.

'How do you know?'

Helen looked Louise in the eye. 'He arrived back from his night away early, and told me he had something to show me. He said he'd done something in honour of our wedding. When he dropped his trousers, his pubes were heart-shaped.'

Louise looked at her blankly, until realisation dawned. 'No! Are you sure it wasn't a coincidence?'

'His bum still has the marks from the caning.'

Stunned, Louise stared at Helen open-mouthed. Eventually she regained the power of speech. 'What did you do?'

'Gave him a hard slap across the face, before realising he probably liked that, so I kicked him in the balls. He didn't seem to like that though.'

Louise thought back to the previous night, when Madam Belle had similarly kicked him between the legs. She thought at the time he'd been hurt, but was that part of his normal treatment? 'I'll just check on Anna,' she said, leaving Helen pouring drinks for them both.

'What do you know about Madame Belle's slave?' she asked Anna, who was baking some finger foods.

'Which one? The one she gave marching orders to last night? She found out he was about to get married. He hadn't told her, and there has to be trust between a dom and a sub. She was less than pleased when she found out his fiancée didn't know about his little hobby. So she's told him to piss off, and had him barred from the Order.'

'What Order is this?' Helen asked, standing in the doorway.

Louise and Anna paused. How much had she heard?

'Helen...' Louise started, before Helen cut her off.

'You knew he'd be there, didn't you!' she said angrily. 'You wanted us to fail, didn't you!'

Helen and wine, thought Louise.

Anna grabbed Helen by the shoulders. 'She knew nothing about the parties until you brought them up. She didn't know anyone who'd be there. You were only there because I sent you the invitations.'

'Anna,' Louise tried to interject, but Anna brushed her aside.

'And I only found out about your fiancée after you'd left last night.'

Helen glared at Anna.

'He was one of Belle's regulars,' said Anna.

'You're a friend of that fucking slut?' Helen spat.

'Belle is very particular, which is why when she found out he was engaged she arranged to punish him before throwing him out.'

'That's why she kicked him in the balls last night?' Louise asked.

Anna looked at her. 'She did that?'

Louise nodded.

'Ouch,' said Anna. 'That's really not her thing.'

'I thought he was enjoying the punishment before then, and the kick took him by surprise.' Both Anna and Helen looked at Louise. 'He even seemed to like her peeing on him.'

'Urgh!' was all Helen could manage. She apparently missed that detail.

Louise spoke before Helen could dwell on that detail much longer. 'So that was staged for Helen's benefit?'

Anna turned to Louise. 'All our party guests are vetted. You'd been vetted, but not Helen, which is why I was in trouble with the Court. When they found out what I'd done they quickly vetted her and discovered who her fiancée was. Madame Belle was contacted to see how she wanted to proceed, and she decided to deal with the matter on the evening. I only found this out from Belle later.'

'What kind of people are you?' Helen glared at Anna, who returned her look.

'The kind of people you wanted to mix with before you committed yourself to a man,' she said frankly.

Louise could see the dilemma in Helen's face; she couldn't protest, as that was true, but she was still quite angry and confused.

'So why was Louise vetted before you sent the invite?' Helen asked.

All eyes were now on Anna. Anna paused, looking at Louise, perhaps for inspiration.

Anna turned back to Helen. 'Because she was going to be invited to join the Purple Court.'

Helen laughed. 'There must be some mistake. Louie's sensible, careful...' Helen struggled to find the right word. 'She's just boring!'

Shocked, Louise glared at her. Anna laughed. 'You don't know your best friend from uni all that well it seems.'

'But I was the one who always went out for a good time, and she was the one saying be careful,' Helen blurted out.

'Sensible is good,' replied Anna. 'But it's not necessarily boring. The whole point of the Courts in the Order is to give us all a safe environment to give vent to our fantasies, and try out new things.'

'I like to try new things,' said Helen, a little defensively.

Anna turned to Louise and winked. She turned back to Helen. 'In that case, I picked up a little something earlier. How would you like to try it out?'

'What is it?' Helen asked. Louise tried to recall all the things Anna had picked up.

'It's a game. All I require from you is your word that you'll continue to participate fully in the game, until it ends.'

'I don't trust you.'

'That's a shame. You wouldn't suffer any harm, and who knows, you might even enjoy it. Louise and I were going to play, before you turned up.'

Helen paused, before emptying her glass of wine. She swallowed, looking at Louise suspiciously.

'OK. I'm in.'

Louise and Helen went back into the lounge, while Anna plated up the snacks she'd made. They opened another bottle of wine and refilled their glasses. Anna came through with a large plate filled with hot delicious looking cakes and pastries, along with some cream, and placed them on the coffee table, before picking up one of her shopping bags and taking out the game.

'I'll just need to prepare things a little first,' she said.

'What are you doing?' asked Helen.

'Writing some forfeits,' Anna replied with a wicked smile.

Louise and Helen looked at each other; Louise smiled, but Helen was still unsure.

'It'll be fine.' Louise tried reassuring Helen.

'Are you sure?'

Louise pushed down the doubt Helen had put in her mind. 'Sure. This is the woman who rescued us from the date rape duo, remember? Now just relax and chill. It'll be fun, I'm sure.'

Anna put a pile of cards face down on the table and set down a small device, with a button on top. 'The game is simple. The box gives a beep at random intervals.' She switched it on to demonstrate; it gave four or five high-pitched beeps before making a low-pitched one.

'As soon as you hear the low beep you have to press the button as quickly as you can. We take it in turns and the slowest loses.'

'And the slowest takes a forfeit card,' said Helen.

'Not quite. The slowest one has a choice to remove an item of clothing, or take a forfeit card.'

'And once you've lost all your clothes, you're out?'

'No. Then you can only take the forfeit.'

'Why can't we decide what the forfeit will be at the time?' said Helen.

'Oh, no. This way none of us has control over what happens during a round, so there's no chance of selecting particular forfeits for particular people. It's all fair.'

'OK then, shall we start?'

'I'll just top up my glass first,' said Anna. 'Help yourself to the food too, though you might want to save the cream for later.'

Helen shot a look at her.

After the first round Louise was the loser.

'So, what are you going to do?' asked Anna.

Louise removed a shoe.

Helen snorted. 'Is that all? Come on!'

'You should remove both shoes,' Anna added.

Louise feigned a huff, and removed her other shoe.

Next round she lost again.

'Something proper this time,' Helen said.

Louise took off her blouse.

Next round she asked if the device was broken, as she removed her skirt.

'Oh, stockings,' Helen said, admiring Louise's legs.

Next to lose was Anna. She was about to take off her shoes when Helen piped up, so she removed her blouse instead. Helen was feeling pleased with herself, but fate changed for her as her blouse came off, followed by her shoes, and then her skirt; she wasn't wearing any hosiery. Then Anna lost her skirt, again no hosiery, but Helen lost the next round. She sat for a moment before taking a drink, standing up, and carefully taking off her bra, supporting her breasts with her arm as she removed them from the cups. She dropped it on the floor before sitting down, still hugging her breasts. Louise and Anna looked at each other, but said nothing.

Then Helen lost again. She rolled back on the sofa and drew off her knickers quickly, sitting back upright again, legs crossed, arm across her chest. 'I suppose that's it then,' she said.

'No,' said Anna. 'Only after the cards are exhausted.'

Helen reached for her drink and downed the wine. Anna topped her glass up.

Anna lost next and kicked off her shoes.

Then Louise, who stood up and slowly peeled off her stockings, bending away from the other girls.

'If I were a man I'd have a hard on,' said Anna dryly.

Louise noticed Helen's breasts heaving, but said nothing, smiling to herself. She topped up her glass and sat back down again, bringing her knees up before her.

Then Helen lost. She took a card and looked at it. She looked between Anna and Louise, before getting up and softly kissing Louise on the lips, taking her by surprise.

'That's the kiss someone on the lips card,' said Anna, hiding a smirk behind her glass.

'What else have you written?' asked Louise.

'Ah, you'll have to wait and see,' she said with a wink.

Helen sat back down, taking another drink.

Anna then lost her bra, revealing her breasts. Then she lost again, but rather than remove her knickers she turned over a card. 'French Kiss.'

Helen looked uncomfortable so she moved over to Louise, and holding the back of her head, pushed her tongue gently into her mouth. Louise happily allowed her in. The kiss was drawn out and Louise almost lost herself in it, until Anna pulled away.

'Let's really go for it,' Anna said to Helen. 'You'll enjoy it more.'

Helen had a strange look on her face; was she jealous?

Louise lost her bra.

'You must be cold,' quipped Anna, looking at her hardened nipples. Louise blushed a little; Anna must've known what she did to her.

She lost again. She was about to take off her knickers when Anna suggested she take a forfeit card instead.

'Cover your breasts in cream; the others lick it off.' Louise laughed, picked up the jug of cream, lay on the floor and poured a little over her breasts, one at a time. With the cold cream dribbling around her nipples she felt them harden a little more. She looked at Anna and Helen expectantly.

Anna stood and grabbed Helen's arm, manoeuvring her to Louise's side. They knelt either side of Louise and leant over her breasts, starting to lick the dribbling cream, working their way to her nipples. Louise tensed as she waited for one of them to reach an erect bud, her anticipation building quickly.

Helen got there first, softly lapping around and over the nipple, while Anna took her time, but once she got there it was worth the wait as her tongue flicked and licked. Louise involuntarily arched her back, taking Helen by surprise, but Anna took advantage of the opening to lick the cream up between Louise's breasts.

As they both knelt upright again Louise noticed the cream on their lips. 'You have cream...' she started, but Anna leant over and pulled Helen in for a hungry kiss, greedily mopping up the cream from her lips. Helen tensed at first, and then Louise saw her body relax.

They parted breathlessly, Helen staring wide-eyed at Anna. Louise's breasts tingled so she rubbed them a little.

'Oh no,' Anna chastised. 'Back to the game.'

Helen returned to it with a new enthusiasm. It seemed that Anna's kisses were something magical, the effect they seemed to have on people.

During the next round Anna purposely lost by not hitting the button. 'What's the forfeit?' she asked as Louise turned over a card.

'For this and the next four turns the loser of each round clips two pegs on themselves, which stay there for a further four rounds.'

Anna reached back for one of her shopping bags, producing a bag of small sprung pegs. She clipped one on each nipple.

Louise lost next so she pegged herself too, her nipples throbbing under the pressure.

Anna lost next, Louise unable to tell whether it was done purposely. Anna spread her legs, took off her knickers and clipped her vagina lips, taking a deep breath as she did so.

Louise lost next, so she clipped the additional clips on her breasts. Then wanting to shock she grabbed more pegs and clipped them in a circle around her nipples.

'Ouch!' said Helen, rubbing her own breasts.

Louise smiled; her tits throbbed, but she found it quite pleasurable. 'I think the cards are stacked,' she said.

Anna feigned indignation, before admitting it. 'Let's just do a couple more rounds and then we can shuffle them,' she said.

Louise lost the next round and her knickers. Now her pussy was exposed she couldn't resist a quick rub, but Anna stopped her.

'There'll be time for that later,' she said.

Anna lost the next round and had to suck someone's nipple.

'Helen's would be easier,' Louise encouraged. Helen looked sheepish, so Anna started by gently fondling her breasts.

'You have lovely boobs,' she purred.

'Er, thank you,' said Helen, not quite sure how to take the compliment.

Louise watched her reaction as Anna started to lick, suck and nibble Helen's breasts, her eyes wide, her mouth open, and she gasped. Louise smiled, and knew she was enjoying the attention when her hand moved to hold Anna's head, as she closed her eyes.

Anna moved away and Helen sobbed a little. 'That's all you're getting for now,' Anna said.

Louise expected her to return to her seat, but instead she pulled gently on Louise's nipple pegs before manoeuvring her tongue between the other pegs to give her nipple a few strong flicks. Louise felt her breasts tingle again.

'See, I could do it even with pegs on.'

Louise sat there, panting a little, and perhaps because she was still reeling from Anna's attention she lost the next round.

'Lick someone's navel.'

Louise got down on all fours and went to Anna. At first she kissed around her tummy button, then licked, before prodding it with her tongue. Anna's toned stomach reacted to the sudden movement.

Louise lost again.

'Lick a pussy.'

'Helen's would be easier,' Anna said, mimicking Louise from earlier.

Louise got back on all fours in front of Anna and pulled her lips apart using the attached pegs, and started gliding her tongue up and down the slit, flicking her clitoris. Anna gasped.

Louise moved to sit back down but Helen interrupted her. 'Feeling a little left out here,' she said, spreading her legs.

Louise exchanged glances with Anna, before slipping between Helen's thighs. She pushed them a little wider apart before pulling her pussy open with her fingers, and then licking up and down a few times. Helen was already moist and Louise could taste her juices. She found Helen's clitoris and teased it with her tongue, gliding around it, flicking it. Helen shuddered, putting a hand on Louise's head, pulling her even closer. Louise eased away, shaking her head and wagging a finger.

Helen lost next. A good spanking was on the cards.

Anna got her onto all fours and she and Louise took turns to smack her arse six times each. Between each slap Helen waggled her buttocks provocatively. She was definitely getting into the spirit of things.

With some relief Anna and Louise unclipped themselves; the throbbing both painful and pleasurable.

Louise sat, poured herself another drink, and popped one of Anna's pastries in her mouth. It was one of the tastiest savouries she'd ever had. 'Are you a chef or something?' she asked. 'These are delicious!'

'Thank you,' Anna replied. 'I'm actually a lawyer.'

'What sort?' asked Helen. 'My...' she tailed off, before adding, 'Oh, fuck him! Let's get back to the game.'

Anna excused herself to go to the bathroom so the girls had a little break from the game, topping up glasses and nipping to the loo. Louise was a little surprised at Helen as she seemed quite comfortable in her nudity; she wasn't covering her breasts with her arm now.

Anna picked up the remainder of the forfeit cards and gave them a shuffle, then lost the next round. 'Insert a butt-plug, only to be removed after not losing three times.' She gleefully went to her bags and produced a vibrating butt-plug with a remote control, and a tube of lube. Helen and Louise watched bemused as she eagerly poured lube on her hand before rubbing it around the head of the plug. Then she knelt up on the floor, reached behind to massage some lube into her anus, and pushed the toy gently in. She manoeuvred herself to be more comfortable, before switching it on. 'Oooh,' she groaned, as she adjusted the control a little.

Louise took the remote from her. 'I think we'll take charge of that,' she said mischievously, briefly turning it up high, giggling at Anna's reaction, and did it a couple more times before deciding it was time to get on with the next round, but when it came to Anna's turn she turned the speed up again, surprising Anna and making sure she lost another round.

'It's going to be like that, is it?' Anna groaned.

'Stop whining and turn over the next card,' Louise giggled.

'Endure a minute of clitoral stimulation from a vibrator,' Anna managed between gasps. Louise looked in the bags and found a large contraption. She turned it on, then off quickly as the thing vibrated excessively.

'I'll do that while you use the remote control,' Helen put in, taking the mammoth toy from her. She parted Anna's legs enough to get the contraption in and switched it on. Anna jumped, her breasts quivering with the vibrations. Helen looked at Louise, who took the cue to turn up the butt-plug, and then alternated it between high and low speeds. Anna started humming.

'I suppose I'd better time this,' said Louise, and just a few seconds later Anna lost control of herself.

'Oh-fuck-oh-fuck-oh-fuck-oh-fuck,' she uttered as she started to buck against the device. Helen took great effort to ensure she was getting the clitoral stimulation, struggling to hold it against her sex. Anna's arms lifted, fingers running through her hair, eyes closed, groaning loudly. Louise noticed Helen seemed to be really enjoying inflicting this intense stimulation to Anna, while she varied the speed of the plug with each movement of Anna's pelvis.

Anna started screaming, thrusting hard against the machine.

'I think that's a minute,' Louise said.

Helen looked at her, holding the vibrator tight against Anna's clit. Louise gave her a look so she released the pressure, only for Anna to grab her hand and push the toy hard against herself. Her body spasmed, shaking rapidly with her moaning. It continued for a few more seconds before she slumped, breathless, releasing her grip on Helen's hand.

'Wow!' Louise whispered.

Anna looked up at her, her hair bedraggled, grinning like a cat that had the cream. When she got her breath back she said, 'I think we'll just have one more round.'

'But there are still a few cards left,' Helen said.

'Let's just have a bigger forfeit,' said Anna. 'Whoever loses gets tied up and used for the pleasure of the other two.'

Helen paused, before agreeing. Louise nodded, not wanting to miss out on more fun.

Anna removed the butt-plug and Helen watched, jaw dropped, as she sucked it into her mouth, licking it greedily. When she put the toy down she murmured to Helen, 'I do like to be really naughty...'

Helen was still open-mouthed.

'Right,' said Anna, standing up. 'Let's play!' She retrieved some more items from her bags, Louise wondering if she'd bought the shop's whole stock. There was a collar similar to the one she'd worn at the party, and two lots of soft rope.

'Can you get your blindfold?' Anna asked her.

Louise went to her room and brought back her blindfold. It didn't occur to her how Anna knew she had one. The items were put on the table. Helen picked up the collar, and looked at Louise.

'Do I get to play with my little mousey again?'

'Or maybe mousey will get her revenge,' Louise replied, with an evil laugh.

Helen lost.

While Anna set about binding kneeling Helen's ankles and wrists with the rope, Louise pushed the furniture to the edge of the room. She heard her phone buzz, and Anna looked over as she viewed her YMV message.

How's your friend?

Louise cheekily typed back. *A bit tied up at the moment.*

The reply came shortly afterwards.

Make sure Anna doesn't take it too far.

Louise couldn't help but laugh. Anna came over and Louise showed her the conversation.

'Cheeky bastard,' she said.

'Who's that?' Helen asked.

Louise was about to respond but Anna got in first. 'Did we say you could speak?' she said sternly.

To Louise's relief Helen smiled and bowed her head, uttering, 'Sorry mistress.'

Anna applied the blindfold to Helen, and then whispered in Louise's ear. 'Put on the corset and your heels.'

They left Helen alone in the lounge while they went into the bedroom to change. Louise put on her corset, and just the feel of it against her skin seemed to heighten her sensitivity. She rolled on the stockings as seductively as she'd removed them, before stepping into her stilettos.

Anna was also putting on a new purchase; several black straps wrapped her body, covering strategic places. She donned a pair of opaque black hold-ups, stepped into her heels and tied her hair back into a ponytail, the overall look severe.

'What shall we do to her?' Louise asked.

'For starters, she can wait,' Anna replied.

They sat on the bed, planning what was in store for their victim. After five minutes they returned to the lounge. Helen was kneeling in the same position, arms behind her back, blindfolded.

'Remind you of anything?' Anna whispered in Louise's ear, who nodded, thinking back to their Master's first visit.

Anna moved to Helen, standing in front of her, legs apart, hands on hips. She looked round to Louise, who made her way to her side, taking up the same posture. Anna pulled the blindfold off and Helen's eyes almost popped out, the two ladies towering over her.

Anna slowly circled her, emphasising each step. 'So, what shall we do for starters?'

'I want to play with those tits,' Louise said lasciviously.

Anna smiled at her, then faced Helen. 'Stand up!' she ordered.

With her arms bound behind her back and her ankles tied together Helen was unable to comply, and began to protest before Anna silenced her with a finger on her lips.

'I didn't say you could speak.'

Helen bowed her head in submission.

'We'll have to punish you for disobedience,' said Louise, and Helen looked up at her pleadingly.

The two grabbed an arm each and hoisted Helen upright, onto her feet. She struggled to balance, so they sat her down on the sofa and sat down either side of her. They fondled her breasts, Louise gently, massaging one, feeling it, whereas Anna was quite rough, squeezing the other, occasionally slapping it, causing Helen to jerk a little with each slap.

Louise pinched a nipple and again Helen jerked. Then she pulled it outward, causing Helen to lean forward slightly, before releasing it suddenly.

'They do feel nice, don't they,' Anna said.

'They do,' Louise agreed. 'And I bet they taste nice too.'

'How about something to go with them?' Anna mused, and wandered into the kitchen, returning with a jar of chocolate spread.

She opened the jar, fishing out a large blob of spread with two fingers, which she rubbed into Helen's breasts. Louise started directing her, telling her she'd missed bits, or more was needed somewhere, until Helen's breasts were caked in chocolate spread.

Anna looked at her fingers. 'Oh dear,' she said, 'I'm going to have to wash my hand.' She grinned at Louise, before turning to Helen with a severe look. 'Lick it clean!' she demanded.

Helen obliged, licking first Anna's palm, and then her fingers and thumb individually, sensually licking up and down each digit before taking it into her mouth, alternating between licking and sucking until Anna's hand was clean.

Louise, a little envious, wiped the chocolate from Helen's mouth with her thumb. 'Her face was dirty, see.' She showed her thumb to Helen.

'And you've dirtied your thumb cleaning her up.' Anna scowled at Helen. 'You'll have to clean her up now.'

Helen leaned forward but Louise moved the thumb back, keeping it just out of her reach until just before she fell off the sofa, when she allowed her to take it into her mouth.

'That's it,' Louise encouraged. 'Lick it clean, you dirty, *dirty* girl.'

Louise moved her hand around, trying not to make it too easy for Helen to continue her work. In the process chocolate spread made its way onto Helen's thighs, where her breasts brushed over them.

'Oh, no!' exclaimed Anna. 'Look at her legs! You really are a dirty girl, aren't you?'

Helen looked at her with a saddened face.

'Aren't you?' repeated Anna, emphatically.

Helen took the cue and replied, 'Yes, Mistress.'

'We'll have to punish her later for her shortcomings, Mistress Improba,' said Louise to Anna.

Anna snorted. 'We certainly will, Mistress Mus. But the first part of our feast awaits.'

They knelt either side of Helen, and holding her arms in place, licked her breasts. Louise started around Helen's side, working her way up and down methodically, whereas Anna started with a lick and a suck of her nipples, then taking random licks, sucks and nibbles around Helen's breast. Louise looked at Anna, her mouth covered in chocolate, and imagined she would be the same.

'Mistress Mus, you have chocolate on your face.'

'As have you, Mistress Improba.'

'Let's clean ourselves then.'

Anna rubbed her face on Helen's belly, leaving chocolate marks across it, and Louise had a wicked idea.

'Stand,' she demanded, and with assistance Helen struggled up. Louise positioned herself behind her and rubbed her face between her buttocks. When she stood back up Anna gave her an approving glance.

'Look, Mistress Mus. It looks like she's soiled herself!'

'Oh, the dirty girl. She really should be punished. Kneel!'

They helped her down again and Louise grabbed her hair, pulling her head back so she was looking up at her. Anna got the jar of chocolate spread and held it out for Louise, who dipped in a couple of fingers and rubbed them between her legs, before pushing them into Helen's mouth for her to lick and suck clean again. She eased her fingers in and out of Helen's mouth, before opening her wider, holding her head still and pushing her hand inside.

'She seems able to take a lot in her mouth,' said Anna, moving to her bags. She produced a strap-on dildo. 'How much do you think she'll manage of this?'

Louise removed her hand and wiped it around Helen's face. 'We'll have to find out. But first I seem to be a little bit mucky down below. I think I need to be cleaned properly.' She stood astride Helen, who started licking up and down her pussy lips, finishing on her clit, which she kissed and sucked. Her tongue moved back to probe inside her a little. Louise breathed deeply, enjoying the sensation of Helen's tongue around her pussy. Anna pushed her head in deeper, and Helen licked more vigorously in response.

Louise felt Anna's hand on her bottom, her chocolate-covered fingers pushing between her buttocks.

'Suck them like you'd suck a big, juicy cock,' Anna coaxed.

Helen's lips slid slowly down Anna's fingers before her head started to bob up and down. Anna removed her fingers a couple of times, inspected them before pushing them back into Helen's mouth. Once she was happy they were clean she looked at Louise.

'Mistress Mus, it seems you have a mucky behind.'

'Have I?' said Louise, looking over her shoulder. 'Then that will need to be cleaned too.'

Again she stood astride Helen, this time facing away from her. With Anna holding Helen's head she lowered her buttocks onto her face and wiggled. She felt Helen's tongue lapping at the chocolate, up and down her crack. She jiggled again and felt Helen's face move, trying to keep in place.

'Let me check,' said Anna.

Louise lifted and felt Anna's hands parting her cheeks.

'It looks like you're clean, but let me just check...'

Louise felt Anna's tongue penetrate her anus, wriggling busily.

'No, she missed some,' she said, thrusting her tongue into Helen's mouth, holding her head in place. She then licked all around Helen's face, spreading chocolate all around. 'Now for the cock,' she said, picking up the dildo. 'It needs some lubricating first,' she said, holding the dildo in front of Helen's mouth, and Helen started to lick the shaft.

'More than that,' Anna urged. 'Open your mouth wider.' Helen obeyed. 'Now let's see how much of this she can take,' Anna said, pushing the dildo slowly into her mouth.

Helen began to move her lips up and down the shaft a little. 'Mistress Mus, could you hold her head still please?' asked Anna politely.

Louise sat by Helen and held her head still as Anna pushed the cock into her mouth. Helen began to gag a little, so Anna pulled it out.

'Well, that's quite impressive,' she said. 'Quite the deep-throat girl, aren't you?'

Helen tried to say thank you, muffled by the dildo.

'Weren't you taught never to speak with your mouth full?' Anna mocked.

Louise went to the table and filled a glass with wine. She walked back, taking a sip. 'Mistress Improba, would you like a drink?' she asked.

'Yes please,' Anna said. 'I am feeling a little dry.' As she held Helen's head and the plastic cock inside her mouth Louise held the glass to her lips while she took a sip. 'Are you feeling thirsty?' she asked Helen.

Helen managed to nod, so Anna pulled the cock slowly out of her mouth and held her head up, mouth open, and looked at Louise, who tipped the glass, pouring the wine slowly. Some went in Helen's mouth, which she swallowed, but Louise made sure some went over her face, dribbling down her chin onto her breasts.

'She is a messy one, isn't she?' scolded Anna.

Louise agreed. 'We should see she's properly punished.'

'She seemed to enjoy having her mouth full,' Anna said. 'Shall we see how much she can take?'

Louise was confused, but agreed regardless. Anna produced another dildo, this time attached to a face mask, and got Helen to lubricate it in the same fashion as earlier. Once lubricated she tested how far Helen's mouth would stretch with both inside. Though it looked a little painful to Louise, Helen seemed to be enjoying it, making moaning sounds as Anna pushed the two cocks in and out of her mouth.

Anna withdrew both dildos. 'I think it's time she pleased her Mistresses,' she said, putting the mask over Helen's head. She untied her arms, retying them in front of her, before unfastening her ankles. She led Helen onto the floor on all fours.

'Mistress Mus, would you like her to please you first?'

Louise sat on the sofa, legs open. Anna led Helen between her thighs and gently guided the cock into Louise, pushing Helen's head so it sank slowly into her. It was a little broader than Louise anticipated, but she made herself comfortable, thankful for Helen's lubrication aiding the entry. She reached down with one hand, rubbing her clitoris, while her other pinched one of her sensitive nipples. She moaned gently, watching Anna donning the strap-on.

'I think I know how to make her go faster,' Anna said, manoeuvring herself between Helen's legs. She rubbed her cock around Helen's pussy lips before pushing it slowly in, Helen stopping the motion with her head momentarily until Anna was fully inserted.

'Did I tell you to stop?' Anna scolded.

Helen began her slow movements again, pushing in and out of Louise. Then Anna started to thrust, pushing Helen further into Louise, who gasped at the first one, which took her by surprise though she was expecting it. From then on the penetration of Louise was instigated by Anna's thrusting, while Helen tried to keep as steady as possible. Louise groaned.

'Is she doing a good job?' asked Anna.

'Hmm... it's nice,' Louise replied breathlessly.

Anna slowed and gently pushed Helen forward so her face sandwiched against Louise's groin. After a few moments Helen pushed back and took a deep breath through her nose. 'I like this one,' Anna mused. 'She has spirit.' She gave Helen a hearty slap across her buttocks, before beginning to fuck her fast and hard with the strap-on. Helen's head bobbed back and forth, pumping the other dildo into Louise's pussy. The vibrations heightened Louise's arousal; she started rubbing her clit faster and pulling her nipples harder. She groaned with each thrust and shivered, feeling the onset of an orgasm. Instinctively she grabbed Helen's head, pulling her close as she started writhing her pelvis, trying to get to the sweet spot, and she found it, holding Helen and her mouth-cock in place while she enjoyed the sensations pulsing through her body. Then she relaxed, releasing her grip on Helen, falling back on the sofa, breathless.

She wiped her sweat-drenched hair from her face and smiled at Anna, who was withdrawing from Helen. She rolled Helen over and started greedily sucking the dildo covered in Louise's juices, while Louise got down on the floor to lick Helen's juices off Anna's strap-on.

'Are you up to giving her a good fucking now?' Anna asked.

Louise was a bit wobbly when she stood.

'I think you should let her do all the work,' Anna suggested, fastening the strap-on around Louise.

Louise sat and Anna unfastened Helen's wrists and removed her mask. Helen knelt between Louise's legs and licked the cock sprouting upward, swallowing it to the point of gagging.

'There's no stopping her now,' Anna noted.

Helen stood up, and straddling Louise's lap she lowered herself onto the dildo, sighing as it impaled her. She held onto Louise's shoulders, starting to rise and fall on the rigid stalk of wet plastic. Louise watched her breasts bounce and jiggle as she picked up the pace, bouncing on Louise's lap.

Louise started to lick and flick the succulent globes of flesh, the nipples hardening against her tongue. She pushed her head between them, enjoying the warmth around her face. She started to squeeze Helen's buttocks, causing her to slow the pace a little. She reached back and sucked one of her fingers, making it wet. She parted Helen's cheeks, massaging her arsehole. Helen began to moan so she pushed the finger in gently, Helen responding with more moans.

'I see she likes having her arse played with,' said Anna, as she knelt behind Helen. Louise felt her lick Helen's crack, so moved her finger away. Anna sucked Louise's finger first, licking all around it before letting her go, returning to Helen's soft and juicy arse. Louise could hear Anna lapping it, and was envious.

Anna stood and retrieved the mask. She held the dildo for Helen, who sucked it in, licking, sucking, swallowing it as she continued to bounce and grind on Louise's lap. Once it was thoroughly wet Anna took it away and knelt behind her. Helen stopped suddenly, and Louise realised what was going on.

'Can you take this one as well?' Anna asked.

Helen rose on Louise's cock, and Louise could see Anna's hand positioning the other dildo between Helen's legs. Helen slowly moved down, her eyes wide open, gazing into Louise's with a glazed intensity, breathing deeply. She took Louise's cock completely, and Anna's too. She started very slowly, cautious and deliberate motions up and down, careful to keep both cocks inside her. Her hands moved to cup Louise's face, and still gazing into Louise's eyes she kissed her, softly yet passionately. Louise eagerly reciprocated, holding Helen's head as their tongues played in their mouths.

Helen moaned, moving a little faster up and down on both dildos, but not too fast, arching her back so her lips could maintain contact with Louise's.

'I wish I had another strap-on,' muttered Anna. 'I'm feeling left out now.'

Helen pulled away from Louise's lips and looked down and around at Anna, holding the mask with its dildo up her arse. She reached out for Anna and pulled her up to her face, gripping the cock tightly in her rear passage, stopping it from dropping out. Anna knelt up and allowed Helen to kiss her. Louise could see their tongues dancing. She squeezed Helen's tits, almost in frustration she so wanted to come again, but Helen was now getting most of the stimulation.

'Let's lie her down,' she said, an authoritative edge to her voice. Anna looked at her in surprise, but moved to help Helen lay on the sofa on her back. Louise raised Helen's legs in the air and pushed the dildo of the mask back up her arse, moving it in and out a little. She then eased the strap-on into Helen's pussy, and Helen moaned in pleasure.

'Sit on her face,' she said to Anna, who wasn't going to argue, slowly lowering herself over Helen's mouth. Helen moved her arms up to hold her legs, giving her space to move a little between her clit and pussy. Louise could see her tongue moving around under Anna, who sighed before leaning forward to lick Helen's clitoris, nudged by Louise's thrusting groin. Anna gasped.

'What's the matter?' Louise asked, maintaining the rhythm.

Anna looked up at her. 'She just pushed a sneaky finger into my arse, the dirty girl.' She sat upright, squeezing her own breasts, moaning with pleasure. Louise started pounding Helen a little harder, and Helen squealed in response to each thrust. To intensify the stimulation Louise started massaging Helen's clitoris with her thumb, all the while fucking her with two plastic penises.

'Shit, fuck!' Helen cried, slightly muffled by Anna's cunt. She shuddered, triggering Anna too. As Helen started to climax Louise pushed into her as hard as she could, and Helen squealed again with each determined thrust before she pushed Anna off her face, and herself away from Louise and the two dildos. She curled up on the sofa, slowing her breathing. Louise and Anna exchanged glances.

'Are you all right?' asked a concerned Louise.

Helen rolled her head around to look at them, her eyes half closed and a broad grin across her face. 'Hell yeah,' she sighed. 'I'm just a fucking dirty slut, and I love it!'

'It seems I've opened the floodgates for this one,' said Anna, and Louise looked at her indignantly. 'OK, it's partly your fault too,' Anna added.

Tired and sweaty they decided to shower before having a late meal. Anna prepared and cooked the food while Louise helped Helen unpack in her spare bedroom. Having eaten Anna reluctantly left for home, as she had to prepare a brief for a client the following day.

Louise and Helen spent the rest of the evening with another bottle of wine, sat

on the sofa, giggling and gossiping. For Louise this was the first time she'd
enjoyed quality time with Helen since leaving Uni, and she loved every minute
of it.

CHAPTER SIX

LABORIS

Louise awoke the next morning and started to make coffee. She knocked on
Helen's door, and popped her head around to see her lying in bed, looking back
at her with an embarrassed expression on her face.

'What did I do last night?' she asked.

Louise was a little irritated. She walked in and sat on the side of her bed. 'You
know perfectly well what you did last night,' she said, a little crossly.

'You're not my mistress,' returned Helen.

'No, I'm not. But you enjoyed yourself. What are you afraid of? What other
people might think? The only people who know are the three of us. You were
so happy last night,' she continued. 'Happier than I'd seen you in a long time.'

'But that was the drink...' Helen began.

'Crap, and you know it is,' snapped Louise.

'Remember it was you who wanted to go to that party. And I saw the way you
looked around the room at what was going on; you wanted to join in. The only
thing stopping you was your impending marriage.'

'I know you, Helen, you always want to do the right thing, to be conventional.
Or that's how you want people to see you. But inside you wish you were more
adventurous, and that comes out when you have a bit to drink.'

Helen sat, arms wrapped around her knees, head down.

'So now you're not getting married, you don't have a fiancé, you can do what
the fuck you want,' Louise continued.

Helen looked up at her. 'What changed for you then? You were always the
careful, cautious one.'

Louise paused; it was true, and it was only the last few months she'd felt a bit
more liberated, though there were still things she wouldn't do. 'I met someone
who unlocked a few doors for me,' she replied.

'Who, Anna?'

'No, but I met Anna through him,' replied Louise.

'Him? So you're not a lesbian then.'

Louise stopped again. She'd thought about her last few exciting times, and
how Anna had been there each time. But she realised that Anna was a friend,
nothing more. And she didn't think Anna was gay either.

'No,' she replied slowly. 'I do like men too you know.'

Helen brightened a little. 'I'm sorry, I don't mean to be a pain.'

Louise hugged her. 'You're my best friend, and I'm here for you, no matter what.' She cupped Helen's face. 'And last night the two of us sat on the sofa, chatting and having a laugh, was like we were at Uni And I loved it.'

Helen smiled. 'So did I. And I did enjoy what we did before it, the three of us,' she admitted, cuddling into Louise, hiding her face. 'I've never done anything like that before, which I'm a bit embarrassed about, but it also makes it more exciting. Do you know what I mean?'

Louise smiled. 'I do.'

Helen sat back up, wiping her eyes. 'So, what's your mystery man like? When do I get to meet him?'

Louise thought for a moment. 'You've already met him,' she said. Helen gave her a questioning look. 'He hosted the party.'

'The man in the mask? What's he like underneath?'

Louise paused again. 'I don't know. But I'm meeting him tomorrow evening.'

'Can I come?' Helen asked.

'I'm sorry, but no,' she replied. 'At least not this time.' She saw the time on the bedside clock. 'I'd better get a move on; need to get ready for work. And so will you,' she said.

'I'm going to take a few days off,' Helen said.

'Take as long as you need. I'm just sorry I can't get the time off myself. Want to meet for lunch?'

Helen agreed, and they arranged for Louise to call her when she knew she could get out.

It was an early and rushed lunch. Helen was, as usual, waiting in the bar waiting for Louise when she hurried in.

'I'm sorry, can't stay for long,' she said. 'We've got a prospective client coming in this afternoon and they want me to meet him.'

'I thought you only dealt with clients once they'd signed up?'

'I do. But this new contract is important to the company and they want me to meet him, as I'll be dealing with the account once they come over. But Andrew's being an ass, as usual, telling me to turn on the charm and show some cleavage to the old guy.'

'Old guy?'

'Yeah. Some fellow by the name of Jefferson Haringay.'

Helen stared at Louise. 'You've never heard of him?'

'I know he's got a lot of fingers in a lot of pies, but I've never had to deal with him before.'

'It could be a huge contract,' said Helen, 'but you have to get past his Rottweiler first.'

'Rottweiler?' questioned Louise.

'That's what David... my fiancé... ex-fiancé... told me the other lawyers call him. Makes most of them run scared.'

'Oh,' was all Louise could manage.

When she returned to the office Andrew was flapping.

'Where the fuck have you been?' he snarled at her.

'I'm entitled to lunch,' she said defensively.

'Not with an important client here.'

'Here?' Louise was told it would be mid-afternoon.

'Yes. He's arrived early. But his Rottweiler's not here yet, so we've got chance to seal the deal with no interference.' Andrew looked at her. 'And as he likes his pretty ladies we want to make a good impression, don't we?'

'I don't do sales pitches, and you know it,' snapped Louise.

'We'll do whatever we have to to get his business,' Andrew said, and Louise didn't appreciate the tone in which he said it. 'He likes cleavage, short skirts and stockings. Can you go and get changed?'

'Andrew, my dear boy!'

They both turned to face the voice.

Jefferson Haringay was an older gentleman, and though slight of frame, he gave the impression of being a large man. He wore a tweed three-piece suit, a yellow cravat, and carried an exquisitely carved cane. There was something of his attire that reminded her of the man in the mask at the party.

'Jefferson!' Andrew exclaimed. 'Sorry, I didn't mean to keep you waiting. Can I introduce you to Louise, who'll be handling your account?' He pushed her forward with his hand on her bottom. Had they been somewhere else she'd have slapped his face, but he being her boss made it awkward; she put up with it as she loved her job and doubted she could get such a position anywhere else.

Andrew led them into one of the meeting rooms and asked his PA, Sally, a busty young blonde who'd obviously been told to wear a short skirt and low-cut top as well, to get them coffee.

He started his pitch to Jefferson, pointing out all the advantages the company could offer, and telling him how Louise had helped turn around the fortunes of several of their major clients. Helped?! She'd done most of the work! Jefferson seemed distracted, and Louise half expected Andrew to push a contract in front of him before his hotshot lawyer turned up.

Sally knocked on the door and started to announce the arrival of Jefferson's lawyer, but was cut short when Anna walked in.

'Andrew!' she said. 'You know Mr Haringay won't sign anything without my reviewing the details first.'

'Miss Collingwood,' said Andrew smarmily, walking to her, hand extended. 'Of course we wouldn't arrange anything without your review.'

Anna walked past him, ignoring his offer of a handshake, and sat next to Louise. 'And who is this?' she said sharply, looking at her.

'Louise Coleman, who'll be working on Mr Haringay's account...'

'If,' Anna emphasised, 'you earn Mr Haringay's business.'

'I'm sure you'll be happy with what we have to offer. Louise, this is Miss Collingwood, Mr Haringay's solicitor.'

Anna turned to Louise, extending her hand in greeting, which Louise took and shook.

'So you're the Rottweiler,' Louise said. She saw Andrew rolling his eyes.

'That is apparently how I'm known in some circles.' She looked over at Andrew. 'I like her. You should be that upfront, Andrew.'

'I'm always upfront and straight,' he lied.

Anna swung in her chair, watching him. Louise saw him loosen his collar; he was feeling uncomfortable under her glare. She smiled to herself.

Anna stood up suddenly. 'Andrew, Miss Coleman, would you mind giving Jefferson and I some privacy for a few moments?'

Andrew didn't want to leave. 'I'm sure we could help explain—'

'I have something to discuss with Mr Haringay which does not concern your negotiations.'

Andrew's mouth seemed to move, but no sound came out.

'Andrew, if you don't mind,' Jefferson said gently.

'Certainly,' said Andrew. He looked over at Louise, who stood up and followed him out of the meeting room, closing the door behind them.

He was agitated. 'Fuck!' he muttered, as he started pacing.

'I've got things to do,' said Louise. 'I'll see you later.'

Andrew grabbed her arm aggressively. 'Unless we land this contract you don't have anything to do,' he said through gritted teeth.

'Andrew, get off!'

'You do as you're told. When we go back in there you do everything to land this contract. Unbutton your blouse. Hitch up your skirt. Flirt. Flaunt your tight little arse,' he grabbed her bum and squeezed. 'Stop being your prissy, frigid, usual self. If need be give the old guy a blowjob; anything to land the contract.'

'That sounds to me like sexual harassment.' Anna was stood at the office door.

Andrew tried to shrug it off with his usual greasy charm. 'This is just banter. We all like a laugh around here, don't we?' He gave Louise a look that said 'agree with me, or else'. Louise did not appreciate being manipulated in such a way. If he wanted a whore to entertain Jefferson, she thought bitterly, why couldn't he get his PA to do the dirty work?

'Louise, if you want representation in a harassment case I'd be more than happy to do it for you.'

'There's really no need,' said Andrew, moving between the two of them.

'Would you represent me?'

The three of them turned to look at Sally.

'I can't afford to pay you anything though,' she added.

Anna walked over to her and put an arm around her shoulder. 'Of course I'd represent you, on a no-win no-fee basis.'

'You'll never work in the City again,' Andrew spat at her.

Louise walked over to join Sally and Anna.

'And I'll see you never work again, bitch!' He glared angrily at her.

'They can work for me.' Jefferson was now in doorway. 'You've been extolling Miss Coleman's virtues and achievements, and I'm sure she could do with an assistant.'

Andrew laughed. 'They can't work for you. There's a clause in their contracts barring them from working for clients.'

'Two points,' said Anna, counting them off her fingers. 'One, you've invalidated their contract of employment because of harassment. And two...' she looked over at Jefferson.

'I'm not your client.'

'But...'

'But nothing, Andrew,' finished Anna.

Jefferson walked over to Sally and Louise, and took their arms. 'Well ladies, allow me to take you out for a late lunch.'

He walked them out of the building surprisingly briskly, and to a nearby restaurant. Anna followed behind. Louise didn't even look back to see the expression on Andrew's face.

Jefferson was an incredibly flamboyant and charismatic fellow. A gentleman, in every sense of the word. He bought champagne by the bottle, which the four of them consumed with gusto. Some might have thought him to be an old school gay, but he certainly enjoyed lavishing attention on the ladies. Their waitress was a very pretty Spanish girl, whom he complimented at every chance. Louise thought that a little over the top, but they received excellent service.

Sally was a surprise to Louise, though. Around the company the rumour mill spread gossip about her and how she got the job. It may well be true that Andrew retained her for so long because of her looks and perhaps some other favours she was providing; most of his PAs left before the end of their probation period. But during their conversation it became apparent to Louise that she was a smart girl, taking in a lot of what was going on around her; more than Andrew realised.

Her phone buzzed. She saw she had several missed calls from him, and a text. She read it; he was offering her a substantial increase with a bonus if she returned to help land Jefferson as a client, and forget the harassment, as it was all just a big misunderstanding.

'Sally?'

Sally looked a little startled when Louise said her name; Louise expected she was only used to her colleagues whispering behind her back and not addressing her directly.

'Yes?'

'Have you heard anything from Andrew?'

Sally checked her phone, but there was nothing. 'No, why?'

Louise showed her the text. 'Are you going back?' she asked.

'Only to pick up my stuff,' Louise stated.

'That's a very generous offer,' said Sally. 'You'd be getting almost the same as he is.'

Sally was sharp.

'He's not being fair to you,' Louise said.

'I don't mind if you take the offer,' said Sally. 'I'd understand.' She gave her a weak smile.

'No,' Louise said resolutely. 'He's not been fair to you, and that's enough of a reason for me not to go back.'

Louise saw Sally tearing up before she leapt up to give Louise a hug. 'I'm sorry,' she whispered in Louise's ear. 'No one's been nice to me before.' She hung on for a few seconds, before releasing her grip and excusing herself to go to the ladies'.

With her suspicions of Jefferson's attire, and Anna appearing, Louise wanted to get a moment alone with Anna to quiz her. The moment came when he went off to the bar area, talking to their waitress, while Sally was still in the ladies'.

'Is that him?'

Anna was puzzled for a moment, then burst out laughing when realisation dawned. 'God, no!' she exclaimed. 'He's a gentle old soul, couldn't hurt a fly.'

'But neither would our guy, would he?'

'He'll inflict pain as part of his role, but Jefferson couldn't even do that. For him women are on a pedestal, to be admired and cherished; a proper old-school gent. He couldn't do what our Master does.'

The conversation was changed as Jefferson returned.

'I have to say, it's very kind of you to offer me a job like that, but...'

Jefferson cut her short. 'Not at all my dear! You do have a reputation for diligence, which is one of the reasons I came to see your company. I could always use someone of your capabilities.'

'I take it you won't be signing up as a client now then,' she said.

'That was never the plan,' he said.

She was confused. 'Then why make the appointment?'

Anna spoke up. 'This is in confidence.' She paused, and Louise nodded in consent.

'Jefferson is looking to gain a substantial stake in the company.'

Louise was speechless. Anna and Jefferson just smiled. Eventually she regained her power of speech.

'Will it still be going ahead now?' Louise thought about the trouble she and Sally were about to cause. 'I hope I haven't ruined anything for you.'

'On the contrary, my dear,' said Jefferson. 'If anything, even the mere rumour of a sexual harassment case, two even, will cause the price to fall, leaving me to take a larger stake.'

It struck Louise that within this man, who exuded warmth and geniality, there lurked a cold, calculating depth. She questioned in her mind whether Anna had been correct in her assertion that he wouldn't hurt anyone.

The afternoon flew by; Anna received a phone call from someone, made her excuses and left, leaving the three of them still drinking. Louise had switched to tonic water as she'd felt herself getting a little tipsy, and didn't want to return home to Helen in a state.

They discussed Louise's potential roles in the organisation; Louise's head swam with the possibilities. They exchanged numbers and agreed they'd meet again the following Monday, not too early, to decide what Sally and Louise would be doing at Jefferson's company.

Sally and Louise returned to the office to collect their stuff. Andrew wasn't about but the rumours had spread sure enough; as Louise walked to her desk the girls in her office stood and applauded. She felt a little embarrassed at the attention. She overheard a few comments as she walked past.

'Nice one girl!'

'About time someone got the pig.'

'Get him where it hurts, for all of us.'

She boxed up her stuff while colleagues popped in to offer encouragement. Why hadn't any of them done something before? Had they all been too afraid?

Then she thought of all the times he'd brushed against her, had a quiet grope, made a suggestive comment, and realised that she, too, hadn't been brave enough or confident enough to stand up to him before. It seemed submitting to her Master had empowered her at the same time.

CHAPTER SEVEN

ULTIO

Louise rushed home; she couldn't wait to tell Helen about the day's events, and to let her know who the Rottweiler was. As she arrived at her door Helen opened it, dressed in her LBD, stockings and heels again. She looked incredibly glamorous.

'I'm glad you're back,' she said. 'I tried calling your office but there was no answer. Come on, we have to go out.' She pushed Louise into the apartment, not even commenting on the box full of stuff she was carrying; she was very excited about something.

'Where are we going?' Louise asked.

'You'll see,' was all Helen offered, and hurried Louise back out and down the street. She wouldn't answer any questions, just saying 'you'll see' in reply. She turned them into a backstreet and down some steps into a cellar bar.

The place was dimly lit, but simply and tastefully decorated. The barman wasn't a tall guy, but was muscular. He looked up as they entered, and put down the glass he'd been cleaning.

'What can I get you ladies?' he asked.

'They're with me, Guy.' He looked over at Anna and nodded, and poured out to liqueurs in small glasses. Louise remembered the taste and looked enquiringly at the barman, who winked. He was much too large in the shoulders to be *him*.

Helen sipped the liqueur. 'That's delicious,' she said. 'But I'll be better off on soft drinks, if you don't mind.'

Louise was taken by surprise.

'That's fine,' he said. 'Non-alcoholic fruit cocktail?' he suggested.

'Sure.'

He turned to Louise. 'And for you? The same?'

Louise was tempted to have another cherry drink, but decided keeping her head would be better. 'The same.'

They got their drinks and sat in the cubicle with Anna, who moved down the bench, asking Helen to sit next to her, and Louise sat blocking both in.

'I hope you don't mind,' said Anna, producing a piece of tape.

'Oooh,' cooed Helen. 'I can't wait.'

Anna taped her mouth, but she played along.

'That stays on until I remove it, understand?'

Helen nodded.

'And you stay there until I say you can go.'

Helen nodded again.

'Regardless of what you might hear.'

Helen nodded again.

Louise took a drink, watching Anna, who was giving nothing away. She'd meant to tell Helen about Anna, but didn't get the opportunity.

Anna's phone beeped and she checked it. She then put her hand on Helen's thigh, holding it in place, and signalled that Louise do the same. Helen looked between them, half amused. Louise saw three smartly dressed men come into the bar and park themselves in the next cubicle. One offered to get drinks for the others, Helen sat upright when she heard one of the voices, and Anna responding by putting her free hand over Helen's mouth to emphasise the point. Helen glared at her, and Louise didn't know what was going on.

When the three men settled with their drinks the girls could hear their conversation clearly.

'So, why did you leave her?'

'I told you, she'd been sleeping around at some of those kinky sex parties behind my back.'

The other two laughed.

'Why didn't you see if she'd let you go too? Have a bit of a swingers do.'

'Nah, not my scene,' he replied.

Louise saw Helen's face changing under Anna's hand; Anna just shook her head and mouthed 'wait'. The penny dropped for Louise.

'So what are you going to do? What about the flat?'

'She's left, so it's all mine now,' he said.

Anna continued to shake her head at Helen.

'I don't think it'll be that easy.'

'I know a few decent lawyers,' he said. They all laughed. 'Once it comes out what a slut she is her reputation will be in tatters, and I'll get everything.'

They heard heels walking over the floor, and then stop.

'Hello David,' said a female voice that Louise recognised, but couldn't place.

There was a pause before he replied. 'I'm sorry, do I know you?'
They heard her sit down. Then they heard a slap.
'Annabelle, don't pretend you don't know me, you little fucker.'
'Look, I think you must have me confused with—' Another slap cut him short.
'Or should I say *Belle*. Madame Belle, to you.'
There was a pause. Louise imagined his mind to be racing, trying to deny all knowledge.
'Look, I'm really sorry but—'
Slap.
'Don't lie to me, David. You know what happens when someone betrays my trust.'
There was another pause.
'Sorry, Madam Belle.'
'And you've been lying to your friends too, haven't you?'
David attempted defiance. 'That is none of your—'
Slap.
'You betrayed my trust, and your fiancée's too.'
'That slut—'
Slap.
'I'll stop you telling lies, even if it means gagging you. What do you suppose your fiancée, or rather ex-fiancée, would say about you spreading malicious lies about her? It wasn't her fucking around at kinky sex parties, was it, David?'
There was complete silence.
'She went to one, and just watched. How many did you attend?'
Anna held Helen's face still while she removed the tape, but kept her mouth covered. The guys remained quiet.
'David, I have two confessions to make.'
'Really?' he said dully.
'You know how you liked to play with my other little slaves, especially the pretty little girls?'
There was another tense pause, before a nervous, 'Yes.'
'And you know how we used to blindfold you before either me or one of my girls would give you and your pathetic cock a delicious blowjob.'
'Yes.'
'Well, it wasn't really me, or one of the girls. We always dragged in one of the TV maids to help.'
'What?'
Louise tried to contain her giggles, but got a glare from Anna.
'What would your ex-fiancée say to that, I wonder?'
'You dare—'
Slap.
'Don't threaten me, boy.'
There was a pause again.
'Helen... have I got her name right?'

'Yes.'

'Helen must be glad to be shot of you. If anything she deserves everything you had because of the shit way you treated her.'

'That has nothing—'

Slap.

'Watch your mouth, boy. You don't know who might be listening.'

Another tense silence.

'So, what would Helen say about your disgusting little habits? Shall we ask her? Helen? What do you have to say?'

Helen climbed out and stood in front of the next cubicle. 'You loathsome little...'

'Look, I'm sorry—'

Slap. This time it wasn't from Annabelle.

'Shut up you filthy fucker!' Helen was angry. 'I want what's rightfully mine.'

David laughed. 'No chance!'

Slap. Annabelle's palm again this time.

Anna slipped out and stood by the table.

'Oh, hello David. Not seen you for a while. It looks like you're in need of good legal representation.'

Louise heard David's voice brighten.

'Anna! Would you take it on? I want to leave this bitch penniless for what she did to me.'

'I'm sorry, sweetie,' said Anna, 'but this "bitch" is my client, if that's ok with you, Helen.'

The other two guys started chuckling. 'Shit, Dave, you're screwed against the Rottweiler!' They shut up suddenly, David giving them a vicious look.

Helen looked at Anna. 'Yes, I would like you to handle this for me,' she said calmly.

Louise had been surprised by Helen not drinking. Now she was surprised to hear what she said.

'Boys. Would you like me to handle you?'

Guy the barman approached. 'Can you folks take this into the back room where it's quieter, then you won't frighten my clientele.'

He led them all through a door, and once in he locked it. Louise watched as Helen took the two men each by the hand and led them over to a bench, where she sat them down.

'You won't do it,' David sneered. 'You were fucking boring between the sheets. That's why I had to find excitement somewhere else.'

Annabelle pushed him down onto a stool and Anna taped his wrists behind his back, while Annabelle taped his feet together.

'You can't do this to me, it's false imprisonment!' he whined.

Annabelle laughed. 'Really? But there's a precedent for me tying you up,' she said.

'How will you prove that?' he said.

'I have pictures,' she said as she taped first his mouth, and then his eyes. 'Now just sit there like a good little boy.'

Anna whispered something to Guy, who disappeared, returning a few moments later with a small package. In the meantime Helen had unzipped the flies of David's two friends, and was alternating between giving each one a blowjob, slowly feeding each cock into her mouth. Anna sat by Louise, who was taking the scene in with some bewilderment.

Helen stood and took a couple of steps away from the men, who sat there wanking themselves. She lifted her dress, revealing a pair of black panties, and slowly drew them down her legs. The guys were staring at her, grinning, anticipating what could come next.

She stepped out of her knickers and turned to face them. Squatting, her hand disappeared between her legs as she rubbed herself, occasionally sliding her fingers into her mouth, licking provocatively, and then returning them between her legs.

'She puts on quite a show, doesn't she?' Anna whispered to Louise.

'This isn't the Helen I know from Uni,' she replied.

'And you're not the Louise she knew from Uni either.'

Fair comment. Things had changed in a remarkably short period of time.

Helen got onto her hands and knees, dress hitched up to her waist, and crawled to one of the guys, between his legs, to start sucking his cock again, her head bobbing, one hand still between her thighs, gently rubbing herself. She then moved to the other guy, doing the same thing before standing up, still rubbing herself. Anna gave her the package.

'Condoms,' Helen said huskily. 'How fortunate.'

She took one out of the packet, placed it on one of the bloated domes, and rolled it down with her lips. After licking it up and down a couple of times she stood and straddled him, gently easing him into her pussy. She sighed once he was fully in, and then began to slowly move up and down, grinding her pelvis around. The other guy watched, dreamily wanking his cock.

After a couple of minutes she looked at him. 'Poor love,' she said. 'Let me give you a little attention too.'

She stood again, took off her dress and bra, releasing her large breasts, and then slipped between his legs. She spat on his cock before licking it, then nestled it between her breasts, cushioning the soft flesh around it. She looked up at him, eye to eye. 'Is that nice?' she breathed.

'Mmmm, yeah,' he drawled.

She stuck her arse in the air and looked at the first guy, condom still on his cock.

'What are you waiting for?' she said, nodding behind her. He took the hint and knelt behind her, slowly pushing his cock back into her. She looked over her shoulder and pushed back against him, sighing again. Then she started to greedily lick and suck the other cock. As one guy thrust into her pussy her mouth was pushed further along the other cock. All eyes in the room, except

David's, were on her, and she knew it. She started to gyrate her hips and move her head around, alternating between licking the cock-shaft, kissing the tip, and taking it in her mouth all the way to its base.

She blindly retrieved the packet of condoms and took one out. After giving the cock one long suck she placed a condom on the helmet, and once again rolled it down with her lips. Once she was happy it was on properly she pushed the guy behind back, stood, and straddled the newly sheathed cock, slowly lowering herself onto it. Once in place she leaned forward, grabbed the free cock, rolled off the condom and resumed her licking and sucking action on it, making loud sucking and slurping noises as she enthusiastically worked.

'She seems to be enjoying herself,' said Anna, watching Louise's face.

'Yes,' Louise replied. She was concerned at Helen's behaviour, hoping she wasn't going to return to her wild and carefree days of Uni; she was a grown woman now, and Louise wouldn't always be around to watch over her. It wasn't so long ago she got drugged; both of them were lucky that time. But in all that time Helen had never done anything this outrageous at Uni; she'd flirted and teased guys, but only had sex with one at a time. And she'd never had sex with people watching.

Louise looked around the room. David was still on the stool, blindfolded, gagged and tied. By one side was Annabelle - Madame Belle - with a hand firmly gripping his shoulder, but watching the action. Guy the barman was by the door, arms folded, eyes alternating between Helen and David.

She looked at Anna, who was looking at her.

'You look worried,' Anna said quietly.

Louise looked over at Helen, who was holding one guys buttocks as she swallowed his cock deeply. 'I hope she'll be all right,' was all she could say.

Anna put a reassuring hand on her arm. 'She will be. She's got you to look after her.'

Louise snorted. 'And who'll look after me?' she said, without thinking.

Anna gave her a hug. 'We will.'

It took a little while for it to sink in. We? Who was we? Anna and Helen? Anna and Jefferson? Before she could voice any questions Anna pulled out of the embrace.

'Watch,' she said, looking over at Helen.

She'd pushed away the guy she'd been giving head to, who had obvious shot his load by the satisfied look on his face. She stood, turned, and after removing the condom from the sitting guy, was blowing his cock even more enthusiastically than before. It was obviously all too much for him as well as he tensed for a few moments, and Louise watched Helen slow her head to a gentler bobbing motion.

When the guy relaxed again Helen stood, put her bra and dress back on and walked over to David. She ripped the tape off his eyes and spat in his face, having saved in her mouth the spunk from both guys, and let David have it.

Louise suddenly felt quite proud of her. Guy threw a towel to Helen, who wiped her face with it. Louise went to her and gave her a hug.

'You were right,' said Helen.

'About what?' asked Louise.

'You don't need to have a drink to have fun!'

She went to the two guys and kissed both on the cheek, saying thank you.

Annabelle untied David's legs and she and Guy led him, still gagged, back out to the bar, the evidence of Helen's prowess dripping from his face onto his nicely tailored suit. Louise wondered about his dry cleaning bill.

The two guys pulled their trousers back up and started following him from the room. One of them paused, and when the other had left he turned to Anna.

'Thank you, Improbus,' she said to him.

'My pleasure, Improba,' he replied with a smile, and left, nodding to Annabelle and Guy on the way out.

Louise looked at Anna. 'You planned this, didn't you?'

'I didn't expect Helen to do what she did, but I thought the confrontation might help her to move on, and I'll make sure she gets her proper share of their properties.'

'David must have known about the Improbus guy though, so why was he lying to them?'

'David isn't a Court member; he was just someone Madame Belle entertained from time to time, only going to the masked balls, so he doesn't know I'm involved, or Jeremy.'

'Jeremy's in the Purple Court too then?'

'No. He's in a different Court, and enjoys causing mischief even more than I do.' Anna winked.

They went over to Helen, who was sitting, grinning to herself, on the bench.

'I have something for you,' Anna said, giving her a key.

'What's this?'

'It's the key to your flat.'

Helen looked at her blankly.

'Some of Guy's, um, colleagues, went over to your place and changed the locks, before he got any funny ideas about getting rid of stuff or trashing the place.'

'What if David goes to get his things and breaks in?'

'He's no reason to. Guy arranged for his wardrobe to be brought over for him so he's no immediate reason to go back. But just for good measure, he's posted one of the other ianitoris there to keep watch.'

Helen hugged her. 'You're amazing,' was all she could say, tears coming to her eyes. 'But if it's all right with you,' she looked at Louise, 'I'd like to stay at yours a little while longer, while I sort out what I'm going to do.'

Louise smiled back. 'Of course. Stay as long as you need to.' They hugged again.

Annabelle returned. 'Well, I didn't expect that, Helen!' she said, laughing. 'You certainly know how to put a man in his place!'

'Well, thank you,' said Helen, uncertainly.

'If you ever want to come and play in my domain, you'd always be welcome.'

Helen looked a bit puzzled.

'Madame Belle has probably the best equipped dungeon I know of,' said Anna.

'I don't know about best, but there aren't many people who know how to do humiliation in such an imaginative fashion.'

Helen blushed.

They exchanged numbers, and after another drink they parted company with Louise and Helen returning to Louise's apartment. Louise finally had chance to recount her day; leaving her job, the offer of a position with Jefferson Haringay, and of course, when she discovered Anna's nickname.

Helen recapped events perfectly in a single sentence. 'Today has been a day for revenge.'

CHAPTER EIGHT

VOX DOMINO

Louise and Helen had a lazy morning, getting out of bed late, lounging around in their nightwear and getting dressed only just before lunchtime. They went out for lunch, followed by some window shopping. Louise watched Helen carefully, but she seemed happy enough.

Come late afternoon they stopped by a coffee shop, having coffee and a cake each. They sat by the window so they could watch the world go by.

'Shall we do something tonight?' asked Louise.

'Such as?'

'Cinema? Show? Something, rather than sit in a pub, or back at the apartment.'

'Haven't you got a meeting tonight?'

Louise thought for a moment, and then remembered. A meeting with her Master. Would she actually see him this time? Her train of thought was interrupted by Helen touching her arm.

'Are you all right?' she asked.

'Sure,' replied Louise. 'I was just thinking.'

They finished their coffees and made their way back. Once home Louise made dinner, before getting changed. She thought about wearing the purple decorated corset, but then thought better of it.

Helen had changed into her nightwear. 'Thought I'd have an evening in watching telly,' she said. Louise sat nervously awaiting the car. Her phone buzzed; it was her YMV app.

There's a black Mercedes waiting outside for you.

She said a quick goodbye to Helen, who wished her an enjoyable evening, before closing her front door.

On the street a black Mercedes was indeed waiting. She climbed in the back, and as soon as she belted herself in the car set off. Though she said hello to the driver he only nodded in acknowledgement, and didn't speak during the journey. Louise was glad there was music on, though opera wouldn't have been her first choice.

Twenty minutes later they stopped in a street around Chelsea. Her YMV app buzzed again.

Take the steps down to the basement flat on the corner.

Louise got out of the car and walked down the steps. The curtains were drawn so she couldn't see inside the front window as she passed it. She rang the bell and the door was quickly answered by the blonde Eastern European lady, dressed in a snug black suit, which only just seemed to contain her boobs.

'Wait here for a moment,' she said, leading Louise into the small hallway. Her voice had an edge to it, or was that just her accent.

Louise waited, noticing the bathroom, while the lady went into the other room, closing the door behind her. She tried to listen, but could only hear music. The door opened.

'You may enter now.'

Louise followed her into the room, where there was a chair in the middle facing a black leather sofa, where the lady sat next to the man in the mask. The lady indicated she should sit on the chair, which she dutifully did.

'Do you remember me?' the lady asked, a little sternly.

Louise hesitated before answering. 'Yes, from the party.'

In a matter-of-fact manner she was asked, 'Is your back sore?'

'Not any more, thank you very much.'

The lady nodded. 'Good. I will be speaking for the Master this evening. You may address me as Vox Domino.'

'Yes, Vox Domino.' Louise subconsciously nodded as she spoke.

Vox Domino smiled. 'Our Master wishes you to know he's pleased with your progress so far.'

'I'm very pleased to hear that, Vox Domino.' Louise was surprised at how easily she slipped into the submissive role.

'He hadn't planned for you to attend one of our events just yet, but someone intervened in that matter,' she said.

Louise wanted to say something in defence of Anna, but the Master put a hand up to silence her.

'But as you are now aware of the Purple Court he believes it only right and proper for you to be given the opportunity to join us.'

Louise was speechless for a moment.

'How much do you know of the Purple Court?'

Louise was struggling to recall what Anna had said, but then decided it easier, and perhaps safer for Anna, to say she knew very little. Vox Domino stood and started to pace around Louise as she spoke.

'As a submissive you will no doubt be aware that the master-slave relationship is about control.'

Louise nodded. Her enjoyment of being at the mercy of someone else was being able to give up control for a time.

'And though the Master appears to completely control the slave, in truth the slave is the one truly in control, placing their trust in their Master.'

Louise nodded. She hadn't thought about it that deeply.

'But how do you know whether you can trust your Master?'

Louise panicked; was she expected to give an answer?

'That is why the Courts of the Order were formed, as a safeguard to us. We can trust the people in our own Order as they have committed to our codes of conduct.'

This made sense to Louise, and she recalled Anna saying something similar.

'However, think carefully, as our codes of conduct apply to all our members, and they also demand a commitment.'

Louise nodded. 'A commitment to the Master.'

'A commitment to the Court.' Vox Domino pointed at the sitting man. 'The Master also must be committed to the Court. In return you will have the full protection of the Court. You can let us know your decision on Friday.'

Louise felt she needed to please her Master somehow, to make her feel worthy of his attention. 'OK, I'll join. What do I need to do?'

Vox Domino turned to look at her, eyes questioning. The Master maintained his stare at Louise, through his mask.

'I would ask that you consider this carefully,' Vox Domino began, before the Master touched her on the arm.

She turned to face him, and moved her ear in front of his mouth. Vox Domino nodded, and stood upright again.

'The Master is pleased you have chosen to join us. He also regrets that you will not be able to properly enjoy the entertainments of our next event, as all members of the Purple Court will be serving the guests in various capacities.'

For a moment Louise wondered if that meant the slaves were all tied up for the whims of the guests, but that seemed to go against the safety ethos.

'The Master will contact you in due course, and inform you of when your initiation will be and how you should prepare yourself. We ask that you not discuss this matter with anyone outside of the Court. Is that understood?'

Louise nodded. 'Yes, Vox Domino.'

'Then the Master thanks you for your time, and you make take your leave.'

Louise sat on the chair a little longer, looking between Vox Domino and the Master. 'But...'

Vox Domino turned, her tone harsh. 'But what? You may go now!'

Louise faltered. 'I thought I would get to spend some time with my Master.'

Vox Domino moved aggressively towards her. Louise leant back instinctively, but the Master intervened, grabbing Vox Domino's arm as he stood. She turned to face him and bowed her head to listen again. Louise didn't think she looked too happy.

'But...' Vox Domino started, before the Master cut her off. She listened again, and nodded in understanding. 'Very well,' she said, straightening up again.

'This is usually my time with *our* Master,' she said. 'But he has asked if I would share with you.' She paused, looking back at him, and then to Louise.

She walked to Louise again and cupped her cheeks in her gloved hands, moving Louise's head to look up into her eyes. 'Why should I let you share my precious time with you?' Vox Domino looked severely into her eyes.

Louise shrugged.

'Do you want to spend time with our Master?'

Louise nodded, quietly saying, 'Yes please, Mistress Vox Domino.'

Vox Domino gave a brief smile, before resuming her severe expression. 'Very well. Stand.'

Louise stood, and her new Mistress pushed the chair away before circling her, eyeing her up and down. The Master sat back down, watching proceedings. Louise looked at him. The Mistress moved around to the front of her, blocking her view of their Master, and putting her palm under Louise's chin, she raised her face so again they were looking at each other, eye to eye.

'I really am putting myself out, allowing you to share his time. I don't like sharing, so you will have to make it up to me.'

'I will try, Mistress.' Louise lowered her head.

'Take off your blouse.'

Louise started unbuttoning it, top down. The Mistress' gaze didn't leave Louise's face. Louise felt her heart racing in anticipation, her breasts heaving. She pulled the blouse off, allowing it to drop to the floor. The Mistress walked around her, kicking the blouse contemptuously to the side of the room. She ran a finger across Louise's bra, around and under her breasts.

'Off!'

Louise reached back to unclip the flimsy garment, and let it drop too. The Mistress gracefully caught it before it landed, and studied it for a few moments.

'Very nice,' she said, before throwing it on top of the discarded blouse.

Her gloved hands stroked around Louise's breasts, a finger traced around her nipples. Louise shuddered slightly, the feeling of the glove material against her skin giving her goose bumps.

The Mistress walked around her again, running her finger inside the skirt's waistband. 'Now this,' she said.

Louise unfastened her skirt, letting it also drop to the floor before stepping out of it. The Mistress kicked it to the side of the room as well, and then started running her finger up and down Louise's side, and then running it inside and around the waistband of her panties.

'Now these,' she ordered.

Louise bent to pull her panties down, stepping out of them. She went to drop them onto the pile of her other clothes, but again the mistress intercepted them. She studied them carefully, occasionally looking at Louise. Louise felt slightly embarrassed, wondering what she could see in her underwear. After a minute's study she dropped them on the pile, and then turned her attention back to Louise, stroking, caressing, exploring again with her finger, the sensuous feel of the glove nice against Louise's skin, making her whole body tingle. She heaved a contented sigh, which elicited a swift slap to her bottom.

'You are here to please me!'

The Mistress parted her legs and hitched up her skirt, pulling the crotch of her silky black knickers to one side, revealing her pussy. With her other hand she pushed Louise down onto her knees and guided her face to her crotch. Louise obediently started to lap at the Mistress' pussy and clit.

'That's better,' the woman said, encouraging her. She stroked Louise's hair as Louise licked around her clitoris, pushing into her pussy, trying to get deeper. The Mistress pulled Louise's face closer, starting to grind against her active mouth.

Louise felt another gloved hand caressing her back and bum. It moved up, and at her neck gently encouraged her to stand. Louise looked to the side to see the masked Master with a hand behind both her and the Mistress, who grabbed her head and kissed her, her lips soft and warm. Aware that her Master was watching she pulled away, opened her mouth slightly, tongue protruding from between her lips, and moved back to passionately kiss the Mistress. She was taken by surprise as the woman seemed to relish really deep kissing, tongue well into her mouth, licking and sucking. Louise's hands seemed to fall naturally at the Mistress' waist and she started to caress her sides. The Mistress responded by stoking the small of her back with one hand and pulling her in deeper, pushing between Louise's shoulders. Louise could only imagine what her Master was thinking, but when she and the Mistress pulled apart she caught a glimpse of an unmistakable bulge in his trousers. She thought she'd have a sneaky grope, but the Mistress caught her hand and pushed her back.

'I will deal with the Master,' she said. 'You are only here to humour him.'

Louise hung her head. 'Sorry, Mistress.'

He whispered something in the Mistress' ear, before moving to a desk.

'The Master is about to remove his mask.'

Louise's brain raced; she'd get to see what he looked like!

'However, you are not yet entitled to his secret, so you will be blindfolded.'

Immediately Louise's eyes were covered and the blindfold fastened around her head. She stood still as she felt hands move around her, massaging her breasts and pulling her into her Master's body. She felt his clothes against her naked flesh and wondered if she'd get to have skin to skin contact with him. She felt his lips against her shoulders, his hands gently tracing down her belly, towards her thighs. She pushed her pelvis back, pressing her buttocks against his erection. Her arms reached back to touch him, but the Mistress grabbed them before she got very far. The woman was interfering too much for Louise's liking.

She held Louise's arms by her side while the Master moved away. She released her hold and walked around behind Louise, who felt a hand stroking her side, before reaching around to her front, tracing a line down to between her legs. She gently stroked around Louise's clitoris; Louise breathed deeply.

'Do you enjoy have your clitoris rubbed?' she asked.

With a sigh Louise answered, 'Yes Mistress.'

The woman pulled her tight to her body, and Louise could feel her clothed breasts pushing against her back. A hand pushed its way to her pussy, stroking her lips.

'Do you enjoy being penetrated?'

Louise took a deep breath. 'Yes, Mistress.'

A finger lingered for a few moments longer, before retreating away from Louise's groin. The Mistress stepped back and Louise felt the hand return, stroking her buttocks, pulling them apart and inserting a finger. Louise adjusted her stance to accommodate the invading digit, which gently massaged her anus.

'Do you enjoy being stimulated here too?'

Louise nodded. 'Yes, Mistress.'

The finger lingered, massaging, before being removed.

'Then I have a few treats for you.'

Louise heard the Mistress walk away, returning and standing in front of her.

'Kneel,' she ordered.

Louise did as she was told. A hand took Louise's and put something into it. She heard the squeeze of a tube and a little dribble of cool gel touched her fingers. She rubbed the lubricant around the object, anticipating what would come next.

'Stick it in your arse.'

Louise knelt up a little, parted her cheeks with one hand and gently eased the device into her rear passage. She felt her anus open, before closing around onto its thinner neck.

'Is that OK?' asked the woman.

'Yes, Mistress,' replied Louise, nodding.

She felt the object begin to vibrate. She remembered Anna had bought something like this, a vibrating anal plug, during their shopping trip a few days earlier.

'Let me know when it begins to get too much,' the Mistress said softly, in complete contrast to her earlier strict tones.

Louise nodded and felt the vibrations slowly increase in speed, to the point where it felt quite uncomfortable.

'Too much,' she said, and the vibrations decreased a little.

'There?' she was asked.

'That's good, thank you Mistress.'

With the butt-plug in place another object was put in her hand; a more familiar shape to Louise, with knobbles around the shaft. She heard the tube of lubricant being squeezed again, and rubbed it all over the dildo. She felt it get switched on, the knobbles seemed to move around the shaft, and then it was switched off.

'Put this inside you,' the Mistress said.

Louise again raised herself a little, placed the dildo on the floor on its base, holding it in place with one hand while the other was opening the lips of her pussy, ready to accommodate it inside her. She lowered herself slowly, a little startled when the dildo kicked into life again, a slow whirring, the knobbles rotating around its shaft and gently massaging the inside of her vagina.

'Is that OK?'

Louise could only manage a nod while she smiled, the vibrations from both devices making her body vibrate and tingle. It was gentle and relaxing; she was sure she'd be able to sit there for hours, just taking it in. She moved her hips a little to enable the dildo to massage different parts of her pussy; she'd have to get herself one!

Then she felt something else being placed in her hand, a more sturdy piece of equipment this time. Once again the lube was squeezed onto it, but then it was place between her legs, on her clitoris. Her hand was guided to the controls, and when switched on the vibration started off slow, so she adjusted the controls to increase the speed, and her pleasure. She threw her head back and began to moan, waves of pleasurable sensations flowing through her.

She felt her nipples being clipped, and then the clips also started to vibrate, causing her breasts to ache deliciously. Her moans increased in volume, along with the intensity of the feelings coursing through her.

She tried to control her breathing, attempting to keep her climax at bay, for now at least. She listened for some indication of what may happen next, and heard the sound of slurping, licking and the squeak of the sofa. It sounded as though the Mistress was performing oral on their Master. It occurred to her that she may be putting on a show for them, so she upped the ante and started to grind her pelvis a little, though not too much for fear of losing the dildo, and bit her lip, with her head facing in their general direction.

'I see you are enjoying the sideshow, Master,' the Mistress said, confirming Louise's suspicions.

Encouraged, Louise moved her hips a little more, using her free hand to stroke, caress, squeeze and draw her nails across the skin of her thighs, belly and chest. She raised her arm to pull her hair up, writhing around not only with the pleasure from the various mechanical devices, but also from the thought of her Master being aroused by her. She imagined what it would have felt like having him inside her instead, that it was his hand instead of hers clawing at her flesh, that it was his body pushing her slowly towards the orgasm she wanted to hold off as long as possible.

The sounds from the sofa changed, now more like someone bouncing up and down on it. Was the Mistress on top, taking his cock, sitting up cowgirl fashion? Or was she on her back, with him pounding into her? Louise imagined she'd be on top, giving him ample opportunity to view her impressive tits bouncing, with the chance to grapple with them for his additional pleasure.

She heard moaning, briefly wondering whether it was the Master or the Mistress, but then she realised it was her, overcome with the sensations her body was experiencing. She turned down the clitoral stimulation, to a level taking her back just below the edge.

She listened for some clue as to what may be happening; she heard a sigh. She tried listening a little harder, but found it difficult to concentrate with so much going on about her body. After a little time she felt a warm pair of breasts pressing against her back, and arms around her.

'I think you're not getting enough,' the Mistress said.

Louise felt the vibrations increase in the dildo and the anal plug, and then she felt the Mistress' hand on hers, pushing the controls on the clitoral stimulator, increasing the intensity of the vibrations. Her breathing became erratic and she began panting. She half-heartedly tried fighting the Mistress, but it was no use; she wanted her climax to come, and it came with such an explosion of bliss. She wailed as the joy pulsated through her. Almost becoming too much she tried to move the stimulator away from her clit, but the Mistress held firm, ensuring she was receiving the full effect of the devices. She screamed and shuddered, the pleasure getting so intense it was verging in pain, but the Mistress still kept the pressure on. Eventually, exhausted, Louise sank forward, at which point the Mistress released her grip and turned everything off.

She gently removed the devices, one by one, still holding Louise, who was still shaking a little from her most intense orgasm. The Mistress helped her up and guided her to the sofa, where she sat. She had cramp in her legs from her time spent kneeling, so she rubbed them to get the feeling back. The Mistress removed the blindfold. Louise sank back into the sofa, and looked around the room.

'He's gone.'

Just like the time he visited her flat.

'But he said he enjoyed your performance, as always,' she added.

'Thank you, Vox Domino,' said Louise.

'You can call me Marta. I'm not Vox Domino now.'

Louise looked at her, confused.

'Vox Domino is a title, and can only be used with the Master present, or with his consent.'

Louise thought for a moment. 'The Master's voice?'

Marta smiled. 'Yes. His spokesperson at a particular time. But you will learn more of this in due course.'

Marta brought Louise a drink while Louise retrieved her clothes and got dressed. She then sat and cradled the glass, sipping from it. 'I'm sorry for intruding on your time with him,' she offered apologetically.

'That's OK,' Marta replied. 'He thought you might want to stay.' Louise turned to face the woman, who laughed. 'Our Master does enjoy the role play. He can be quite imaginative.'

Louise downed her drink and stood, a little wobbly still. 'I'd better be getting back.'

'Have another drink.' Marta returned Louise's glass to her hand and refilled it. 'The car should be back in about ten minutes, after dropping the Master off.'

Resignedly Louise sat back down, and watched Marta getting dressed into jeans and a T-shirt; a complete contrast to her earlier smart attire. Her curiosity got the better of her. 'So, you know what he looks like?'

Marta looked at her for a moment before answering. 'Yes.'

Louise waited for more, but Marta wasn't forthcoming. 'So, what's he like?'

Marta just smiled.

'Will I ever get to see him? Properly, I mean.'

Marta shrugged. 'Who knows?'

There was a knock at the door. Marta went to answer it. She came back moments later.

'Your car is here,' she announced. Louise downed her drink and stood. She walked to the door but was intercepted by Marta, who kissed her on both cheeks. 'I'll see you at your initiation,' she said. 'I'm sure you'll enjoy it.'

'Thank you,' Louise replied, before leaving the flat.

She climbed the steps carefully, and got into the car. On the journey home her imagination ran overtime. Why did he keep his face covered? Why had she not heard his voice? Was he disfigured? Was he someone famous?

It didn't seem too long before the car stopped and the door opened. She got out, thanked the driver, and then made her way back to her apartment. As she entered she heard giggling coming from the lounge. She walked through to find Helen and Anna on her sofa. Anna stood.

'So, did you meet him?' asked Helen.

'Yes,' replied Louise.

'You were quite some time,' said Anna. 'What happened?'

'I...' Louise paused, thinking back to her instructions. 'I'm not allowed to talk of it,' she finally said.

Anna's eyes widened. 'Wow! So you're joining us!'

Louise's mouth opened, but she couldn't think what to say. She ended up just nodding.

'Was Marta there?'

Louise nodded again.

Anna laughed. 'That explains why you were so long,' she said.

Louise blushed. She went to get herself a glass from the kitchen and joined the other two, pouring herself a drink from the open bottle on the table. She downed about half before dropping into the sofa. She gave her glass a puzzled look. 'What kind of wine is this?' she asked.

'Non-alcoholic,' replied Helen, apologetically.

'Drinking games are out of the question, I'm afraid,' joked Anna.

Louise smiled. 'Probably for the best,' she said, pushing off her shoes and putting her feet up on the table. 'Have you met him yet?' she asked Anna.

'Friday.'

'I hope it'll be all right.'

'Don't worry about it. What's the worst that could happen? They're not going to throw me out. They'd have done that by now if they were.'

There were a few moments' silence, which Helen broke.

'When will I get invited to join? I don't want to miss out on all the fun,' she said with a grin.

Anna laughed. 'You'll still be invited to the parties, if you wish. But I don't think you realise how privileged you are.'

'Privileged? How so?' Helen poured herself another drink.

'It isn't everyone that gets invited to assist Annabelle.'

'You have though, haven't you?'

Anna shook her head. 'No. But if she likes you, you may be invited to join her Court.'

'Oh really?' Helen gloated a little.

Feeling weary Louise downed the remaining liquid from her glass, and stood. 'I'm sorry, girls, but I'm off to bed.'

'We'll keep the noise down,' promised Helen.

'Even if I have to gag her,' added Anna.

They had a giggle, and Louise left them to it. She didn't hear what they got up to, as she was out as soon as her head hit the pillow.

That night she had vivid dreams; she cried out... and woke up.

'Is everything OK?' Helen was in her room, looking concerned.

'Yes, I think so,' replied Louise, groggily.

'You cried out,' she said, by way of explanation.

'Oh, sorry for disturbing you,' apologised Louise.

'You didn't. I was having breakfast.'

Louise looked at the time. It was almost ten. 'It's a good job I'm not working today.'

CHAPTER NINE

CONSERVATOR

Over the next few days Louise and Helen got to see a film they'd wanted to watch at the cinema, get last minute tickets to an afternoon performance of a stage show, and visit some of the museums and palaces they'd never got around to seeing.

Anna called Helen, and asked to see her Friday afternoon at her offices, regarding the distribution of assets from her relationship with David. Helen and Louise arranged to meet up afterwards in a Holborn pub, not far from Anna's office, and then they'd make plans for the evening there.

Louise arrived at the pub to find Helen sat with a man. Helen stood and waved, so Louise made her way over.

'Louise, this is Lucian. Lucian, this is my best friend Louise.'

Lucian stood and shook hands with Louise. 'Pleased to meet you,' he said, with a nod of his head.

To Louise's estimation he was late-thirties, early-forties, short dark hair, receding, a little overweight though not obese, wearing a dark three-piece suit and a tasteful tie. She eyed him suspiciously.

'Can I get you a drink?' he offered.

Before she could refuse Helen chipped in. 'I'll have a fresh orange juice, no ice.'

'And for you?' He looked at Louise intently.

'The same,' she said shortly.

Lucian walked off to the bar to order the drinks.

'Who's he?' she hissed.

'My knight in shining armour,' replied Helen.

Louise had heard this before from Helen, usually an early indication of more trouble to come. 'What's that supposed to mean?'

Helen recounted the tale. She'd been sitting at the bar waiting for her, having got out earlier from her meeting with Anna than expected. Anna really had everything sewn up, and all Helen had to do was give her consent to proceed, which she did.

She'd resisted the urge to order wine to celebrate, and instead went for an orange juice. At which point some obnoxious guy sat next to her, talked about how she should let her hair down, have something stronger, and maybe spend the evening with him. Helen refused, and refused, and refused, but this was one of those guys who didn't take no for an answer.

Then Lucian showed up, walked over to her and greeted her like an old friend. When he leant over to kiss her on the cheek he whispered in her ear, 'If you want rid of this fellow play along. As soon as he's gone I'll leave you to it, and you can get on with your evening in peace.'

Helen had looked up at him as he moved away, stood, and wrapped her arms around him, saying loudly, 'I've not seen you in simply ages. How are you doing?'

Obnoxious guy had scuttled into a corner, while Lucian and Helen sat down at a table.

Lucian returned with the drinks.

'I see your *friend* has just left the bar, and as you have another friend to offer support I'll allow you two ladies to continue with your planned evening. Allow me to apologise for any disruption of service.' He bowed, and Helen laughed.

'No please,' she said. 'Stay with us a while.' She put on her poshest accent. 'It's not often one meets a true gentleman, you know.'

'I'd hardly call myself a true gentleman, though I do try,' he said modestly. 'But I'm sure you and your friend have things you wish to catch up on.'

'No, please stay,' Louise said. 'I apologise for my cold reception earlier, but my friend,' she looked at Helen, 'has a habit of attracting trouble, and I assumed the worst. For that I am sorry. Now please stay, and allow us to buy you a drink in return for your act of kindness.'

'I couldn't possibly accept a drink,' he replied, holding his palm up to emphasise his words. 'But I cannot refuse the offer to spend time in the company of two very attractive ladies.'

Helen made space beside her, and he sat.

'So, what do you do?' asked Louise.

Lucian looked a little uncomfortable. 'Well, er, it's a little difficult to explain,' he started. 'I supposed the easiest description would be just to say I work with Information Security, but I'd rather not discuss work, if that's all right with you.'

Helen's eyes just looked at him. Louise wondered if it could work; he was hardly her usual type. And although it struck her that Helen had developed a taste for sexual adventure in the past week, she didn't see this man as the sexually adventurous type.

Then again, looks can be deceiving, as Louise herself knew only too well.

The three of them chatted about all sorts of things, but never anything too personal to any of them. He didn't ask how they knew each other, what their jobs were, how long they'd lived in London. Instead they spoke about the news, holiday destinations, music, theatre and films. Whenever the conversation began to encroach on anyone's personal details he subtly manoeuvred the conversation away.

Louise was a little relieved, but also intrigued. Information Security he'd said; could he work for the government?

When he finished his drink he stood. 'Well, thank you ladies for your company and conversation. It's not often I have an intelligent chat with strangers I've met in the pub, so please accept my appreciation. I'll allow you to go off and enjoy the rest of your planned evening.'

Helen stood and held his arm. 'Please don't go,' she said. 'We don't have anything planned, and I've enjoyed our conversation too. As this place is getting busy, shall we go back to ours and continue our conversation?'

'That sounds lovely, but I really don't want to impose,' he replied.

Helen looked at Louise, who stood and finished her orange juice.

'You're more than welcome,' she said. 'It'd be nice to have someone to talk intelligently with. I've only had Helen for the last few days.'

Helen punched her on the arm and Lucian laughed.

'Then at least allow me to bring a bottle of wine back with us,' he said. 'There's nothing like good wine and good company.'

He bought two bottles, and together they returned to Louise's apartment. Helen showed him through to the lounge while Louise fetched three glasses from the kitchen and took them through. Lucian opened the bottle but Helen refused, asking Louise for a soft drink instead.

'It isn't drugged,' he said.

Louise and Helen looked at each other, before Helen explained.

'When I have too much to drink I usually end up in trouble,' she admitted. 'So

I've stopped.'

'That's a very sensible precaution,' he said. 'But you can enjoy all things in moderation. And besides, both your friend and I are here to ensure that you don't drink too much and get yourself into trouble.'

Helen relented. 'OK. I'll have one.'

Lucian poured out three drinks.

Louise got a text message from Anna. *Are you at home?*

Yes. Why?

Mind if I come round?

See you later.

Louise looked at her phone thoughtfully. Wasn't it tonight Anna was seeing him?

'Problems?' Lucian asked.

'Oh, no,' she replied. 'Just a friend.'

They continued conversing on a range of topics, mostly amusing, never too serious. About quarter of an hour later Lucian excused himself to the bathroom.

Helen leaned over to Louise and spoke quietly. 'What do you think?' she whispered conspiratorially.

'He seems like a nice enough guy.'

'Do you think we should give him a treat, after him rescuing me?'

Louise stared at her, hoping she didn't mean what she thought she was intimating.

'I bet he's never had a threesome.'

Louise's fears were confirmed. 'Helen, don't you think...?' She was interrupted as Lucian returned to the room.

'Shall I leave until you finish your conversation?' he asked.

'No, no, that's fine,' said Helen, patting the seat beside her.

Louise hoped she put across to Helen her reluctance to get down and dirty with a stranger; reading subtlety wasn't Helen's strong point.

The doorbell rang. Relieved at the interruption Louise stood and let Anna in. She didn't look too happy.

'What's the matter?' Louise asked, but before Anna answered they heard Helen and Lucian laughing in the lounge.

'You have visitors?' Anna asked.

'Just Helen, and some guy who rescued her from an obnoxious prick in the bar.'

'I'll leave you to it,' said Anna, turning away.

'No, please,' said Louise. 'Helen wants us to have a threesome, and I'm not so keen.'

Anna laughed. 'So now she's your pimp?'

Louise closed the front door and led Anna through to the lounge. Helen stood to welcome her.

'Anna! Meet my knight in shining armour, this is...'

'Lucian.' Anna finished Helen's sentence. 'What mischief are you up to?'

'Anna!' Lucian laughed, standing to give her a hug. 'You know all about mischief. But I'm innocent of all charges on this occasion.'

'So you didn't set up the situation to meet these ladies?'

'Actually, no,' he said. 'And as well you know, I would only set up situations for your Master.'

'Oh, an actual coincidence,' mocked Anna.

'I'm afraid so. Some chap making a complete arse of himself, bothering dear Helen here.'

'How gallant.' Anna strutted past him, heading for the wine bottle.

'You know each other?' Helen asked.

'He knows all about you too,' said Anna plainly.

'Anna, dear, you make me sound like some sort of stalker.'

'What do you mean?' Helen looked at Lucian suspiciously.

'Lucian vets all the Court members and party guests. He knew who you were all along.'

Lucian shrugged. 'It's true, alas. But I could hardly be on first name terms until we were introduced. It wouldn't be proper.' He looked at Helen. 'But when I saw you being bothered by that chap, I had to do something.'

Helen thought for a moment. 'I'm glad you did.'

She gave him a peck on the cheek, taking him by surprise.

'Right! How about a game?' Helen suggested, filling her glass again and dropping back into her seat.

'A card game?' asked Lucian.

'Strip poker?' Helen giggled.

Lucian blushed a little at her suggestion. 'How about cribbage?' he suggested.

'How do you play?' asked Louise, after the others had shrugged.

Lucian talked through the rules, giving examples. Then he suggested they have a game together, first pair up to 121. He and Helen played against Louise and Anna. Before they started Helen asked about having forfeits for the losers; Lucian looked a little uncomfortable.

'I would imagine you've seen just about everything, but what's your fetish, Lucian?' Anna asked.

He paused. 'I'm not so keen on some of the more, um, extreme activities. I don't like inflicting pain. But I do like to watch.'

Anna smiled. 'In that case how about, if we lose, Louise and I put on a little show for you. And if you lose, Louise and I get to spank your arses.'

Helen looked at Louise and giggled. Lucian looked at Helen, and agreed to the terms. Play began. The game scoring was close, with Louise keeping tabs. Helen had just counted her hand, and the totals were 117 for Helen and Lucian, and 120 for Anna and Louise.

'Looks like they'll win in the next hand,' said Helen resignedly.

'You still have the box to count, my dear,' said Lucian.

Helen took the four cards and placed them face up, one by one. 'Four of Hearts. Three of Hearts. Nine of Hearts. King of Hearts. Nothing!' She slumped back.

'But with the Queen of Hearts turned up before,' Lucian said, 'that scores us five points for all five cards being hearts.'

Helen sat up and looked. Then she smiled, before looking over at Anna and Louise. 'I suppose that means...' she began, but Anna had started stroking Louise's cheek, gently turning Louise's head toward her. She moved in to kiss her; a couple of short soft kisses on her lips, before moving in for a longer kiss, her tongue working Louise's mouth. Louise relaxed and allowed Anna to lead the way. She felt Anna's hand stroke her neck, before unbuttoning her blouse from the top downwards. She felt her way to Anna's shoulder, and started to undo Anna's blouse as well. A few moments later both were sat with their blouses open, shrugging them off their shoulders.

Louise glanced quickly at Helen and Lucian. He was sitting cross-legged, possibly hiding a hard on, whilst Helen watched Anna and Louise with a smirk, her hand again stroking Lucian's thigh.

Anna moved in again, stroking Louise's arms, kissing her again. Louise stroked Anna's arms in return, mirroring Anna's moves. They unclasped each other's bras, freeing their breasts, before caressing each other's, all the while kissing passionately. Louise's pulse raced.

Anna moved, kissing Louise's neck, down to her breasts. She kissed around Louise's areola, stroking the other breast with her hand. Louise looked at Lucian and Helen, her eyes half closed. Helen was unzipping Lucian's fly. She gasped as Anna bit her nipple. Anna continued to work her magic with her tongue, while Louise continued to watch Helen as she freed Lucian's cock from his trousers, and began to stroke it gently.

Anna's hands moved down to Louise's skirt. Louise lifter her hips to allow her room to pull off her skirt and panties, before Anna stood to remove her own. She then got down between Louise's thighs, licking around her clitoris. Louise watched Lucian and Helen again, Lucian running his fingers through Helen's hair as she licked up and down his shaft.

Louise ran her fingers through Anna's hair. Anna responded by moving back up to kiss her. Louise could taste her juices on Anna's lips. She pulled her head back and nodded towards Lucian and Helen.

Anna looked, and then stood up, hands on her hips. 'I was hoping to have your undivided attention,' she said. 'But it seems you're being distracted.'

'But such a sweet distraction, I could hardly refuse.' Lucian grinned.

'I think we need a change of rules,' she said.

Helen raised her head to watch Anna leave the room, before looking at Louise, who shrugged in response. Anna returned moments later, blindfold in hand, which she placed over Lucian's eyes.

'Stand up,' she ordered, helping him to his feet. She stroked his neck with the backs of her fingers.

'What now?' he asked.

Anna laughed. 'Well, with three beautiful ladies in the room you couldn't go wrong, could you?'

'With you, Anna, nothing's that simple.'

'How well you know me,' she replied. 'So, any one of us may do something to you. But you have to say which one of us is doing it.'

'Sounds nice. What happens when I guess right?'

'You get a treat.'

'And if I'm wrong?'

She slowly circled him before answering. 'Either you have to treat us...'

'Or...?' he asked.

'Or we get to punish you.' She silently indicated to Helen to strip off, which she did quickly and quietly.

'OK,' Lucian replied, uncertainly.

Anna moved Helen and Louise to stand by the sofa, then whispered in Helen's ear. Helen walked quietly over and kissed Lucian on the lips before standing back.

'I do like your perfume, Helen,' he said, smiling confidently.

'Is she a nice kisser?' Anna asked.

'Indeed she is,' Lucian replied.

'Helen, would you indulge him a little longer this time?'

Helen moved back to him, held his head while she kissed him again. After a few moments his arms wrapped around her, hands feeling the naked flesh, exploring her figure until Anna put a stop to it.

'I think that's enough of that,' she said, pulling his hands away from Helen, who stood back, joining Louise.

'Now I think you should keep your arms by your sides, unless we say otherwise. I don't want you getting an unfair advantage.'

'Very well.'

Anna whispered in Louise's ear. 'Take his jacket off.'

Louise hung back for a moment, before walking behind Lucian and easing off his jacket.

'That, I think, is Louise.'

She stopped, staring at Anna, wondering what she'd be expected to do.

'Give him a bit of a shoulder massage, before helping him off with his waistcoat and tie.'

Louise did as Anna said, rubbing his shoulders and neck, before moving to his front and unbuttoning his waistcoat, taking it off, and then loosening and removing his tie.

'Thank you,' Lucian said.

She moved back to where Anna and Helen were. Anna waited a few moments before stepping behind him. She reached around to unbutton his shirt, kissing his neck sensuously. She stopped when she got halfway down.

Lucian waited a moment, before answering. 'You wear a distinctive perfume, Anna.'

She sighed, and continued to unbutton his shirt and kiss his neck. Lucian's chest swelled in reaction to her soft kisses and he sighed with pleasure.

Anna pulled his shirt off. 'I think you're having it too much your own way,' she said.

'Says she, who blindly obeys a masked man.'

She went to Helen and whispered again. In response Helen went to her handbag, retrieved her perfume and passed it to Anna, who squirted herself, Helen and Louise with it. 'Now who will undo his trousers?' she asked rhetorically.

Helen let out a sound with her hand up, obviously eager to carry this out, but Anna held up her hand and walked over herself. Standing behind him she reached around and unbuckled his belt, slowly unzipped his fly and unfastened the button. She let the trousers drop to his ankles before slowly peeling down his boxer shorts.

'Ah, dear sweet Helen.'

Nobody replied. Anna waited before giving him an almighty slap across his buttocks.

'What?' Lucian retorted.

Her lips by his ear, Anna spoke softly. 'I'm afraid you're wrong.'

The surprise on his face was obvious. 'You sprayed yourself with Helen's perfume.'

'Clever boy, but not clever enough. It was that or a clothes peg on your nose.'

He laughed. 'Fair play.'

Anna walked back, took Louise by the arm, and led her to just by Lucian. Anna started to circle Lucian's nipple, before moving her head close to start to lick it, occasionally grazing it with her teeth.

'Ah!' said Lucian confidently, 'that would be...' Louise moved in, flicking his nipple with her tongue, '...two of you!' he finished, in a different tone.

Anna and Louise continued for a short while, licking, flicking, and caressing his nipples with their fingers. Then Anna signalled Louise to move back.

'I'll say Anna and Helen.'

Anna bent down and bit his bottom.

'Ouch! Well I'd be half right!' he insisted.

'But you got the one person not involved wrong!' Anna slapped him across the buttocks, then she and Louise returned to Helen's side.

Anna made a hand gesture, to which Louise stepped forward, gently stroking Lucian's semi-erect manhood from base to tip and back again. It responded by continuing its upward journey. She stopped after a minute or so.

'Er,' Lucian paused. 'I'll guess Louise.'

For a moment nobody said or did anything. Lucian's face began to show doubt, but then relief and pleasure as Louise recommenced the stroking, making him even harder, with her other hand stroking his balls, before finishing with a quick lick from base to tip, to which Lucian's whole body responded.

Pleased with herself she returned to the other girls. With no consultation Anna walked behind him, crouched down, her hands parting his buttocks, and

Lucian's reaction showed he enjoyed Anna's rimming technique. Louise could only imaging what she was doing, but was familiar with the effect.

'That could only be Anna,' he said confidently.

She reached around and grabbed his cock, massaging its length up and down, before moving around to tickle his balls with first her fingers, and then her tongue. Lucian began to groan, at which point she stopped and returned to Helen and Louise.

'What next?' whispered Helen.

'Lie down!' ordered Anna, and Lucian got down on the floor, on his back, cock pointing upwards.

'Do you want to sit on his face?' Anna whispered to Louise, who shook her head in response.

Anna looked at Helen, who nodded, but before she could move Anna had gone over to Lucian. Standing astride his head she moved slowly, down to a kneeling position, then lowered her pussy onto his face. She smiled as they heard Lucian's tongue licking her. He began to raise his hands but Anna slapped them down. A muffled laugh could be heard, and Anna raised herself enough to allow him to speak.

'I was going to say Helen, but that was an Anna slap!'

She sighed, lowered herself again, allowing him to continue licking, and bent over, taking his cock into her mouth, giving it a few deep sucks, her cheeks hollowing. His hands wavered, fingers clenching and unclenching, before gently stroking Anna's sides.

'Do you think I could join in?' Helen whispered to Louise, but before she could do anything Anna stood, went to her handbag and extracted a packet of condoms. She skilfully unrolled one over his cock with her mouth, then returned to Helen and Louise before speaking again.

'You've done well so far, Lucian. But now for your final test. Get it right and you will be treated. If you're wrong, then you have to treat our every whim.'

Lucian smiled. 'As you wish.'

Before she could do or say anything more Helen stood over him, squatted, and held his penis in place while she lowered herself onto it. Both of them gasped as he entered her. She carefully went all the way down, pausing for a few moments with him fully embedded. Then her hands on his chest she started slowly sliding up and down, the squelching noises indicating how turned on she was.

'If I'm right can I remove the blindfold and move my arms?' Lucian asked.

Anna placed a hand on Helen's shoulder, who reluctantly stopped all movement. They waited.

'Helen.'

Anna bent over him and removed the blindfold, making sure she blocked his view of Helen.

'Lucian, I'm sorry to say...' she paused, '...you're correct.'

She moved away allowing him the full view of Helen straddling him. His smile widened.

'I'm very pleased to make your acquaintance,' he said.

'I should hope you are, kind sir,' replied Helen, before gyrating on him, palms still on his chest for support. His hands started on her thighs, stroking and squeezing, before caressing up her sides and coming to rest on her breasts. His thumbs circled her nipples before tweaking them, and then he massaged them with his palms, stroking gently as she continued to work on his cock.

'Does it make you tingle inside?' Anna whispered to Louise.

Louise smiled. 'A little, yes.'

She felt Anna's hand stroking her thigh, and then moving between her legs, moving ever so slowly upward. She turned to face Anna and kissed her. Anna's lips felt cool and soft. They lingered for a few moments, before sitting down on the sofa. Louise caressed Anna's hair while Anna went back to stroking her thighs, slowly edging towards her pussy. It ached in anticipation of the touch. Louise moved to try and get Anna's fingers closer, but Anna removed her hand.

Louise pouted but Anna whispered in her ear, 'Go and sit on his face.' Louise shot her a scowl, but Anna urged, 'Go on.'

After a moment's hesitation Louise got up and stood over Lucian, who looked up at her. She bent and kissed Helen on the lips. Helen's hands moved up to Louise's shoulders, and she gently pushed her tongue into Louise's mouth. Lucian's breathing became louder and deeper. They broke off and looked down at him, then as Helen leant back a little, her hands now supporting her on Lucian's thighs, Louise lowered herself onto his face. His hands moved to hold her thighs, and his face moved to meet her, at first teasing her clitoris, and then as she sat further down his tongue penetrating her, darting in and out, his hands gently squeezing her soft thighs. She gazed at Helen, gyrating on his cock.

Anna knelt behind Helen and wrapped her arms around her, squeezing her breasts and kissing her shoulders and neck. Helen began to groan, and Anna's hand dropped to squeeze her buttock. Helen turned her head to the side and they kissed a slow, sensuous kiss.

Louise found herself subconsciously gyrating in time with Helen's movements, and then she started to moan.

'I think you two are enjoying yourselves too much,' said Anna.

'No such thing,' gasped Helen, her brow furrowed with pleasure. 'You're only jealous.'

'That'd be it,' said Anna. 'I'd like in on a bit more of the action.'

Lucian pushed Louise upward slightly, to give himself enough room to speak. 'This is the first time I've been treated to ladies fighting over me,' he mumbled from the warmth of Louise's groin.

'I don't want to stop,' pleaded Helen.

'Why don't you try his tongue for a while?' suggested Anna.

Helen looked dubiously at Louise.

'It really is rather nice,' Louise murmured, eyes half closed.

'OK...' Helen conceded.

Somewhat listlessly they both stood, Louise moving away to allow Helen to lower herself onto his face, immediately gasping blissfully.

'Oooh, I do like that,' she said with a twinkle in her eye. She wiggled a little on his face.

Meanwhile Anna lowered herself onto his cock, writhing up and down with a vengeance, riding hard and fast. She grabbed Louise, pulled her close and kissed her, tongue working as hard and fast in Louise's mouth as her pelvis was working on Lucian. Louise felt another pair of hands pulling her, so she broke away from Anna and kissed Helen again, whose hands were all over her, stroking and squeezing and nipping. Anna prised them apart and leaned to Helen for a deep kiss, then began to alternate between the two of them, first Helen, and then Louise, back and forth, her kissing becoming more heated each time, getting more breathless with each exchange.

Then she leaned back and started moving her groin even faster. Lucian's fingers found their way between her legs, stroking and massaging her clit. Suddenly she lunged forward, pushing Helen off his face, and started kissing him passionately as she continued to pummel his groin. Helen and Louise watched as she panted through the kisses, before slowing down, making the kisses gentler, and then stilling to a halt. She sat motionless for a little while, before getting up.

Lucian's cock was still erect, so Helen got him to stand as she sat back on the sofa, leading him between her legs. He carefully entered her, lifting her legs a little to accommodate him. Helen sighed with his first thrust, then as he got into his rhythm she looked at Louise and beckoned her over. Louise moved to straddle her face and lowered herself. Helen began by teasing her clit, before pushing her tongue into her pussy.

Anna moved behind Lucian and reach between his legs. Louise imagined she was massaging his balls, but as Helen began to moan through her pussy she thought that perhaps Anna was doing something to her instead. As Helen's tongue worked she felt herself getting wetter; a combination of the girl's saliva and her own juices.

Helen moaned again. Louise knelt up and looked down at her face; she was happy, gasping in time with Lucian's thrusts. So Louise climbed off the sofa and was intercepted by Anna, who held and kissed her.

'You've been a bit neglected,' Anna whispered in her ear. 'I'll make it up to you later.'

Helen's squeals were getting more intense. Anna and Louise watched, arms around each other. Helen's breasts jiggled with each of Lucian's thrusts. She moved her legs and wrapped them around him, limiting his stroke length, and he fell forward. She grabbed his shoulders with both hands and pulled him over her, kissing him feverishly. He got back into his rhythm, groaning through their kisses, Helen moaning with each thrust, both building in intensity.

Her eyes closed tightly, her face contorted, her body shuddered, and then she went eerily silent, holding her breath, her whole body tense, before she let go, and with a sudden scream she hit her climax.

Her orgasm triggered Lucian. His movements slowed, becoming harder and deeper as he grunted with each thrust.

Suddenly Helen pushed him away. 'Oh no, no, no!' She rolled off the sofa onto her knees and pulled the condom off Lucian's cock, stroking it a few strokes before engulfing it in her mouth.

Anna got down beside her, coaxing his balls, taking it in turns to suck his cock. He stiffened, and Anna managed to have him when he shot his first load. She moved off and wanked him over Helen's breasts. Her hand slowed as Lucian began to relax a little, and Helen stood, semen oozing in her cleavage and coating her breasts. She ran a finger down the trail, and seductively sucked her finger clean. Not to be outdone Anna licked his discharge from Helen's breasts, before kissing Helen again, the two of them giggling.

Lucian caressed Helen and she kissed him, a long and sensuous kiss. He gave Anna a peck on the cheek, and smiled over at Louise. 'Well thank you ladies for a memorable night,' he said.

'Always the gentleman,' said Helen, and he gave her a polite nod.

'But would you excuse me while I go and freshen up a little? I think I'd feel a little uncomfortable travelling home in my current state.'

Helen took his arm. 'Won't you stay?'

'I wouldn't want to impose.'

She looked him in the eyes. 'I'd really like you to.'

He took a deep breath. 'I don't want to outstay my welcome, though I do enjoy your company.'

'Then you're staying, if you don't mind sharing a bed with me.' Helen fluttered her eyelashes at him.

Lucian smiled. 'An offer I could hardly refuse. But I'd still like to freshen up.'

She led him by the hand to the bathroom, leaving Anna and Louise in the lounge. Anna started picking up her clothes.

'Don't think you're leaving me to play gooseberry,' Louise said.

'And where would I sleep?'

'You promised to make it up to me, so you're coming to bed with me.' She stroked a finger against Anna's soft cheek before adding, 'And who said anything about sleep?'

CHAPTER TEN

NON DORMIUNT

Helen and Lucian returned, showered and dressed again, Helen in her nightwear, Lucian in his shirt and trousers. Anna had put her underwear back on, whereas Louise had changed into her nightwear, and made drinks for all. They sat back relaxing in the lounge. The conversation was varied, but during a brief lull Louise decided to find out what was bothering Anna before.

'So what happened earlier? You didn't seem too happy when you arrived.'

Anna's face changed, and she looked over at Helen and Lucian. 'I'm not supposed to discuss it.'

Louise eyed her briefly, before Lucian chipped in, 'She's been promoted.'

Anna glared at him.

'It would have happened sooner if it was up to me,' he added.

'Isn't that a good thing?' asked Louise.

'Enjoyed where I was,' Anna replied.

'Unfortunately times change, and the Court, and the Order, have changing requirements.'

Anna looked again at him.

'Only two people know the Court and order rules better than you. That's why you were such a good Improba.'

'So why should I have to change?'

'Because you couldn't stay in that role forever, and because we need you more as an arbitra now.'

'Arbitra?' Helen said. 'Just like...'

'The lady on the door,' finished Anna. 'Yes. They're our "police" force.'

'Surely that could be fun. Do you have to dress up as policewomen?' Helen joked, but Anna wasn't impressed.

'It means more responsibility,' said Lucian. 'But the only person qualified to deal with the issues is you.'

'What issues?' Anna demanded.

Lucian paused before answering. 'It will be discussed with you at a time of your Master's choosing. Now let's not ruin what has otherwise been a wonderful evening.'

Helen and Lucian retired to her room, leaving Anna and Louise alone. Anna was pensive, so Louise interrupted her thoughts. 'I hope you're thinking about what you're going to do to me.'

Anna looked up and smiled. 'I'll show you.' She grabbed Louise's arm and pulled her into Louise's bedroom. She stripped her and tied her arms and legs to the corners of the bed. 'I'll be back,' she said, as she went out of the room.

Louise waited for what seemed like an age before Anna returned, and when she did she was completely naked, and had her bag with her. She smiled at Louise's quizzical expression, put the bag on the bedside table and knelt astride her shoulders, her knees sinking into the soft mattress, then began to lower herself onto the spellbound face beneath her.

'I thought you were supposed to be pleasuring me,' Louise protested.

'For your impudence you will pleasure me,' Anna said. 'Don't you like licking my pussy?'

Louise raised her lips to meet her, and began to lick between her legs; Anna tasted of cherries, so Louise started to lick enthusiastically around her pussy and clit, making her very wet. Then she eased her head back a little and blew, her breath cooling Anna's wet skin.

Anna giggled. 'I think I need something a little more,' she said. She reached into her bag, producing a dildo gag. She knelt up and fastened it around Louise's head before rubbing lube over it, and then lowering herself slowly onto it. As she moved up and down Louise could do very little but try and keep her head still. As Anna continued to do her thing on the dildo Louise could smell cherries mixed with Anna's juices, the erotic aroma getting stronger.

Anna made a few noises of frustration before sitting right down. Louise's nose nudged between Anna's soft buttocks. She felt Anna lean over to the bag again, retrieving something else from it. She heard the buzz as Anna turned it on, and then felt the vibrations around her chin; Anna was giving her clit some additional stimulation.

She had the urge to grab Anna's thighs and pull her in closer, tighter, but bound as she was she unable to; she just had to sit tight until Anna had finished.

Anna's pelvis jerked suddenly and Louise took it as a cue to start pumping the dildo into her. She pushed her head back into the pillows before pressing up into Anna, being rewarded by a moan. She continued, though her jaw was beginning to ache with the vibrations.

The scent of Anna's juices and the cherries became even stronger and she pushed harder with the dildo, and then she felt the vibrations slow, and a pause in Anna's breathing. For a few moments all she could hear was the vibrator slowing down, and then it stopped. She felt the dildo pull, as Anna's muscles contracted, and then Anna leaned forward, one hand reaching under her to keep the dildo still as she lifted herself off it and knelt beside Louise on the bed.

Louise looked at her, still unable to speak. Anna smiled and stroked her cheek before taking off the gag. She gave Louise a lingering kiss, and Louise tasted cherries again. She then watched as Anna licked her own juices off the dildo and the vibrator, then lay next to her on the bed.

Louise felt a little exasperated, a little frustrated, a little neglected; Anna had just used her for her own pleasure. But she thought better of saying anything, as she was still tied up and at Anna's mercy.

She hadn't known Anna for long at all, so how had she let herself get drawn in so quickly and deeply. She thought of Helen, in the next room, with a virtual stranger. Had she put not only herself but her friend in danger? She tensed a little, but then relaxed as Anna started to stroke her face, moving down her neck, her breasts, her sides and her thighs. She breathed deeply, then turned to speak, but Anna put a finger to her lips, starting to kiss her way from Louise's forehead down to her toes, which she kissed one by one, licking between them, taking them into her mouth and sucking.

Anna then kissed her way back up her legs, crossing between each one, ensuring every inch of both had been covered. On reaching the tops of Louise's thighs she continued upward, softly kissing and licking Louise's belly. She toyed with Louise's breasts and nipples, kissing them, and continued up, her whole body moving up, brushing against Louise's skin.

She kissed Louise's throat, finishing on her lips, her body covering Louise, her hands stroking up and down her arms and flanks as she kissed her. Louise closed her eyes, enjoying the sensations, her reservations gone.

Anna lifted her head, smiled, and after a moment's pause resumed the kiss. Louise felt a hand running through her hair, and then gripping it, pulling her head back. She let out a gasp, her eyes widening as she looked into Anna's eyes. Anna kissed her throat, grazing her skin with her teeth. Louise rolled her head to one side to give Anna fuller access, and Anna spent dreamy moments kissing and grazing Louise's neck and shoulder.

Louise sighed and closed her eyes as she felt Anna's hands moving down her body, softly stroking her skin, making her tingle. She moaned quietly and Anna moved her kisses down, following the strokes of her hands. As she approached her nipples Louise arched her back up, pushing her breasts towards her. Anna took a nipple into her mouth, sucking it, gently at first, then a little harder, occasionally flicking it with her tongue. Louise moaned a little louder, her nipple hardening at Anna's attention.

Anna stroked and tweaked Louise's other nipple until it was just as hard, and then gave it a few kisses, licks and flicks for good measure, before continuing down, kissing around her naval, and continuing down.

Louise felt a pause in activity, and opened her eyes to see Anna climbing between her legs. In readiness she lifted her pelvis a little. Anna squeezed her hands under her buttocks, kissing the insides of her thighs, alternating from one to the other, slowly making her way up. She kissed around Louise's clitoris, gently sucking it into her mouth and licking. Louise gasped as she felt a finger enter her. Anna pushed another finger in, sliding the two in and out, massaging gently.

She removed them and Louise watched her slipping them into her mouth, sucking the juices. It turned Louise on even more and she moved her hips, groaning, wanting more. Anna pushed her tongue into her, licking, her nose rubbing against her clit. Louise felt a finger massaging around her anus and lifted her pelvis again to accommodate it. Her eyes widened when Anna pushed inside, massaging her rectum. Louise tightened and relaxed around the finger, making the most of the sensations.

Anna sat up and reached for her bag, retrieving her vibrating butt-plug. She squeezed some lubricant over it before pushing it gently into Louise's arse. Louise lifted again and closed her eyes, savouring the entry. Once in she lowered herself, and Anna switched it on. Louise winced, feeling the vibrations flow through her abdomen. Anna resumed her tonguing of her pussy and fingering of her clit. Louise ground her hips, holding on for as long as she could, but she orgasmed quickly.

Eventually her bliss subsided and she relaxed, lowering her buttocks into the mattress. Anna sat and massaged the feeling back into Louise's legs, untying them as she did, then Louise used their freedom to pull Anna into a warm cuddle.

'Thank you,' she whispered.

'But I still haven't untied your hands,' said Anna, with a wicked smile.

Louise sighed a happy sigh. 'Perhaps another time. I'm tired now.'

'Me too,' agreed Anna, untying her wrists.

They showered and returned to bed, cuddling under the duvet. It had been a while since Louise had slept with a warm body beside her, and the first time it was a woman. She fell asleep quickly, feeling fully refreshed when waking in the morning. She looked at Anna, still sleeping. She watched her for a while, trying to analyse her feelings. Despite her strong affection for her she was still devoted to their Master, whoever he may be. Then she wondered what his feelings for her were. Could she have someone else in her life while he was around, or until she found out?

Anna stirred and rolled over. She opened her eyes and smiled at Louise. 'Morning,' she said languidly. 'Sleep well?'

Louise smiled in return. 'Surprisingly well,' she replied. 'How about some breakfast?'

Anna moved in closer to Louise, ready to kiss her, her hand making its way down between Louise's legs.

'That's not quite what I meant,' Louise giggled.

They both looked up when they heard footsteps outside the door, and a quiet knock.

'Are you awake?' It was Helen.

'Yes,' answered Louise.

'Not interrupting anything am I?' beamed Helen, looking around the door.

Louise felt herself blush.

'How did you enjoy your night with Lucian?' asked Anna.

Now Helen blushed. 'Breakfast will be ready in about five minutes,' she said, changing the subject before ducking back out of the bedroom.

Louise and Anna got dressed and went through to the kitchen, where Lucian was preparing breakfast.

'Hope you don't mind,' he said. 'I thought I ought to repay your hospitality somehow.'

'Eggs Benedict,' said Anna, looking over his shoulder. 'Did you make the sauce yourself?'

'Of course,' he snorted.

He plated up and served it to the breakfast bar, which the four of them sat around.

'Looks delicious,' said Helen.

Louise cut into the muffin, spilling the yolk. It spread the glorious yellow colour around her plate, which she mopped up with the muffin and bacon.

'Any plans for today?' Helen asked generally.

'I have some business to attend to,' answered Lucian.

'That's a shame,' she said, a little forlornly.

'We can have dinner tonight, if you wish,' he suggested.

Helen brightened up. 'That would be lovely.' She looked at Anna and Louise. 'So what about during the day?'

'I'm open to suggestion,' Anna replied, as Louise's phone began to ring.

It was Sally. 'Do you know the dress code for work?' Louise asked. She didn't want her new assistant wearing the short skirts and low tops she wore for their previous employer. She moved the phone away from her mouth for a moment. 'Anna, do you know if there's a dress code at Jefferson Haringay's place?'

'Business suits if you deal with externals. Smart casual otherwise.'

'Any ideas what Sally and I will be doing?'

Anna shrugged. 'I only find out what Jefferson's up to when he needs legal advice.'

Louise lifted the phone back to her ear. 'A suit would be best, to start with.'

Sally sounded a little despondent.

'What's wrong?'

'The smartest clothes I have are the clothes Andrew insisted I wore,' Sally explained, 'and I don't really feel comfortable in those.'

Louise was a little relieved to hear that. 'Then let's go shopping today, and buy ourselves new suits we can both feel comfortable in.'

Helen looked up at the mention of shopping, whereas Anna raised an eyebrow quizzically.

'But I couldn't afford...'

Louise interrupted Sally. 'As you'll be my assistant I want us both to look our best, so I'll buy. No arguments,' she added firmly.

There was a pause before Sally thanked Louise profusely, the relief in her voice was apparent. Louise felt good about herself. They arranged to meet before lunch in town.

Louise hung up the phone.

'Is that our day sorted then?' said Helen.

Louise laughed. 'I suppose so.'

Anna shook her head. 'This is one shopping trip I don't want to miss,' she said.

CHAPTER ELEVEN

VESTIBUS QUERUNT

They met Sally around Piccadilly Circus. After introductions Helen took her by the arm and led her off. 'Before you buy anything else, let's get you a bra that fits.'

Sally began to protest, but Helen stopped her.

'We'll get you measured properly, and then get you a bra that feels comfortable.'

Anna and Louise followed behind as Helen led Sally to Rigby and Peller. Louise watched on bemused as Sally was measured, and an array of large-cupped bras were brought out for Helen's choice. Sally blushed a little when she noticed the prices, but Anna told the assistant she'd take care of the bill, before persuading Sally to choose four bras she found comfortable. Louise noticed that Anna had a surreptitious feel of Sally's breasts with one of the bras on, while asking Sally if they felt comfortable.

Then off they went to find somewhere for lunch. Being Saturday everywhere was busy, but Anna managed to find somewhere a little quieter, with a table available for the four of them.

After lunch Louise took them to a ladies' outfitters for the suits, where she bought herself a light grey jacket and knee-length skirt. Sally, in complete contrast to her previous work attire, went for a black trouser suit. Anna commented that it was a pity to hide such lovely legs, but Sally had had enough of skirts, for now at least.

Then shoe shopping; Sally again going against previous type by getting flat-soled shoes. Louise, ever conscious of her smaller stature, found the highest heels she could comfortably walk around in.

Late afternoon saw Helen hurry back to meet up with Lucian, so the three others wound up in a wine bar, having a meal together. Anna's phone rang, and with some exasperation she dug it out. Her face changed when she saw the number. She excused herself, going outside to take the call.

Sally leaned over to Louise and quietly asked, 'Is your friend gay or something?'

Louise gave her a look over her wine glass. 'What makes you ask that?'

'She was getting a little...' Sally paused, searching for the words, '...touchy-feely. Do you know what I mean?'

Louise smiled to herself. 'I think she's just a very sensuous person,' she replied, after some consideration. 'Would it be a problem?'

Sally sat back. 'Oh, no, no,' she said emphatically. 'I just wondered, that's all.'

'Talking about me?' Anna had returned, and grinned wryly as Sally visibly blushed.

'She was wondering about your preferences,' Louise said.

Anna looked at her, and then at Sally. 'I take it you don't mean preferences in wine.'

Sally squirmed a little under her gaze. Anna sat down next to her. 'Would you mind if I made an observation?'

Sally looked at her blankly for a moment. 'OK...'

'You're more intelligent than people realise, and you're gorgeous...' Sally blushed again, 'but there seems to be one thing you're lacking.'

Sally looked between Anna and Louise. Louise thought she knew what Anna was getting at.

After getting no verbal response from Sally, Anna continued. 'Confidence.' Sally hung her head a little, and Anna smiled. 'But you do "cute-shy" very well.'

Sally's eyes moved around, avoiding Anna's gaze.

'In all the shops we've been in you were going to defer to what the shop assistants suggested, and they're there to serve *you*.'

Sally nodded, her eyes beginning to water.

'You could benefit from some assertiveness training.'

Again Sally meekly nodded.

'I can teach you.'

Sally and Louise both looked at Anna.

'It might be a little unorthodox, but if you can spare the odd evening it'd be worth your while.'

Sally looked at Louise, who shrugged. 'It's up to you. It would certainly be an interesting course.'

'How much?' Sally eventually asked.

Anna laughed. 'We'll get some others to pay for the privilege,' she said, a little enigmatically.

With some trepidation Sally agreed, and they arranged their first session for during the week. They left the wine bar, and Sally went home with her shopping.

'Have you any plans for tonight?' ask Anna.

Louise shook her head, a little curious. 'Helen's not around, so I thought I'd be having a quiet night in. You?'

'I'm preparing you for next Friday.'

Louise's curiosity increased. 'What's happening next Friday?'

'Your initiation into our Court.'

They returned to Louise's, with Anna picking up a bottle of wine on the way. They opened it and sat on the sofa, each with a glass in hand.

'I'm intrigued by your assertiveness training,' said Louise.

Anna smiled. 'I have a plan,' was all she would say on the subject. 'But let's talk about next Friday.'

'What's going to happen?'

'It'll be a surprise, but it's just a ceremony with guests present, so nothing too shocking or intimate goes on, no impromptu gangbangs or torturing.'

Louise was a little relieved, but still a bit apprehensive. 'What should I wear?'

'It doesn't matter. You'll be getting changed when you arrive.'

'Where do you meet?'

'A car will pick you up at a quarter to eight.'

'Do I need to bring anything with me?'

'No.'

Louise paused. 'I thought you were supposed to be preparing me?'

Anna laughed. 'I'm thinking of a name for you.'

'What do you mean?'

'We use pseudonyms in Court, to give us some anonymity, and to separate Court life from normal life.'

'And yours is Improba?'

'No. That was my role. I have an idea for a name, but I'll have to run it past our Master.'

'As long as it's not mus...'

Anna laughed again. 'No. It isn't.' Her tone of voice changed suddenly. 'Now strip and get on your knees.'

Louise took her cue and changed her attitude to subservient, quickly undressing and then kneeling on the floor in front of Anna, looking up at her expectantly. It had seemed a while since she was last in this situation.

Anna looked down at her as she slowly sipped her wine. When she stood Louise's eyes followed her around the room as she topped up her wine glass and returned to her seat. She crossed her legs. swinging her foot close to Louise, who sat as still as she could and waited.

Anna picked up a magazine and started to read it. Louise cleared her throat, but Anna just glared at her over the top of the magazine. Louise remained quiet, watching.

After a quick flick through the pages Anna started again from the beginning, reading each page carefully for several minutes before slowly and deliberately turning the page. Time seemed to slow down for Louise, and each turn of the page seemed to take an age. She shifted a little to relieve the cramp that was starting in her legs.

'Keep still!' Anna said sternly, peering over the periodical.

Louise dropped her head, meekly replying, 'Sorry Mistress.'

Anna watched her for a few moments, before returning to her reading. A few moments later her phone bleeped. She retrieved it from her bag and put it down beside her. She pressed a button and a synthetic voice spoke.

'Puellam paras?'

'Ita vero, mei domini,' replied Anna.

'Mihi exhibes!'

Anna picked it up, and Louise noticed that the light on her camera was on. Anna held it up so Louise was in the view range. Louise bowed her head. She wondered whether she'd be expected to respond in Latin at some point, or would she be expected to learn it as a second language. She found herself wondering again what she'd gotten herself involved in. Then it dawned on her; their Master had control of Anna's phone. Did he have the same control over *her* phone? Could he listen in, or even watch at will?

'Louise.'

She was startled by the mention of her name. She quickly regained her composure. 'Yes, Master.' She looked directly at the phone's camera. There was a slight pause.

'You are aware you are to be initiated on Friday.'

'I am, Master.'

Again there was a pause.

'We use some Latin phrases in Court. Have you ever studied it?'

'I'm sorry, no, Master.'

She noticed there was a pause before each comment now, perhaps to allow him time to type.

'Anna, can you place her in position?'

Anna stood and replied, 'Yes, Master.'

Standing beside the kneeling Louise she ordered her to lean forward, her arms resting on the seat she'd previously occupied. Louise complied, and was given Anna's phone.

'Hold it so you're looking into the camera.'

Louise looked into the lens, thinking about him watching her on the other side of the link. She felt a little excited by the thought. The phone spoke.

'We will teach you a few phrases you'll need during your initiation. You will be rewarded or punished as required. Do you understand?'

'Yes, Master.'

'Good. If you please me you will be rewarded.'

Louise felt Anna's finger stroking between her thighs. She moved her legs to allow more access, and Anna began to gently caress her clitoris. Louise's body tingled at the contact. She closed her eyes and sighed.

'Louise!'

The contact stopped abruptly and she opened her eyes and moved the phone back for the camera lens to see her.

'At all times you must face the camera. For this infraction you will be punished.'

Anna slapped her backside hard, making it sting. The slap seemed to echo. Louise jolted, but managed to keep eye contact with the camera.

'Do you understand?'

'Yes, Master.'

'Good.'

There was a pause before he spoke again. Louise ensured she stayed perfectly still.

'When in Court, or on Court business, I am addressed by members of the Court as mei domini.'

'Yes, mei domini.'

'Good. Anna, premium pullae das.'

Anna resumed rubbing Louise's clit, and with her other hand she stroked Louise's inner thighs. Louise resisted the urge to close her eyes, and instead gazed intently into the camera lens.

After a few minutes Anna stopped, and Louise said, 'Thank you, mei domini.'

'To say thank you, you should say, ego tibi gratias ago.'

Louise took her time to repeat the phrase. 'Ego tibi gratias ago,' following it with, 'mei domini.'

'Premium puellae das.'

Anna's hand resumed its work and Louise sighed, grinning into the camera lens. After a few moments the voice from the phone spoke, prompting Anna to stop again.

'I'm impressed by your pronunciation. Are you sure you haven't studied Latin?'

'I haven't, Master.'

Louise's response elicited a smack across her buttocks. She turned to look, to which Anna slapped her again and indicated she should look back into the camera.

'You should address our Master as mei domini,' Anna reminded her.

'I'm sorry, mei domini.'

After a pause the voice continued. 'To apologise you should say "me paenitet".'

'Me paenitet, mei domini,' Louise repeated carefully.

In the time it took for the Master to respond she was wondering whether she'd be expected to hold a complete conversation in Latin by Friday.

'You will pick up other phrases whilst in Court, or aula, but these phrases can be used if you are addressed directly. So how do you address me?'

'Mei domini,' replied Louise.

'How would you thank me?'

Louise paused a moment, before speaking the phrase slowly. 'Ego tibi gratias ago, mei domini.'

'Good. If you make a mistake, what would you say?'

'Me paenitet, mei domini,' she replied, still slowly.

'Excellent. The ianitoris will complete your final preparations when you reach Court. Do you wish to be picked up from home or work?'

Louise paused before answering. 'From home, please... mei domini.'

A few moments later the voice continued. 'A car will you pick you up from home at seven-fifteen. You need not bring anything else. Do you have any questions?'

Before Louise could speak Anna cut in. 'Domine?'

'Yes Anna?' replied the voice.

'I was told she'd be picked up at a quarter to eight, mei domini.'

'We have a few things to do that evening, so we decided upon an earlier start.

The appropriate communications are being sent out today.'

'What time should I be there?' she asked.

'We need to prepare you too, so seven o'clock, prompt.'

'Very well, mei domini.'

'What time will it finish?' Louise asked. She had visions of it going through the night, and wondered about getting home afterwards.

'You both will be staying behind after Court has finished, but you should still be away by ten-thirty. We will, of course, ensure you get home safely, or to a destination of your choice, should you choose to go on somewhere.'

Louise thought hard before saying, 'Ego tibi gratias ago, mei domini.'

'Very good. Keep practising, and you'll do well.'

'I'll get a book and read up a bit, mei domini,' Louise volunteered.

'You don't need to go to that trouble, but if you do you need to know that Vs are pronounced as double-Us.'

Louise was a little confused.

'S-A-L-V-E would be pronounced *sal*-way, which is our greeting; hello and goodbye,' said Anna. Louise dare not turn away from the phone. 'It's salvete for more than one person.'

'Thank you, Anna. You have both pleased your Master today.'

'Thank you, Master,' said Anna.

'I believe you have been getting on rather well of late.'

Louise felt herself blush, while Anna stayed silent.

'Louise, as you have done well today I think a reward is definitely in order. Anna, would you see to it that she receives an appropriate reward?'

Louise could make out a restrained laugh in Anna's voice when she spoke.

'Certainly, Master. It would be my pleasure.'

Louise felt Anna's hands on her arms, gently pulling her upright. She followed her direction and stood, ensuring she continued to look into the camera lens. Anna turned her around and sat her down. She pushed Louise's knees apart before getting down between them.

She started off by stroking the inside of Louise's thighs with the backs of her fingers, slowly up from the knees, almost to the tops, and back down again, one thigh at a time. After several strokes up and down her hand moved further on, to Louise's belly. Louise gasped at her touch. She traced patterns around her tummy, slowly meandering up to her breasts, circling her nipples, and all the while gazing into Louise's eyes. But Louise maintained her look into the lens, her eyes half closed.

'What's Anna doing to you?'

Louise started to move the phone to show him, but she was interrupted.

'No. I want to see your face as you tell me.'

'She's stroking my tummy.' She felt a little strange, having to narrate what was happening to her, but she also found it exciting. She jolted a little when Anna pinched one of her nipples.

'Gently, Anna,' said the voice from the phone.

'Sorry, Master,' Anna replied, with a mischievous glint in her eye. She then returned her attention to Louise's thighs, this time slowly plotting her way up with soft, lingering kisses, swapping sides every few seconds. Louise's breathing quickened as she tried to will Anna on to reach her. Her breathing deepened, becoming a little irregular as Anna reached halfway. She wondered if the Master would speak again, but the phone remained silent, the only sign of his presence being the light of the camera.

'What's she doing now?'

'She's kissing my thighs.'

'Do you like that?'

'Yes,' she answered, a little breathlessly.

Anna seemed to slow in her progress; Louise's anticipation building in intensity. She started shifting her hips, until Anna's hands clamped her thighs in place, pushing them further apart as she got closer to the top. Three-quarters of the way there and Louise felt she might scream if it were to take any longer. She was beginning to tremble.

'What now?'

'She's still kissing my thighs. She's taking her time.'

Anna laughed, and at last pushed Louise's legs as far apart as they'd go to give her full access to Louise's pussy. She licked, skirting around the tops of Louise's legs, before a few flicks on her clitoris. Louise felt her eyelids drooping, but didn't care how she looked on camera; she only wanted the full satisfaction that she hoped Anna would bring.

'What is she doing to you?'

It took her a few moments to reply. 'She's playing with my clitoris.' She felt a little embarrassed saying it.

Anna's tongue was as good as ever, and she held Louise firmly to prevent her bucking in reaction to her oral skills. After a good few minutes' work on Louise's clit she pushed her tongue deep inside, before withdrawing, and then thrusting in and out.

'And now?'

Louise was breathing deeply as she replied. 'She's tonguing me.' She let out a whimper when Anna stopped, but lay back again when she recommenced tonguing her clit, a finger slowly pushing into her, massaging gently. Louise moaned.

'Is that good?'

'Mmmm, yes,' she replied, her eyes almost closed.

'What is she doing?'

'She's... she's licking my clit, and fingering me.' She was startled when a finger started massaging around her anus.

'What's she doing now?'

'She still licking and fingering me, and fingering my...' she thought for a few moments, searching for a suitable word, before she settled on, 'arse.'

'Do you like that?'

She blushed as she answered. 'Yes.'

As Anna continued Louise couldn't help herself and closed her eyes as the sensations overcame her. She felt her arm droop a little, but didn't care, she just wanted to climax. Her breathing quickened, she began to moan as her abdomen quivered, the intensity growing inside her. She didn't know how much more she could take, and it didn't take long to tip her over the edge. She screamed and Anna eased off, allowing her orgasm to subside. Louise's breathing slowed, and she opened her eyes and looked back into the camera lens. She didn't have to wait long for a response.

'You seemed to enjoy that.'

She eventually answered him. 'Yes,' she said, breathlessly.

'Now I know what you like I might do it for you sometime,' the voice said.

'If it pleases you, Master,' she replied.

'Thank you both,' the voice resumed. 'I will see you on Friday.'

'Thank you, Master,' they both replied, and the camera light went out.

Louise handed the phone to Anna, who put it back into her handbag. On shaky legs Louise stood, and made her way to the bathroom. She quickly showered, dried and put on her robe. As she stepped out of the bathroom she froze as she heard a key in the front door, and the door opened. She hoped Helen hadn't brought Lucian back.

Helen walked in, alone. She closed the door and looked at Louise. 'Are you all right?' she asked.

'Yes,' said Louise. 'But I wasn't expecting you back tonight.'

'I didn't expect to be back. He said he had to go out and attend to some business.'

Louise hoped she hadn't been given the brush off already. 'Oh, OK.'

They walked through to the lounge and Helen dropped onto the sofa, pulling her shoes off. Anna gave her a look.

'How did you enjoy your evening with Lucian?' she asked.

'It was wonderful. He's quite a cook, you know.'

'I wouldn't know,' replied Anna.

'Are you seeing him again?' asked Louise, before she could stop herself.

'We're having lunch during the week, and then he said he'll make sure he's free next Saturday just for me.'

Anna looked at her. 'And?'

Helen shrugged. 'And what?'

Anna sighed. 'What was... dessert like?'

Helen looked confused. 'It was a very chocolaty pudding. Delicious actually.'

Anna rolled her eyes.

'I think Anna is trying to find out if you had sex with him,' Louise said, trying to be helpful.

Helen blushed. 'No, he was a perfect gentleman,' she replied.

'Didn't seem much like a gentleman last night,' Anna quipped.

Helen turned purposefully to Louise, avoiding Anna's gaze. 'We were talking about antiques...'

Louise wondered how the conversation between Helen and Lucian could possibly include antiques, especially after the games the previous night.

'...and he was telling me about his friend who collects weird Victorian type stuff.'

'Oh?' Anna said, suddenly interested. Louise looked at her, and suddenly realised what she was thinking; they both thought they knew who the friend might be.

'Did you know the Victorians invented ice cream, jelly and vibrators?' Helen said.

'Really,' Anna said. 'Vibrators, eh? They must have been clockwork or something.'

Helen missed the tone of Anna's voice and continued. 'His friend has a steam powered one.'

Anna and Louise looked at each other.

'Steam powered? Now that could be interesting,' said Anna.

Louise winced at the thought. Would it get hot and burn?

There was the familiar buzzing; all three grabbed their phones.

'It's Lucian,' said Helen. 'He's installed this application which lets us keep in touch. We can message each other whenever we like. He seems a bit security conscious.'

Anna and Louise looked at the app on Helen's phone. It was the same YMV app they had, but she could send messages.

'Did Lucian mention what else it could do?' asked Anna.

'He said if I'm in trouble I can press a button and it'll let him know where I am.'

Anna and Louise looked at each other again. It seemed that Helen was moving further into their world.

Anna helped herself to another drink, while Louise was impressed that Helen went for a juice. There used to be no stopping her when it came to an open bottle of wine, but of late that had changed. They chatted for a while longer, and then Anna stood to leave.

'Please don't go because of me,' Helen said.

'I need to catch up on some work tomorrow, so it's best if I stay home tonight. There are a couple of very important cases amongst them,' Anna added seriously, 'relating to arseholes.'

'Arseholes?' Helen questioned.

'Indeed. One is a lady who had one as a boyfriend, and one for a couple of girls who had one as a boss!'

'That is important,' Louise agreed, smiling. 'You'd better get off then. See you Friday.'

'I'll call into the office during the week,' Anna said, then went, leaving Helen and Louise alone.

'What's happening Friday?' asked Helen. 'Can I come along?'

'Er, sorry, no,' Louise said, a little awkwardly.

'This is Court business, isn't it? That's why Lucian isn't available Friday.'

Louise nodded. She hadn't thought Lucian would be there. Who else would be? She'd not stopped to consider what might happen, but she'd just have to trust Anna and her Master.

Sunday was a quiet day. Louise started cleaning her apartment. It seemed like ages since she'd last done it, and as she didn't know what the next few days in her new job would bring she wanted to get it out of the way.

Helen mucked in too, and by lunchtime Louise was happy with the results of their efforts. The afternoon saw them off to the gym, Louise working out on the equipment while Helen swam. Both finished off in the steam room, with Louise wondering what it might be like to have sex in there, before ruling it out as an option, as it would be too hot and steamy.

Though Louise had kept thinking about her initiation, after dinner she realised she was starting a new job the following day. She made sure everything was ready, sorting out her recently acquired suit, underwear, shoes and her case. A new job, so not much to put in it, but she did put in some assorted stationery, not knowing what would be provided. She considered putting in one of her toys, but decided against that; she wanted to make a good impression, and didn't think nipping off to the loo for a quick play would give the right impression.

After watching some television and having a hot milky drink she went off to bed, falling asleep as soon as her head hit the pillow.

CHAPTER TWELVE

NOVO OPUS

Helen was already up and dressed by the time Louise got up the following morning. Helen wished her luck before departing for work. Louise took her time getting ready and had a leisurely breakfast, something she was sure wouldn't happen again for a while.

Outside it was a grey, rainy London day, not the most cheerful of days to start a new job, but she did look forward to the change of scene and wondered just what Jefferson had in mind for her. Sally was waiting outside the office, sheltering from the elements under the entrance canopy. After exchanging greetings and compliments on how they looked in their new suits, they entered the building.

At reception they were directed up to the top floor, and were met by an attractive black woman, who introduced herself as Tina, Mr Haringay's personal assistant. As she turned and led them to the boardroom Louise had to admire the wiggle as Tina walked, enhanced by the tight pencil skirt and heels she wore.

They sat next to each other in the empty boardroom for a few minutes before Jefferson arrived. He breezed in, followed by a man carrying a couple of box files. Louise and Sally stood, but Jefferson waved them down again.

'Ladies, this is Peter, who'll be helping you to get settled into your new roles. Peter, this is Louise and Sally. Louise will be heading up the Australasia project.'

Louise was taken by surprise by the 'heading up' comment. Peter offered his hand to each in turn, which Louise and Sally shook. Jefferson signalled to Tina before taking a seat next to Louise. Tina brought in a tray with a coffee pot, milk jug, sugar bowl and four cups on it. She closed the doors as she left.

Jefferson began by describing his company's current interests, and how he wanted to break into the Australasian markets. They'd tried before, and Louise noticed that Peter was a little negative about their previous attempts. She was pleased to see Sally taking notes as they both listened intently. Jefferson was hoping she would be able to make inroads into the markets there, and Louise was taken aback a little, as she'd only been used to dealing with Western Europeans.

After an hour's briefing Jefferson left the three of them, Louise with the remit of putting together a proposal, and Peter with assisting her in getting what she needed, and getting acclimatised to their way of working. And she had less than two weeks to do it. They spoke for a while and she quizzed Peter on the previous attempts, Sally still taking notes.

Peter then gave them a tour of the building, eventually getting to her office, which was on the floor below the boardroom, Jefferson's office and Peter's office. She had a sturdy wooden desk and a dark table with four chairs around it. Sally had a desk just outside her door, and she immediately set about organising stationery in drawers. Peter placed the box files onto Louise's desk, showed them both how the telephone system worked, and then left them to it. As soon as he'd gone Sally entered.

'Would you like a drink, Miss Coleman?' She flashed Louise a cheeky smile.

'Certainly,' she replied. 'And let's keep it to first names, Sally.' Louise realised she didn't know Sally's surname.

She started unpacking the box files on the table, and had made a start on looking through them when Sally returned. 'Let's see what we have here then,' she said.

Sally paused at the door. 'You want me to go through this with you?'

Louise looked up. 'Why wouldn't I? Bring through your notes from before.'

Sally retrieved her paperwork and sat next to Louise. Together they started poring through the documents, referring back to the notes taken from the conversations with Jefferson and Peter.

It didn't seem long before Tina knocked on the open door. 'We're ordering lunch. Would you like anything?'

Louise looked at her watch; was it lunchtime already?

Tina ran through the available options that she could recall, and promised to drop a menu in for them. They ordered soups and a sandwich, and were pleasantly surprised when less than half an hour later Tina came down to say the food had arrived. She showed them to the kitchen, and they sat and had their lunch. A few people introduced themselves, until Peter arrived, when he pointed out or introduced various people as they passed. He asked how they were getting on, and reminded them to let him know if he could help with anything. Louise asked about how they did their research, to which he explained their sources.

After lunch they returned to Louise's office and got back to work. A young man knocked on the door and strolled in with a pair of laptops for them. He introduced himself as Phil, in his early twenties by Louise's estimation. He also didn't hide very well his attraction to Sally. She smiled and was polite, but it was obvious to Louise that she wasn't interested in the way he'd like. He also appeared later in the afternoon with a mobile phone for Louise. After showing her how it worked he left, but not before a lingering glance in Sally's direction, which she didn't return, feigning engrossment in her task at hand. When he left Louise closed the door.

'Not your type?' she asked.

Sally looked up. 'Not really. And I'm trying to avoid the relationship in the workplace thing.'

Louise felt for her, wondering what their former boss had put her through.

They kept the door closed for the rest of the afternoon as they read through the files Peter had passed on, only popping out occasionally for coffee or toilet breaks. Louise found Sally to be very helpful, understanding much of what they'd been given, with Louise only explaining a few points. She'd also picked up on things, and together they compiled a list of questions about what they'd done to date. When they checked the time it was almost eight in the evening.

'I'm sorry for keeping you late,' Louise said.

'That's fine; it's been nice getting involved like this,' Sally replied.

'You go off, I'll see you in the morning.'

'I'll help you clear up.'

'You don't have to.'

'I really don't mind,' Sally insisted.

While they were getting the files and their notes in order, Louise's phone buzzed.

'Don't you need to get that?' Sally asked.

'No, it can wait.'

'It's OK. You see to that and I'll file these.'

Louise looked at her phone; it was a message from him.

How was your first day in your new job?

She wondered a little who'd told him, but just sent a message back. *It was good, thank you.* Feeling a little cheeky she added, *How was your day?*

My day was interesting. Are you home?

She was a little surprised; normally he seemed to know where she was.

I'm still at the office, she replied.

That's a shame. I shall see you Friday then.

The YMV closed off again, giving her no option to reply. She looked at her phone pensively.

'Nothing bad I hope?'

Sally's comment broke her out of her thoughts. 'No. Nothing really.'

'I hope he's worth it,' Sally offered.

Louise found herself saying 'so do I' to herself.

The next few days seemed to fly by. Louise was absorbed completely with her task, finding Sally incredibly helpful with research, and some unexpected insight. Peter, however, seemed more of a hindrance. Whatever she suggested he said they'd already tried and it hadn't worked.

Helen was a little miffed at Louise's late finishes, spending the first couple of evenings home alone. She'd had a rushed lunch with Lucian, due to having to get back to her work, but kept in frequent touch with him via her YMV connection. Despite his busy schedule they also managed to fit in a dinner on Thursday.

Anna called in to see Louise and Sally at the office on the Thursday, with an update about their case against their former employer. It seemed following their leaving several people had come forward to complain about Andrew. As a result he had been suspended, with an impending disciplinary. The company was also keen to keep it low profile, so were very willing to negotiate a settlement. Anna was playing it cool, holding back for a better offer. Sally thought the existing one was more than enough, but she deferred to Anna.

When Sally nipped out to refill the coffee pot Anna closed the door. 'There's something I forgot to mention,' she said.

'Something to do with Andrew?' Louise asked.

'No. Tomorrow evening.'

Louise had forgotten about it. 'What?'

'You need six things to confess.'

'What?'

'Nothing serious, just little things. Say you left the cap off the toothpaste, or something similarly trivial.'

'Great!' Louise said, frustrated.

Sally came back in, and seeing Louise's frustration asked if everything was all right.

Louise laughed. 'I'm fine. Just a personal thing. It's nothing to worry about.'

Anna left shortly afterwards, leaving them to get back to their work.

On Friday Louise found herself making deliberate mistakes; she walked into someone in the corridor, when finding Peter's office unoccupied she rearranged the items on his desk and removed the staples from his stapler, and even put the toilet seats up in all the ladies' cubicles.

She treated Sally to lunch out. When ordering she deliberately chose something from another day's menu. She was a little disappointed, however, when the waiter arrived with the meal she'd ordered.

'You're in a funny mood today,' Sally observed.

'What makes you say that?'

'I saw you move stuff around on Peter's desk, and then I heard some of the girls talking about the ladies' toilets, which I think you did too.'

'Does anyone else suspect?'

'No. What's going on? It's not April the first you know.'

'I have a, er, function tonight, and I have to, er, talk about something. So I'm doing some things to talk about.'

Sally gave her a strange look. 'It seems a bit odd to me,' she said.

'Me too,' Louise replied under her breath, before taking another mouthful of her meal.

'Will he be there?'

Louise looked up from her food, slowly emptying her mouth. 'Who?'

'The guy who messages you.'

'I think so, yes,' she said cautiously.

'Are you trying to impress him?'

Louise paused before answering. 'Possibly.'

'Is Anna going too?'

Louise was taken aback by Sally's perception. 'Perhaps.'

'Are you ever going to give me a straight answer about it?'

Louise grinned. 'Maybe.'

Sally threw her napkin at her. Louise was surprised, but also glad that Sally was relaxed enough to do that with her.

She mentally counted her misdemeanours during the day; she should have more than enough for the evening.

That evening.

Louise took a breath, which luckily Sally didn't notice. It was that evening, and she'd have to be sure they were out of the office by six.

Louise looked up at the clock; it was almost six. 'Shall we call it a day?'

'Shall we go for a drink?' Sally suggested.

'I'm sorry I don't have the time,' Louise said.

'Oh.' Sally was a little downcast.

'What's wrong?'

'I didn't fancy going straight home tonight.'

'Oh.' Louise had an idea and got out her phone. She dialled Helen's number. 'Hi Helen. Have you anything arranged for tonight?'

'I thought you were...'

'I wondered if you'd take Sally out; it's been a busy week and I think she needs to wind down a bit.'

'Oh, OK then. I'll meet you back at yours.'

'Thanks Helen.' She turned to Sally. 'That's sorted then. You can have drinks with Helen.'

'But...'

Louise interrupted her. 'No buts. I think you've earned it.'

They filed their paperwork away and left the office, returning to Louise's apartment. Helen was already there.

'How's your first week at the new job been?' she asked Sally. 'What's your new boss like?'

Sally laughed at the last comment. 'It's great. Interesting. I get to use my brain, instead of dressing up.'

'There's nothing wrong with dressing up,' Helen put in. 'For the right occasion. By the way, you look great in that suit. Is that one we got last weekend?'

'Thanks, yes it is.'

From Sally's initial uncertainty when she entered Louise's apartment, Helen had managed to gain her trust and have her exuding confidence with a few phrases. Louise wondered whether Anna's 'assertiveness training' would have the same effect.

Louise gave her apologies, went to the bathroom and showered. As she was drying off she heard Helen and Sally call 'bye' before the front door closed behind them. She went through into her bedroom and picked out a skirt, blouse, and shoes that didn't have much of a heel on them. She wasn't sure what to expect, but didn't fancy the prospect of toppling off high heels.

Once dressed she made her way to the kitchen and poured herself a drink; with Helen in her teetotal phase they hadn't got any alcohol in. Her phone buzzed.

'Your carriage awaits.'

She laughed to herself as she left her apartment. Sure enough when she got outside a car was waiting; she recognised the driver. She nodded to him, and as soon as she was belted in they were off.

Louise wasn't as nervous as she thought she'd be; perhaps she was getting used to being driven around to face the unknown. She looked out of the tinted windows, watching the shops and houses go by. She knew this area of London pretty well, and realised after a while they were going in circles. Was this a ploy to try and confuse her, to get her disorientated, lost? After a few minutes the driver's phone buzzed. When they stopped at a set of lights he turned to her.

'Can I ask you to wear this, Miss?' He threw a blindfold onto her lap.

'Of course,' Louise replied, putting it on. The car pulled off and she felt a right turn, a bit of a drive before a left, and then the car slowed. After a few moments she felt it moving forward, and then stop again. A few more moments later the door opened.

'Can you move over this way, Miss?' She felt the driver's hand on her arm, gently guiding her out. 'Mind the step,' he said as she twisted around and dropped her feet to the ground. She carefully stood. 'This way,' he said, guiding her by the elbow.

She carefully stepped in the indicated direction, following his lead. They stopped, and she heard him open a door before they moved on. They stopped again, and she heard the familiar rumble of a lift. The bell rang and she heard the doors opened.

'This way, Miss,' he said again. She stepped forward and they stopped again. She heard the doors close and she felt the lift lurch upward. A few seconds later the lift stopped, and the doors opened.

He led her out, turned to the left, and then a few more steps before stopping. He knocked on a door, and for the first time she felt a little anxiety. She hoped she'd dressed appropriately. She heard the door open and was led through. As soon as it closed behind her the blindfold was removed.

'I'm sorry about that Miss,' the driver said apologetically. 'We don't want people to know where we meet until they're properly a member.'

'That's understandable,' she said. She looked around. The room was wood panelled, with a pair of large doors on one side and a single door ahead of her. Besides her and the driver there were three other men in the room. The driver was in a conventional black suit, but the three others were dressed as she'd seen the doormen dressed at the party. One of them stepped forward.

'Salve,' he said.

She thought before answering. 'Salvete.'

He smiled at her. 'You've been primed well,' he said. 'Most people forget.'

'And are they punished for it?' she joked.

'Of course,' he said, seriously.

One of the other men handed her a grey smock and led her to the single door.

'Could you put this on please, Miss? No underwear. If you put your shoes and clothes in the basket we'll put it into a locker for safekeeping.'

She entered the small room and the man closed the door behind her. She looked around; there was a toilet, sink, small bench with a basket on top, and a mirror on the wall. She undressed and carefully folded her clothes, placing them on top of her shoes in the basket. She sat on the toilet, emptied what little was in her bladder before putting the smock on. She didn't expect it to be flattering, but as she looked in the mirror it wasn't too bad, shaped a little for her figure.

She picked up the basket of her stuff, stepped over to the door, and paused. Should she just open it, or should she knock first? She stood there for a few moments, beginning to feel nervous. What would happen if she got anything wrong? Her thoughts were broken by a knock on the door.

'Is everything OK, Miss?'

She felt a little relief. 'Yes, thank you. I'm ready.' She pulled the handle and opened the door.

'They're nearly ready for you,' said the main man, leading her to the double doors. Another of the men had his ear to one of them, listening to whatever was going on inside.

Louise noticed her chauffeur had also changed, into clothes as the other men were wearing. She saw one of the men was holding a grey hood and some soft rope. The main man noticed her gaze.

'I'm sorry, Miss. There's a little more preparation yet before you go in.'

'I'm not surprised,' she said.

He gave a little laugh. 'You'll be fine.' He took the basket from her and passed it to one of the others, instructing them to put it in one of the lockers. Then he tied her wrists in front of her and carefully placed the hood over her head.

She stood barefoot, in the grey smock, hood, wrists tied, and wondered again what she'd got herself into. She heard the double doors open, and then heard a female voice.

'Major Ianitor. Puella paratus est?'

The man who'd 'prepared' her replied. 'Ita vero. Puella paratus est, Madame Orator.'

She felt the rope tying her wrist gently pulling her forward, and the Ianitor placed his hands on her shoulders. As he gently pushed her he whispered in her ear.

'Don't worry. Just relax and enjoy the experience.'

CHAPTER THIRTEEN

INITIATA

She followed the direction of pull with uncertain steps. She tried to listen out for any clues as to what was going on, but could only hear music quietly playing. After several steps she felt a hand resting on her left arm, holding her still. A female voice to her left, the person Louise thought to be holding her arm, spoke.

'Members of the Purple Court, before you stands our latest novice for admission.'

Another female voice, by her right this time, responded, 'Major ancilla. Who sponsors her?'

'The Master of our Court, Dominus Victor.'

Victor. Was that his name? But Anna had told her real names weren't used.

'It is customary for a novice's sponsor to present them to Court. As the sponsor is the Master of our Court, who is to act as his proxy?'

Louise heard footsteps walk up to her right side.

'I do.'

She recognised Anna's voice. Madame Orator spoke again. 'Mistress Vulpes, are you to act as the proxima domino?'

'I am,' Anna replied.

Mistress Vulpes? Was that something to do with vultures?

'Has the Master agreed a suitable recompense for you acting thus?'

'He has.'
Louise wondered what Anna's reward would be.
'Does puella have a name?'
Anna paused. Louise waited to see what she'd decided upon.
'Beatitas.'
Under the hood Louise rolled her eyes. *Beatitas?* Sounded a little like 'beat its ass'; is that why Anna chose it? At the end of the evening she would be having words with Anna. She expected sniggers from whoever was around, but there were none; the only sound was the quiet background music, her breathing, and then a few footsteps towards her. She felt a hand on her shoulder.

'Puella Beatitas. You stand here before the aula purpurea, awaiting entry. Beyond this there is no return. But first you must demonstrate your commitment to serve the Court, and the order to which the Court belongs. Mistress Vulpes. Please lead puella Beatitas through the obligation.'

Anna dictated to Louise what to say, and Louise repeated the words, affirming that she would undertake the whole ceremony, to serve the Court and its Master, and to never reveal details of the ceremony, Court or Order to anyone outside.

'Madame Orator,' Anna spoke aloud, 'Puella Beatitas is ready to proceed.'

The Orator pulled the hood off Louise to the sound of stamping. As Louise adjusted to the dim light she noticed people seated to her left and right. Some were stamping, others banging canes and walking sticks on the floor. Ahead of her hung a large white sheet with a purple crest upon it. There was a lot to take in. A woman stood close by, Louise guessed to be Madame Orator, dressed in a black and purple ankle-length dress, with a black corset with purple piping over it. She also held a staff, with a carving on its head that Louise couldn't quite make out, and a gold chain around her neck with what Louise thought to be amethyst hanging from it, obscured a little by her smooth blonde hair hanging down over one shoulder.

Louise turned and saw Anna, also dressed in a black and purple dress, without a corset. Anna smiled and gave her a reassuring squeeze of her arm.

The banging ceased when the Orator raised her hand, turned and spoke aloud to Anna. 'Mistress Vuples, before we can accept puella Beatitas she must be approved by those who govern our Court. Please oversee the cleansing of puella Beatitas, so she may be presented to the Dominae.'

Anna stepped forward and took Louise's arm before speaking. 'Major ancilla, see to it that puella Beatitas is properly prepared to be presented to Court.'

A woman dressed in a white smock, with two sets of purple piping around the collar, stood in front of them, and bowing to Anna she replied, 'It will be done, Mistress Vulpes.'

She clapped her hands twice and eight women stood, all dressed in white smocks with a single line of purple piping around their collars. Six had sheets. They circled Louise, Anna, the major ancilla and the two other women, and held up the sheets, shielding them from sight of the rest of the Court.

The two remaining girls had buckets, sponges and towels. They took Louise by surprise when after untying her hands they pulled off her grey smock and washed her body with the sponges, before drying her off. Once completed the major ancilla dressed her in a plain white smock, putting white slippers on her feet. Once Louise was dressed the women broke the circle, first lining up before them, and curtseyed to Anna, before returning to their seats behind Anna. The major ancilla stood nearby.

Anna moved close to Louise's left side and held her arm. 'Aulicae! Bear witness that puella Beatitas has been prepared in readiness to be accepted into Court.'

The Orator stood by Louise on the other side. 'Mistress Vulpes, I accept your petition on behalf of the aula purpurea. Puella Beatitas can now be presented to the dominae.'

With Anna holding one arm and the Orator the other, they guided her forward to the sheet, pausing just before it as it was raised to reveal six ladies standing in a line in front. All were dressed similarly, black and purples dresses, in different styles, with purple corsets with black lacing and lining, and long purple gloves. A couple of them wore face masks, but one she recognised: Marta. She didn't wear a mask, and stood out as the shortest of them, even in her tall stiletto boots.

The Madam Orator made a short speech to the effect that the members of Court were prepared to accept Louise, puella Beatitas, as a new member, and sought approval from the Master of the Court.

A slim yet busty brunette stood forward. Her dress was low-cut, not quite knee length, and she wore laced ankle boots. Her face was obscured by a face mask. 'Madame Orator, can you confirm the puella been cleansed and made ready for presentation?'

'She has, Madame Vox Domino.'

'Who is her sponsor to join the Court?'

'Mistress Vulpes is acting as proxima domino, Madame Vox Domino.'

The Vox Domino turned to face Anna. 'Mistress Vulpes.'

Louise felt Anna stiffen. 'Yes, Madame Vox Domino?'

'Dominus Victor thanks you for your services. You may hand over your ward to my care.'

Anna held up Louise's arm, and this vox domino lady took it, replacing Anna at her side. Louise saw Anna curtsy to the ladies, something that surprised her, before moving off to sit down.

'Don't worry; we'll look after you,' the Vox Domino whispered in Louise's ear. 'He doesn't bite,' she added, 'much.'

Louise stifled a nervous giggle.

'Sisters,' the Vox Domino spoke aloud, 'let us present puella Beatitas to our Master.'

Two of the ladies stayed in place, while the others made two lines facing Louise, the final place being made up by the Orator. The Vox Domino moved forward, gently pulling Louise alongside her. As they got to the first two ladies they stood aside facing inward. The same happened with the next pair, and the final pair. Louise thought of this as some sort of honour-guard.

With the final two stepping aside a pair of curtains were revealed, purple with gold trimming, and the same crest, this time embroidered on each side. Louise looked up, and saw it was hanging from a small canopy similar to those seen above four poster beds.

Her escort had stopped. 'When the curtains are opened curtsy as low as you can,' she whispered into Louise's ear again.

The final pair of ladies pulled one curtain each, moving around the back of the ornate chair within, where her Master was seated. Louise, vox domino and the other ladies all curtsied, staying down.

He rapped the floor three times with his staff. The other ladies arose, and Louise followed their lead. She looked him in the face, or rather, in the mask; he was wearing the same mask, with a three-piece suit, hat and gloves. She thought she saw an approving nod, and she smiled in response.

The vox domino moved to his side. He turned to her, speaking into her ear.

'Dominus Victor is pleased to see you before him this evening,' she said.

'Ego tibi gratias ago, mei domini,' Louise answered slowly.

The Vox Domino raised an eyebrow, but the Master just nodded, before speaking into the Vox Domino's ear again.

'The Master commends you, and will ensure you are rewarded for your efforts.' She paused, and Louise wondered whether she was expected to speak, but the Vox spoke again.

'The Court requires all its members give devotion to their Master, which you will do later. All members are expected to serve the Court in various capacities. As a newly joined member you will be expected to perform your servitude as a member of the ancillae.'

She turned slightly, facing the major ancilla, who Louise had forgotten was still there.

'Major ancilla.'

The major ancilla stepped forward and curtsied. 'Yes, vox domino?'

'It is your duty to oversee the work of the ancillae. The Master requests that you oversee the instruction of puella Beatitas. You are prepared to accept the Master's wishes?'

'Ita vero,' she replied.

'Major ancilla, place the badges of office on puella Beatitas.'

The major ancilla stood in front of Louise, and put white wristbands with a purple stripe on her wrists, before speaking. 'It is the Master's desire that you be my charge. From now on you will be known as ancilla Beatitas, and will serve the Court with the other ancillae.'

She stepped back beside Louise. The Master whispered again into the vox's ear.

'At this point,' she began, 'it is usual for the new member to be taken to the

Master's private chambers to show their devotion. However, there are things that ancilla Beatitas must be made aware of. Major ancilla, would you escort ancilla Beatitas to her seat in Court amongst the ancillae?'

The major ancilla took Louise by the elbow, and led her to a seat at the opposite end of the hall to the Master. They turned and faced him, and curtsied before sitting.

The dominae had all sit, the current vox and Marta sat each side of him, and the other four in front. The Orator had moved to the right side of the room, and sat next to a similarly attired man.

Louise had a proper look around. She spotted Lucian, who gave a small wave and a nod. She also saw Mistress Annabelle with a small entourage around her, dressed in pink, including the men. She could also make out a group of people wearing kimonos.

The Master's staff pounded the floor once, and the Vox Domino stood.

'The Master recently attended a meeting with other Masters and Mistresses of the Order, and things were brought to light that may affect some of the members of this, and other Courts. The Master Arbiter and Ianitor for the Order is here tonight, and the Master wishes him to address the Court directly.'

'Madame Orator. As the representative of the members of Court, will you allow this change from protocol and allow him to speak?'

The Orator stood and spoke.

'Aulicae. Dominus Victor has already spoken to me on this matter. I believe it is in the best interests of our Court to allow this break in protocol, and hear what has to be said by the Master Arbiter.'

The Orator sat.

The Vox Domino continued. 'The Master requests that the Master Arbiter takes the floor to address the aula purpurea. May the aulicae take note that our normal protocols do not apply while the stranger has the floor.'

The Master rapped the floor three times with his staff; Lucian stood and made his way into the middle. He bowed to the Master before speaking.

'Ladies, gentlemen and friends of the Purple Court. I thank you for allowing me to speak, out of turn, as it were. However, the rulers of the Courts in the Order felt it appropriate that I come and address you myself, rather than via the usual channels, so you may ask questions directly.

'Some of you are aware that some of our members have lost their phones. At first we believed this was the normal mobile phone theft we get in and around London. However, we now believe that members of the Order are being targeted specifically.'

'What makes you think that?' someone called out.

Lucian took a deep breath before answering. 'Because attempts have been made to try and compromise the YMV system.'

A murmur arose, but abated when the Master knocked once with his staff.

'Couldn't you use the GPS to trace them?' the same person called out.

'The phones are being fed a false signal, so the GPS function doesn't work properly. This is another reason we believe it is a deliberate attempt.'

The murmuring started again, interrupted by the Master's staff.

'What do we use instead of the YMV system?'

'You can continue to use the YMV system as normal; it is quite safe. But if you lose your phone you must let either your Master, or one of the arbitras know as soon as possible.'

'Is it just from one Court?'

'No. To date there has been one gone from the Purple Court, two from the Court of Humility, two from Electra, and two from the Aqua Vitae Court.'

'Don't you know who's doing this? What are we going to do about it?'

Louise thought she saw Lucian roll his eyes.

'We have our suspicions, which the Masters, Mistresses and Arbiters have been made aware of. But we have no real proof as yet. Once we do we will contact the authorities with any information we have.'

Someone laughed. 'Yeah, I'm really sure they'll help! I say we deal with this ourselves, because nobody else will. That's why we have this Court system after all, to look after ourselves.'

The Master's staff hit the floor three times and everyone turned. He looked a little agitated, and spoke into the Vox Domino's ear. She stood and spoke, slowly and carefully.

'The Master reminds us that the Order was set up to give us all a safe environment to engage in our own interests, with likeminded people. The law is the law, and we are not vigilantes, and would take a very dim view of any member of Court who went against his wishes.'

Louise wasn't sure whether she was conveying her own annoyance or the Master's when she spoke. The response was an uneasy silence. The Vox Domino spoke again.

'Master Arbiter, thank you for bringing this to the attention of our Court. Unless there are any further questions we shall continue with this evening's agenda.' She and Lucian looked around, but no more questions came, so Lucian bowed to the Master and returned to his seat.

The Vox Domino spoke. 'Madame Orator, please continue with the Court agenda.'

She sat, and the Madame Orator stood and nodded. 'Thank you.' She paused to read a scroll she had in her hand.

'Master. We have received a grievance from the Court of Humility. Do you wish to hear their petition?'

All eyes turned to the Master, and he nodded.

'The Emissary of the Court of Humility here tonight to present the petition. Mistress Bella; please take to the floor.'

Annabelle stood and made her way into the middle, followed by a masked man. He was wearing a dog collar, and Annabelle held the leash. 'Thank you, Madame Orator,' she began. Her slave knelt beside her.

'Ladies and gentlemen of the Purple Court.' She turned to face the Master and nodded to him as she said, 'Master of the Court.' She began to slowly pace the floor. Louise could easily imagine the sense of anticipation her slaves would feel, hearing those stiletto boots getting closer. 'Your last hosted event was an enjoyable evening, for which I thank you for the kind invitation.'

Annabelle turned and continued her pacing, and Louise realised that now as she spoke she was heading towards her, smiling as she strode.

'However, it was marred by the loss of one of my slaves.'

Louise held her breath as Annabelle came close to her, within a step, before she turned and stopped.

'As the hosting Court I hold you responsible for this, and demand some form of recompense.' She turned her head back to Louise, winked, and then strode to her original position, where her slave still knelt.

Louise was a little anxious. She wondered if she was expected to perform some act for Annabelle; the thought both worried and excited her.

The Orator stood. 'Master. Our Court has enjoyed a good and mutually enjoyable relationship with the Court of Humility. Is it your wish we offer the usual recompense?'

The Master gestured with his hand and nodded.

Two women who'd been sitting near the dominae stood and walked over. They were dressed similarly, and each had a whip hanging by their side. They took a member of the Court out and pulled her to the middle of the room. She was dressed in a grey tunic with a purple waistband. Louise recognised her as the arbitra who'd meted out punishment to Louise for Anna's indiscretion. She thought briefly about her marks, which hadn't bothered her since a couple of days after the incident.

Meanwhile an ancilla stood and was taking a small padded table over to them. It was put down and the ancilla returned to her seat. The grey-clad girl was bent over it and the two arbitrae, as Louise recalled their title, tied her thighs and arms to it.

One arbitra stood to one side, while the other approached Annabelle. 'Mistress of the Court of Humility. We offer our improba for your retribution.'

Improba? Louise remembered that had been Anna's title. And this girl had been an arbitra. She seemed to recall Lucian mentioning that Anna was being made an arbitra; had they swapped places?

Annabelle walked slowly around the improba, as though inspecting her. She stopped and crouched down, holding the improba's head up and looking her in the eye for a few moments. She stood suddenly and beckoned her slave. He stood and walked to her. She held out a hand and from a pouch he produced a hood, which Annabelle placed over the improba's head, fastening it with some white cord around her throat.

She then strolled again around the girl. Louise noticed her steps were more pronounced now as she walked. Occasionally she'd stop, only moving on when the girl's head moved. Annabelle was playing a game, with the improba as her captured prey. At one point she stopped and lifted the skirt, revealing the improba's grey panties. She bunched up the back of the panties to reveal the full flesh of her buttocks. When the improba moved her head around she restarted her circling, slowly pacing around the girl.

She signalled again to her slave, and he retrieved a case from where they had been sitting. He stood and opened it. Louise moved a little to see if she could glimpse what was inside, but to no avail.

Annabelle stopped by the improba's rear and considered the contents of the case, before taking out a riding crop. She swished it through the air a few times before returning it to its place in the case. She then took out a black paddle and hit the girl's rump. The improba grunted, taken by surprise.

Annabelle walked around to the girl's head, quickly unfastened the hood, pulled it up and gripped her chin, pulling it up so she could look her again in the eye.

'Master Victor,' she said loudly and severely, 'your last improba knew her place, but this one hasn't the same class or character. Do you wish me to break her in for you?'

Louise saw the Master whisper into the ear of the Vox Domino before she spoke.

'The Master suggests you proceed as you see fit, to ensure good relations between our Courts.'

Annabelle stared for a moment longer into the improba's eyes, before releasing her chin and standing. 'Very well then.'

She signalled her slave again, who brought a bag to her. She took out a strap-on dildo, and to Louise's surprise put it on her slave. She positioned him in front of the improba and guided the dildo into her mouth. Louise could hear something being said to the improba, but couldn't make out what it was.

When the improba gagged she held her slave for a moment. 'Stay there,' she ordered him, before returning to the rear of the girl. She picked up her paddle and swung it around, hitting the girl, who jerked forward with the momentum, causing her to gag again. For the next hit she held firm. Annabelle returned the paddle to the case and removed her gloves. She ran her fingernails up the improba's thighs, and Louise saw the girl shudder a little.

She moved to the girl's head and pushed her slave out of the way, withdrawing the dildo quickly from her mouth. She gasped in relief, but Annabelle grabbed her chin again and gave her a loud slap to one cheek.

Louise noticed a look of anger flash across the girl's face. Annabelle just smiled and dismissed her slave, who collected the things they'd used, packing them away, before returning to his seat. Annabelle grabbed the improba's hair and pulled her head up to face the Master.

'Not as resilient as the last one, but she shows promise,' she said, before roughly releasing the hair. 'Thank you, Master Victor, for allowing me the privilege of breaking your new improba in, a little.'

The Master nodded and waved in acknowledgement, and Annabelle returned to her seat, winking at Louise as she briefly looked over.

The Vox Domino spoke. 'The Master wishes to thank the Court of Humility's representative for honouring our time constraints this evening. However, he was impressed by the good use of that short time.'

Annabelle nodded in response, and smiled.

The Master nodded to the Madame Orator. She stood, nodded in return, and banged on the floor once with her staff.

'Members of the aula purpurea! Following the departure of Fidelia from the ranks of the arbitra, there is a requirement to fill this role as soon as practicable.'

She turned towards the Master. 'Master. Who do you propose to fill this role?'

Louise already knew the answer before the Vox Domino stood to speak.

'Madame Orator. Members of the aula purpurea. The Master has asked to appoint Mistress Vulpes to fulfil the vacant arbitra role.'

There was a quiet murmuring among some of the members, but Louise couldn't make out what was said.

The Orator stood and walked over to where Anna was sitting. Anna stood, and the Orator took her arm and led her to the middle of the room. Two of the arbitrae stood and moved to face Anna and the Orator. The Orator and Anna turned to face each other.

'Mistress Vulpes. A Court arbitra assists in keeping the peace within the aula, both while the Court is in session, and outside. This role comes with its own privileges, and restrictions. An arbitra is bound to the Court and Master, the rules of the arbitrae, and to the greater Order.

'The Master has requested that you relinquish your freedoms as one of the aulae, and serve the Court as one of the arbitrae. Do you accept the Master's request?'

Anna's face was serious when she answered. 'I do.'

The Orator and Anna both turned to face the two arbitrae. The Orator took Anna's arm and held it up in front of one of the arbitrae.

'Major Arbitra, I pass over to you Mistress Vulpes, presently of the aula purpurea, willing to renounce her freedoms of the aula in order to serve.'

One of the arbitrae took Anna's hand and spoke. 'I thank you, Madame Orator, for your presentation. Vulpes has now renounced all her claims and freedoms to general membership of the aula purpurea, in order to be bestowed with the honour and penance of the arbitra.'

The Orator let go of Anna's hand and stood back, before returning to her seat. Louise was wondering why all the ritual and ceremony was necessary, but was nonetheless intrigued with what was happening.

Then the Master stood, followed by everyone else in the room. Louise followed their lead. He stepped forward and put out his right hand in front of him. Anna held out her left hand, and the major arbitra proceeded to wrap purple cord around their arms, speaking as she did so.

'Vulpes, I bind you to the Master and the Court. As arbitra you will act as the Master's right hand, meting out discipline when required, and ensuring order in

Court.'

The other arbitra had produced a corset similar to the ones they were wearing. She put it around Anna's waist and tightened the laces at the back. She wedged her knee into the small of Anna's back as she pulled them, and Anna rocked a little with each tug.

The Major Arbitra spoke again. 'As this garment binds you, you are bound to the role of arbitra; you are bound to our rules, bound to the Court, and bound to the Order. Do you understand the terms of this agreement?'

'I do,' Anna replied.

The other arbitra had by now finished tying Anna's corset, had loosened the bindings to the Master, and was standing to one side.

The major arbitra continued. 'Then I give you this, the symbol of your office in our Court.'

She gave Anna a whip, which Anna hung by her side.

'Aulicae! I present to you Arbitra Vulpes.'

Many people stood up, and the major ancilla encouraged Louise to do the same. Altogether they spoke.

'Salve, Arbitra Vulpes.'

Anna faced the Master. 'Dominus, I thank you for this honour and promise to serve you, the Court, and the Order as best I can.'

The Master nodded, and everyone sat again.

The Vox Domino stood and walked over to Anna. 'The role of arbitra demands a lot. In recognition of this we give each of our arbitrae an assistant from the ranks of ancillae. Do you have a preference?'

Louise had a bad feeling.

'I would like ancilla Beatitas as my assistant,' Anna replied.

There were some murmurings around the room. Louise glared at the back of Anna's head.

'Major Ancilla!'

The major ancilla stood and took Louise's arm, gently pulling her to stand, which Louise did. She leant over to her and whispered. 'Don't worry, you'll be fine.'

It didn't help ease Louise's discomfort.

They walked to the Vox Domino and Louise's arm was passed to her. The Vox Domino spoke again.

'It is highly unusual for an ancilla to be initiated and given a role in the same evening, but this has been agreed by the Master, and you will receive instruction from both He and Arbitra Vulpes.'

She took hold of Anna's right hand and placed it by Louise's, as the major arbitra wound the soft cord around their arms.

'You are now bound to each other, to serve each other, and to serve the Master and Court.'

Anna grasped Louise's hand. 'Ego tibi gratias ago, mei domini.'

The cord was unwrapped from around their arms.

'Major Arbitra, see to it that your new office and her ancilla are prepared to prove devotion to the Master.'

'It will be done, Dominus.'

The two arbitrae led Anna and Louise to a small room off the chamber, where two men dressed as ianitors were waiting. They put wrist straps on them and fastened them to ropes hanging from the ceiling, before the Ianitoris and the arbitrae left, by different doors, leaving Anna and Louise standing, not quite hanging, in the middle of the room.

'What now?' asked Louise.

'They'll close the meeting, everyone else will leave while the Master comes in here to allow us to prove our devotion.'

'And what does that entail?'

Anna smiled. 'Nothing you haven't already experienced. It'll just be the Master, Marta, and us. You just need to confess, take penance and prove devotion to him, and then do it again for me.'

Louise closed her eyes. She was confused, dazed and didn't know where to begin. 'Beatitas?'

Anna smiled. 'It means intense pleasure.'

'I don't get it.'

Anna laughed. 'You don't know how you look when you orgasm.'

Louise blushed. The conversation didn't continue as the door from the chamber opened and in walked Dominus Victor, the Vox Domino, and Marta. Louise shot Anna a glance, who just smiled.

The Master took a seat behind a wooden desk, which looked just like the one Louise had been treated on at the party. Marta perched on the front edge of it, cross-legged. The Vox Domino stood in front of Anna and Louise.

'Vulpes, it's been a while,' she said as she stroked Anna's cheek.

'Domina Aurora. A rare pleasure.'

Aurora smiled and gave Anna a lingering kiss, which Anna seemed to enjoy. She then turned to look at Louise. She'd removed the mask she was wearing earlier.

'Beatitas, welcome to our world. Your Master has told me much about you.' She stroked Louise's cheek and neck, watching, as if examining her.

'Thank you, Domina,' Louise replied.

Aurora smiled. 'Before we get started, would either of you like a drink?' She walked over to the desk, undoing her corset and dress as she did, allowing them to fall. She stepped out of them and turned to face Anna and Louise. She was now only wearing high-heeled ankle boots, stockings and black knickers. She was slim with long legs, and her ample breasts supported themselves. Louise had guessed she'd be around the late thirties, and her body was very well looked after.

'If you don't mind,' Anna said.

'Yes, please,' Louise responded.

The Master poured water into two glasses and placed straws in them. Aurora picked them up and brought them over, allowing Anna and Louise to drink. Louise didn't realise how thirsty she was, and quickly drank it all.

Aurora returned the empty glasses to the desk and picked up a glass filled with red wine. 'I do find sitting through those meetings thirsty work,' she said. 'Especially when I have to do all the talking.' She glanced at the Master, who just shrugged in response. She looked back at Anna and Louise. 'Still, there are some perks.'

She motioned to Marta, who got off the table and followed her to Anna and Louise.

'Let's start with ancilla Beatitas,' she said. Marta moved behind Louise, and Aurora held Louise's head still, facing her.

'Ancilla!'

'Yes Domina?' Louise responded.

Aurora smiled. 'Do you have something to confess?'

Louise's mind went blank, before she recalled the events of her day. 'I rearranged everything on a colleague's desk when he was out of the office.'

Aurora smiled. 'Madame Intenta.'

Marta raised Louise's smock and smacked her bottom. Louise's buttocks tingled.

'Do you have anything else?'

'I deliberately ordered a meal I knew was not available.'

Aurora paused before speaking. 'Did they serve it to you?'

'They did.'

Aurora nodded, and Marta smacked Louise again.

'If you want to cause disruption you need to do it properly,' she said.

'I will remember that in future, Domina.'

'Anything else?'

Louise felt a little embarrassed. The only thing she could recall now seemed trivial. 'Yes, Domina,' she replied.

'Well?' Aurora's voice became a little stern.

'I left the toilet seats up in the ladies' lavatory.'

Aurora looked at her, puzzled, before putting her hand to Louise's groin and having a feel. 'Not just one seat?' she asked.

'All of them.'

'How many?'

Louise swallowed. 'Six,' she lied.

Aurora chuckled before speaking again. 'Madame Intenta.'

Marta smacked Louise's bottom a little harder, and a little lower, so she caught the tops of Louise's thighs. Louise writhed a little, enjoying the tingling sensation.

Aurora turned to the Master. 'I think we have a possible Improba here,' she said. The Master nodded. 'And speaking of Improba,' she said, walking to Anna, 'from naughty step to teacher's pet!'

'His Master's Choice,' Anna replied.

Louise felt this was some kind of joke between them, and she had no idea what it could allude to.

'And what do you have to confess?'

'I turned up to Court wearing no underwear,' Anna replied.

Louise raised an eyebrow.

'I thought that was the norm in Court. Or is that only for the men? A poor attempt. Madame Intenta.'

Marta smacked Anna's bottom with a paddle.

'Do you have anything better?'

'I took a case from one of my colleagues, while he was out shagging his assistant.'

'Really? Is he married?'

'Yes.'

'To his assistant?'

'No.'

'An open marriage?'

'Not to his wife's knowledge.'

'I'm sorry, but that is just what he deserves,' Aurora said, walking around Anna shaking her head. Louise heard the paddle slap Anna's bottom. Anna jerked in response.

'Haven't you anything juicy? Original?'

'I'm teaching ancilla Beatitas's assistant to be a dominatrix.'

Louise's head snapped around towards Anna, who continued to face forward.

Aurora caught sight of Louise's expression and laughed. 'Really? Is this true?'

Anna nodded. 'Yes. I suggested she take assertiveness training, and thought learning to be a dominatrix would be the ideal way.'

Louise caught sight of Marta giggling, and when she looked at the Master his shoulders were shaking, a hand covering his mask. Anna was biting her lip. Louise was just speechless.

'Will she be joining us anytime soon?' Aurora asked.

'No,' said Anna. 'She's only twenty-two.'

Louise was a little relieved; the thought of someone from work knowing about this side of her life bothered her. Aurora stepped in front of her gaze.

'Would you like to administer this punishment?' she asked.

Louise took a deep breath, and shook her head. 'No, Domina.'

Aurora raised her eyebrows. 'How restrained.'

Louise heard the slap of the paddle against Anna's buttocks, and then Marta made her way back to the desk, perching back on it before taking a drink.

Aurora tilted her head and stroked Louise's cheek again. 'So now you need to prove your devotion to the Master. And as I'm the Master's Voice, I suppose I get to choose the form of that devotion.'

Louise looked over to him, and he indicated for Aurora to continue, whereupon she leaned in to Louise and slowly sucked her earlobe, then whispered, 'He likes a good show, you know.'

Aurora moved over to Anna, put her arms and a leg around her, and pulled her close before kissing her. Anna closed her eyes. Louise couldn't watch for much longer as Marta moved to her, similarly clinching her, and licked up her throat before pushing her tongue deep into her mouth. Louise, with her arms tied above her head, could only close her eyes and enjoy the sensations. Marta used her hand to tilt Louise's head the other way, continuing the kiss, probing inside her warm mouth with her tongue. Marta tasted of orange, but the taste had a bit of an edge.

She lifted Louise's smock and let it hang from the clasps around her wrists. Apart from the slippers Louise was naked, and Marta began to explore her body with cool fingers, starting at her neck, slowly stroking downward, sometimes following up with soft kisses from moist lips, around Louise's pert breasts, tweaking the nipples, making them harder and ache more.

Marta stroked lower, meandering downward, followed by her tongue. Moving down to Louise's lower belly Marta kissed with soft kisses, her hands reaching around to her buttocks, squeezing, pulling them gently apart and running a finger between them.

Louise glanced at Anna; she and Aurora were kissing, tongues obviously involved, Aurora holding Anna's head with one hand and stroking between Anna's legs with the other. She looked at the Master, sitting back, one hand on the desk, the other on top of his walking cane. She half expected him to be playing with himself, but he wasn't; he was just watching.

Marta stood and unhooked the wrist straps. She pulled Louise to the desk, and after making her lie back in front of him she knelt up on it and lifted her skirt as she lowered herself onto Louise's face. Louise licked Marta's pussy. She was wet already, and smelled sweet. Masculine hands stroked her tummy and breasts. His touch was light and soft, and caused her skin to tingle. She felt for Marta's clitoris with her tongue and tried to concentrate on it, lightly licking and flicking.

She felt a warm tongue making its way up her thighs, each in turn, teasing her. She knew it was Anna, and felt more hands playing with her breasts, teasing her nipples, massaging them, occasionally brushing over them. She arched her back when Anna reached her clitoris, resulting in hands pushing her back down onto the desk, holding her still. She gasped, pausing her licking, prompting Marta to bear down on her until she resumed. Her tongue began to ache, but she continued to work on Marta. Soon she involuntarily let out a groan, muffled by Marta's groin. Anna's licking stopped and Marta climbed down from the desk, looking down at her.

'I think it's my turn,' Aurora said, taking her place over Louise's face, slowly lowering herself onto it. Louise resumed licking; this time Aurora's sweet pussy. She felt a hand on one of her breasts, and then a tongue on the other. Nails ran up and down her thighs. She wondered what the Master was up to, but that was answered by Aurora's sultry tones.

'You still like my breasts then, Master?'

Louise imagined him fondling Aurora's ample breasts while she sat on her face.

Aurora moaned. 'So, you like your newest little slave girl tonguing my pussy? Have you ever wondered what it would feel like to have her tongue licking up and down your shaft, taking it into her luscious little mouth? Wouldn't you like to fuck that juicy pussy of hers? She is your devoted slave after all, and I'm sure she'd do anything to please her Master, as she's the good little slave you've been telling me she is.'

There was silence, apart from the lapping of Louise's tongue inside Aurora's pussy. Louise tried to listen for any clue of what was happening.

'Or do you prefer to watch nowadays? When was the last time you had a good fuck?'

After a few moments Aurora lifted herself off Louise's face, and stood at the side of the desk. Louise looked around. Anna, it seemed, was feeling as awkward as she did, and Marta was looking a little angry. The Master grabbed Aurora by the wrists and pulled her to the ropes where she and Anna had been tied. He fastened her wrists together and hooked them up, but Aurora just laughed.

He picked up a paddle and swatted her buttocks a few times. After the first she thrust her pelvis, raising her buttocks to meet it.

'Are you warming me up for a good fucking?' she goaded after he'd finished. Her buttocks were red and she clenched and released them a few times, teasingly.

He walked over to Louise, still lying on the desk but watching him. He gently stroked her cheek with the back of a gloved hand, and then slowly traced down her body. She shivered as he finished at her thighs. She wasn't sure of his expression, hidden behind the mask, but she thought she saw a wistful quality, perhaps a longing, in his eyes.

The room was silent as he began to massage her gently between her legs. She winced as a seam ran over her clitoris. He stopped and examined the glove, then after giving her a seemingly apologetic look, he signalled to Marta.

'Ancilla, Arbitra, the Master dismisses you,' she said, unfastening their wristbands. They both put on their clothing and left by the door through which they'd been led in.

The Master opened one of the drawers in the desk. She didn't see what he withdrew as he looked up and paused. He nodded to her, so she moved out of the room and Anna closed the door behind them.

The hall looked different now it had been cleared of other furnishings.

'Is that what normally happens?' Louise asked.

'No, but I think Aurora was testing the Master's patience,' Anna replied.

They went out of the hall and into the changing room. There was a lady sitting, waiting, wearing jeans, a tight sweater and high heels. She stood as they entered, and Louise recognised her as Annabelle.

'So, how did it go?' she asked.

'Not as usual,' replied Anna. 'The devotion was cut short. It seems Aurora has something on her mind.'

'She only comes to this Court occasionally, and doesn't visit the other Courts with the Master. It's always Madame Intenta by his side. She doesn't even come to the events your Court organises. I'm surprised she's still a member.'

'She's worried she'll be recognised,' Anna continued. 'But everyone knows she did porn, and we've all seen some of it.' She paused. 'She not been since the gate-crashers.'

'What gate-crashers?' asked Louise.

'A couple of guys, avid fans, let's say, found out she'd be at one of our evenings and managed to get tickets. They expected a free fuck with their favourite porn star, I suppose. She hasn't been since to avoid such occurrences.'

'Is that when Lucian started vetting ticket holders?'

'I think so.'

Annabelle looked at Louise. 'So what did you think of tonight's events?'

Louise thought for a moment. 'It was different.'

The door opened and in strode Marta. She smiled at Louise as she walked over to a locker, and spoke as she emptied the contents. 'Hey, are you OK?' she asked.

'Yes, why?' Louise said.

'Well it's not normally like that. It's been a strange night and,' she paused, 'and Aurora's being strange too.'

'How so?'

'That's not how the devotion's supposed to go,' said Anna.

'What's supposed to happen?'

'You were supposed to show devotion to me as well as the Master.' Anna looked at Marta. 'And you're out sooner than I expected.'

'I think Aurora wanted him to show his devotion to her,' Marta replied.

'And I'm sure he's not just showing her his devotion either,' Annabelle said, in a smutty tone.

'So what's wrong with her?' Anna asked.

'I don't know, but it's between her and the Master,' Marta said, a little curtly.

Louise felt she was sending out the message not to ask any more about it. 'So, how do I show my devotion to you?' she asked Anna.

'At a time convenient for me,' Anna answered.

The three of them changed into their normal clothes and continued chatting between themselves and Annabelle.

'So, how's your friend Helen?' Annabelle asked.

'She seems to be doing well,' Louise replied.

'Do you think she'd like to come and play sometime?'

Louise caught Annabelle's meaning. 'I think she's a bit preoccupied with a new man in her life,' she said.

'Really? Anyone we know?'

Louise looked at Anna. 'Lucian,' she replied.

Annabelle stared at her for a moment. 'Not Lucian from...' a quizzical expression covered her face.

'Yes,' Louise nodded. 'Him.'

Annabelle looked at Anna, who just shrugged and nodded. 'But I thought...'

'Is she blonde with big breasts?' Marta interjected.

Louise looked at her. 'Yes. Why?'

Marta played with her own sizeable assets, grinning. 'He likes breasts.'

The three of them stared at Marta, who just shrugged and put her bra on, carefully placing each breast in place.

'Well, this *has* been a night of revelation,' Annabelle said.

Chapter Fourteen

Ad Domum

Anna shared the ride with Louise back to her apartment. It was the same driver as had brought Louise earlier. She recognised the area as soon as the car left the building, and watched the streets go by.

They rode in silence for a few minutes before Anna spoke. 'What's bothering you?'

Louise turned to look at her. 'What am I getting myself into?'

Anna watched Louise intently, but said nothing.

'Is this some kind of cult, or what?'

'No,' Anna said with a laugh. 'Most definitely not.'

'Then why the ceremony? I felt like a sacrificial lamb in that room.'

Anna placed a hand on Louise's arm. 'It was supposed to be a special night for you. Something for you to remember, and a common experience with all the other members of the Court.'

Louise snorted. 'I got involved with *him* because he made me feel special. I enjoyed his attention, whether he was talking to me, teasing me or tormenting me. Then he came to see me, and he doesn't seem to have as much time for me as he did.'

Anna spoke softly, gently stroking Louise's shoulder. 'It seems things have changed in the last few weeks, and he has other things to attend to.'

'So now I've committed myself to the Court he'll have less time for me?'

'I'm here.'

Louise gave a faint smile. She leaned over and hugged Anna. 'I do enjoy your company, but I guess I joined to get to know *him* better.'

Anna smiled. 'Smitten?'

Louise blushed and shrugged, looking away. She did feel something, but had hoped for something more in return.

'You may be seeing a little more of him now though,' suggested Anna.

'How so?'

'There are things going on which he has to deal with. He wanted my help with some of the problems, which is why I was given my new role.'

'What things?'

'You'll find out, just as I will. But you, as my ancilla, will be attending meetings with me, some of which he'll be present at.'

'It's not the same. I won't have his undivided attention.'

'I think the only person getting his undivided attention at present is Miss Angel.'

Louise shot Anna a glance. 'Who?'

'That's Aurora's old professional name; Georgia Angel.'

The name seemed vaguely familiar to Louise, but she made a mental note to look it up later. They pulled up outside her building.

'Do you want me to come in with you?' Anna asked.

'No, I'll be all right.'

'By the way, we have a Purple Court event weekend after next, and I've been given a task I'll want your help with,' Anna said, a little enigmatically. 'But I'll tell you nearer the time, and after you've shown your devotion to me.' She winked.

Louise laughed to herself and got out of the car. 'More secrets,' she said.

'Call them surprises,' replied Anna. 'They're much more fun. We'll be bringing someone's fantasy to life, but I'll give you the details during the week.'

Louise had her own fantasies that she might like enacted, but she wanted Him to be a part of them.

She waved Anna off and went inside. Helen was there, curled up on the sofa, mug in hand, watching TV.

'So, how'd it go?' she asked.

Louise hesitated.

'Don't tell me, it's a secret,' teased Helen.

Louise smiled. 'It was... unusual.'

She went into the kitchen to make herself a drink. As the kettle was warming up she went back to the lounge. 'Have you heard of Georgia Angel?'

Helen looked at her with a raised eyebrow. 'What, the MILF porn star?'

Louise was a little taken aback by the response. 'Well, I suppose so.'

'She was a bit adventurous. Did all sorts of porn; fetish, bondage and stuff. Why do you ask?'

'Oh, no reason.' Louise returned to the kitchen, but could feel Helen's eyes following her. When she returned with her coffee Helen continued the interrogation.

'So, was she there?'

'Who?'

'Georgia Angel.'

Louise paused. 'Perhaps.'

'And?' Helen looked at her expectantly.

Louise thought she should turn the tables. 'How do you know who she is?'

Helen wasn't fazed. 'An old boyfriend of mine was a bit obsessed. I drew the line at wearing a brunette wig.'

Louise laughed. 'And I thought gentlemen prefer blondes.'

'He was definitely not a gentleman!' Helen retorted.

They giggled, and snuggled on the sofa to watch the end of the film Helen was watching.

The next morning Louise wandered into the kitchen to make coffee, and was startled to see Lucian.

'Morning,' he said brightly.

Louise faltered. 'I didn't know you stayed the night.'

'He turned up early this morning,' said Helen, who was dressed.

Louise silently mouthed at her 'you could have warned me', but Helen just shrugged.

'So, how did you find last night?' Lucian asked.

Louise hesitated.

'She wouldn't tell me about it either,' said Helen. 'I suppose it's all a secret.'

Lucian gave Louise a slightly concerned look. 'Did everything go all right?' he asked.

'You were there, weren't you?' Helen said, slightly suspiciously.

Lucian turned to her. 'There are parts that are shared solely between candidate and Master, so that's a private affair.'

Helen gave Louise a cheeky smile. 'Oh, really? Did you get to see him?'

Louise shook her head. 'He kept his mask on.'

'Oh, kinky!' Helen exclaimed.

Louise was conscious of Lucian studying her expression before he said, 'I think that's between Louise and her Master, and we shouldn't pry any more.'

Helen tilted her head and raised both eyebrows at him, but he shook his head in response. She gave up and went through to the lounge.

Lucian put a hand on Louise's shoulder. 'As long as you're enjoying it you can remain a part of it,' he said. 'When you don't, then you can leave. There's no pressure.'

'OK,' Louise said.

'Do you know what you're doing at the next event?'

She thought back to the journey home. 'Anna said I'd be helping her do something, but she hasn't said what just yet.'

'I'm sure you'll enjoy it. Do you think Helen would like to come? I was thinking of inviting her along.'

'You could ask her,' suggested Louise.

Lucian and Helen went out for the day, leaving Louise to her own devices. She spent some of the time cleaning up, and some time looking up Aurora, or Georgia Angel, on the Internet, watching some of her films. Dated from around ten years earlier she thought she'd aged very well, and looked just as good in the flesh as on film, though sometimes the acting had something to be desired, but then again, nobody watched these films for the acting.

Louise felt a little jealous; it was supposed to have been her special night and she'd taken over. The evening was an anti-climax overall. And if she was going to be spending her time at the next event as Anna's assistant, then she was unlikely to get His exclusive attention.

An email arrived; it was from Him.

I must apologise for last night. My friend doesn't attend our evenings very often, but she always likes to be the centre of attention.

That may explain her former career choice, Louise thought.

Rest assured I will be personally supervising your training, and ensuring the correct discipline is administered. You will be hearing from me to make arrangements. Make sure you are available at the appropriate time, otherwise punitive action will be taken.

Louise had mixed feelings. She was relieved and yet unsettled. He hadn't forgotten her, at least. But with her being in a new job, one she was beginning to enjoy, she hoped they wouldn't clash.

The rest of the weekend passed fairly uneventfully. Louise had expected to hear from her Master or Anna, but she heard from neither. She'd thought about calling Anna, but instead chose to go over her work from the previous week.

Helen spent it with Lucian, arriving back early evening Sunday. Lucian apparently had to be up early to catch a train. Louise wondered why Helen hadn't stayed over, but didn't ask; Helen was happy, and she didn't want to ruin it.

She returned to work early on Monday, and Sally had beaten her to it; apparently Louise wasn't the only one enjoying her new job. Sally spent most of her time in Louise's office rather than at her desk, and it wasn't until Louise noticed Phil, the IT guy, hanging around outside that she twigged.

'Is he bothering you?' she asked.

Sally looked up, out of the office window to where Louise was looking. 'Not really,' she replied, shifting a little uncomfortable as she spoke. 'He keeps appearing in the kitchen when I'm there, and asking if I need anything. He seems a bit... creepy.'

'Would you like me to speak to him?'

'No, that's OK.'

So much for Anna's assertiveness training, Louise thought to herself.

Peter came in shortly afterwards and reviewed their progress, to which Louise began to take exception. It was as if he thought Louise was being reckless in her proposals. He came in again on Tuesday afternoon, asking her to be more cautious, but Louise was confident in what she was doing; she had, after all, made a lot of money for her previous employer, and didn't see this as any different. She was relieved when Peter spent all of Wednesday in his office, not interrupting or criticising her.

It was also Wednesday when she heard from Anna via the YMV app. She had to visit her place that evening for the start of her "training".

About time, Louise caught herself thinking, wondering why she felt a little irritable.

'Problem?' Sally asked, as she entered the office with their coffees.

Louise looked up. 'Oh no, just a personal thing.'

She felt irritable for the rest of the day. A couple of times she snapped responses to Sally's questions, but quickly apologised. Sally was beginning to tread carefully around her, which just made Louise more tense. Partly because of her mood, but also because of her evening appointment, she left at five o'clock on the dot. Sally stayed to get more research ready for the following day.

She got back to the flat, and after showering, changed into comfortable clothes, as she had no idea what was expected of her. She was beginning to feel a little excited, imagining all kinds of ways in which her "training" may be administered. As she opened the door to leave she bumped into Helen.

'If you're off to the gym hang on and I'll join you,' she said.

'No, I'm seeing Anna,' Louise replied as she squeezed past.

'Oh, can I come along?' she asked.

'It's, um, just me,' Louise replied, a little breathlessly.

Helen regarded her for a moment, and smiled a little. 'OK, have fun,' she said.

'Thanks.' Louise hurried off and made her way to Anna's place.

Despite making her way through the homeward bound masses on the underground, she arrived in good time. She pressed the doorbell and waited. There were no sounds coming from the flat. She checked her phone again for messages.

'You're early,' said a stern voice.

Startled, she looked around to see Anna walking up the corridor. She began to smile but Anna tapped her ear. Louise noticed her Bluetooth earpiece, and took a moment to realise He must be talking to her. She bowed her head. 'Sorry... arbitra.'

'As my ancilla I am your mistress, and you must address me as such.'

'Yes, mistress.'

Anna stood as though considering her. Louise wondered if He was giving her instructions. Anna then unlocked the door to her apartment. She stepped in and opened the door to the room Louise had first visited.

Louise entered the apartment, wiped her feet, and went through into Anna's playroom. Anna followed her through, closing the door behind her. She switched on her computer, before turning to look at Louise. 'You need to disrobe.'

'Yes, mistress.'

Louise took off her shoes, pulled off her top and bra, before stepping out of her leggings and knickers. Anna handed her a smock, similar to the one she'd worn at Court, which Louise put on.

Anna ran an application and Louise noticed some webcams around the room lit up. A few moments later the speakers crackled into life, and the familiar computer voice spoke as Anna left the room.

'Good evening ancilla Beatitas. I trust you had a good day today.'

'Yes thank you, Master.'

'Your mistress is not properly prepared and attired. You will need to wash and clothe her.'

'Yes Master.' Louise looked around, and noticed Anna's arbitra clothes were hanging up.

'Please face forward.'

Louise turned back to face the computer. Anna returned with a bowl and sponge. She laid it down in front of Louise and stood by her side.

'You will need to disrobe your mistress before washing.'

'Yes, Master.'

Louise moved behind Anna and slipped her suit jacket off, slipping it on a hanger which was one of two on a hook on the back of the door. She moved to Anna's front and carefully unbuttoned her blouse, pulling it out from the skirt when she reached the waistband. She unbuttoned the cuffs before moving around to gently pull off the blouse. She hung it on the other hanger, then went to unclip Anna's bra.

'Skirt next,' said Anna, firmly.

'Sorry, mistress,' Louise replied, obeying. She didn't let it drop, but lowered it to her feet. Anna stepped out of it and Louise hung it up with the jacket.

Anna was wearing a black bra, black knickers, black stockings and suspender belt, and was still standing in her black stilettos. Louise wondered whether she went to work wearing these things, or whether she had changed at some point. Wherever their Master was he must have had an erection by now, watching beautiful Anna being undressed by another woman.

'Now the bra,' said Anna.

Louise unclipped it and gently eased the straps off Anna's shoulders. Anna gave a soft sigh. Louise reached around and carefully removed the bra cups from Anna's breasts. She allowed her thumbs to brush Anna's nipples, expecting to be chastised, but instead Anna pushed her bottom back against her. Louise got the message.

Knowing where Anna got her lingerie from she resisted the urge to just discard the bra, instead hanging it again on the back of the door. She crouched and slowly started to pull Anna's knickers down, lightly stroking her thighs and calves as she did. She liked the feel of Anna's stockings. Anna breathed out slowly as Louise got lower. Louise felt the tension rising, the anticipation of what may come.

Anna stepped out of her knickers and Louise hung them up. As she turned back she noticed Anna watching her with a smirk. 'Are you always so fastidious with clothing?' she asked.

'Sorry, mistress,' Louise replied. She carefully unhooked Anna's stockings and removed her suspender belt, casually dropping it to the floor. And then she started on the stockings, rolling the left one down, brushing Anna's thigh, who inhaled deeply, her eyes closed, a contented look on her face.

Finishing at her ankle Louise looked up at Anna, who placed a hand on Louise's shoulder to steady herself while lifting her foot, allowing Louise to remove her shoe and the stocking.

Anna replaced her foot on the floor and kicked off her other shoe. Louise rolled the right stocking slowly down the thigh, Anna casually stroking Louise's hair. Down slowly to the ankle, and again Anna supported herself on Louise's shoulder while the stocking was removed.

Anna stood naked. Louise picked up the sponge from the bowl and squeezed the warm soapy water out. 'Where would you like me to start, mistress?'

'From the neck, downwards.'

Louise moved behind her, and holding up her hair, she sponged around her neck, reaching around to the front. Anna bent her head slightly to accommodate. Louise then moved to her shoulders, and Anna held her hair up as she did, straightening one arm at a time as Louise sponged them, moving towards the wrists.

She then started washing Anna's back, slowly drawing the sponge down. Anna wriggled a little as the dribbles worked their way via the small of her back. Louise continued to slowly stroke downwards and watched the dribbles run between Anna's buttocks.

Anna raised her arm as Louise worked down her side, and then around to Anna's front. Dipping the sponge in the bowl again she started from the wrist, squeezing the sponge slightly to release soapy water down to Anna's breasts.

She moved around to the other side, and Anna raised her arm to allow access. Louise knelt to wash her buttocks, allowing more liquid to drip down them from the sponge. She took her time, and with her free hand gently stroked the back of Anna's thigh. Anna moved her legs apart to allow her between, and Louise washed the insides of her thighs and then continued down her legs, backs of her knees and calves, moving around to the front.

She washed Anna's pubic hair, moving her head a little closer, smelling the sweet scent of Anna's pussy...

'Ladies!'

They froze, looking at the computer.

'Please concentrate on the job at hand. We haven't much time.'

With a sigh Louise hurriedly washed down the front of Anna's legs. She stood and picked up a towel folded on the computer shelf, and dried Anna briskly before hanging the towel over a radiator. She then picked up Anna's clothes and dressed her, putting on her knickers and slip before carefully putting on the corset. All that remained was the whip. Louise picked it up and returned to Anna, wondering where to put it. Anna relieved her of it and tied it to the side of her corset.

'At last,' the computer voice said. 'Arbitra Vulpes, offer your ancilla a seat.'

Anna took a folding chair from one corner and placed it behind Louise. 'Sit,' she ordered.

Louise did she was told. She realised she hadn't been using the Latin she'd been taught.

The computer spoke again. 'We will be hosting an evening soon, and as a member of our Court you will be expected to assist.'

'Yes, Master.'

'Arbitra Vuples has been asked to arrange one of our private sessions, and you will be assisting her.'

'Of course, Master.'

'Vulpes, is there anything Beatitas needs to know beforehand?'

Anna stood next to Louise as she spoke. 'She'll need to bring a smart business suit with her.'

Louise looked up at her. This was different from the time she visited with Helen, when they'd been made to wear cat and mouse outfits.

'But not your best one,' Anna added.

Louise was curious, but knew better than to ask without permission.

The Master went on to explain the etiquette; what was expected of members of the hosting aula, what was expected of the ancillae, and also dealing with unacceptable behaviour of guests towards aulae and other guests. Arbitrae and ianitors would be on hand to resolve any difficulties, and though as hosts they were there to ensure the enjoyment of guests, they didn't have to do anything they didn't want to. Guests chose their fantasies, and hosts chose to what extent they participated. She would, as with other participating hosts, be driven to and from the event, and she'd be notified of the time once the ianitors had arranged their schedule. Though she appreciated what they were talking through was important, she couldn't wait for the real fun to begin. She was tingling with anticipation.

'Do you have any questions?'

Louise wracked her brains for a sensible one, but all she could think of was her impending experience. 'No, Master,' she eventually replied.

There was a pause before the computer spoke again.

'Then I must ask you to leave as there are things I must discuss with my arbitra.'

Louise sat for a moment, stunned. 'Very well, Master,' she replied. She stood and glanced at Anna, who looked equally surprised and possibly disappointed. They nodded at each other before she collected her clothes and left the room. She changed in the hall, and could hear through the door.

'Arbitra Vulpes, you are aware that as arbitra you do have additional duties and responsibilities to the Court?'

'Yes, Master.'

'We will discuss some of these matters shortly, but first, how are your preparations going for your programme?'

'They're mostly in hand, Master. But I wondered if I may borrow your desk?'

Louise didn't hear the reply as she left the apartment, dressed in her own casual clothes, leaving the smock folded up on the floor by the door to Anna's playroom.

She returned home, frustrated, and hoped Helen wasn't in so she'd be able to relieve herself in private without having to be careful of disturbing her temporary flatmate. But she was disappointed when she arrived to find Helen and Sally there.

'Everything go all right?' Helen asked.

'Yeah, sure,' Louise snapped back.

'Coffee?'

Louise paused and tried to relax a little before answering. 'That would be good, thanks.'

Helen went into the kitchen and Sally stood. 'I'm sorry for calling in,' she said, 'but I thought you ought to know.'

Louise looked at her quizzically.

'Peter came in after you'd left...'

'And?'

'He's looked through our work, and is insisting that we run the final report through him before submitting it to Jefferson. I mean, Mr Haringay.'

'Like hell I will,' snapped Louise, and Sally was a little taken aback. 'I'm sorry, I didn't mean to snap at you.'

Helen came back with Louise's coffee. 'Here you go, pet.'

'Thanks.' Louise took the drink and slumped into a chair. Helen sat and motioned to Sally to do likewise again.

'How did you get on this evening otherwise?' Louise asked.

Sally reached into her bag and pulled out some papers. 'I found this, which I thought could be interesting.'

She passed them over to Louise, who glanced through the pages. She reached the last and looked closer, and then reread the whole document more carefully. When she finished the second read she put it down and smiled.

'Good work, Sally. We'll have to rewrite some of our report tomorrow, but I'm sure Jefferson will be impressed with what we've got.'

Sally smiled back. 'Thanks boss.'

'Peter hasn't seen this, has he?' Louise asked. She didn't know what he was playing at, but she was damned sure he wasn't going to take credit for their work.

'No. He came in just before I discovered it.'

'Then we'll work hard tomorrow and hand it to Jefferson in the evening. Our work, not watered down by Peter.'

The three of them started chatting about other things, and Sally left half an hour later. Louise headed off to bed shortly afterwards and tried to relieve her frustration, but unfortunately couldn't quite get there, perhaps because she was having to stifle herself with Helen being within earshot. Still frustrated she eventually drifted off to sleep.

CHAPTER FIFTEEN

IRA

The following day Louise and Sally arrived at the office early and began collating their intelligence, rewriting the report they'd started a few days earlier. At lunchtime Sally arranged for sandwiches and coffees to be brought to them, so they could work through. They didn't see Peter at all during the day, much to Louise's relief.

It was almost seven when they finished. They'd printed off a couple of copies and worked through them checking for typos, making sure all the references were correctly identified, and generally reviewing the document.

'We'll drop it off with Tina to pass on to Jefferson, and then nip out for a meal,' Louise suggested.

Sally was fine with that. They grabbed their coats and bags and went to Jefferson's office. He wasn't around, but Tina was.

'Here's the report for Jefferson,' Louise said, handing it to her.

'But Peter's already given it to him,' said Tina, not taking the document.

'What?' Louise said.

'He came down earlier and gave it directly to Jefferson before he left for the day. He's going to read it overnight.'

'Bastard!' Louise cursed. She turned to Sally. 'I'll see you down in reception shortly. I'm going to have a few words with our *colleague*.' She spat the final word in disgust. 'And then we'll go off for that drink.'

She stormed off to Peter's office.

There was no one around on the floor but she could make out a light shining through the closed blinds of his office. She marched up to the door, thrust it open, and banged it closed. Peter looked up.

'What the fuck do you think you're doing?' she yelled.

He opened his mouth to answer but didn't get chance.

'I was asked to do a job and you're hell bent on stopping me. Are you trying to make me look stupid or something?' she seethed.

Peter rose from his desk. 'No, I didn't want you to get fired.'

'What?' She was incredulous.

'We don't like to take chances like those you proposed, and I didn't want you to get fired after only just starting.'

'But this is my job, to make assessments and recommendations.' Louise realised she hadn't been given too many specifics of her job, but she was already in full flow. 'I'll pass my recommendations on and it's up to Jefferson whether they're followed or not. If I'm going to be fired it should be because of what I've done or not done.'

Peter walked up to her. 'I'm trying to protect you.'

Louise slapped him. 'I don't need your protection.'

'I'm sorry,' he said, a little meekly. Louise felt guilty at lashing out. 'But there's nothing I can do now. Jefferson has the report and will already be reading it.'

Louise balled her hands into fists, fuming.

He put a hand on her shoulder but she just brushed it off. 'I'm sorry,' he said again. 'Could I at least buy you dinner?'

'Trying to buy off the little lady, are you?' she snapped. Memories of her previous mistreatment at the hands of her former employer went through her mind, and Peter seemed no different, undermining her and then trying to patronise her.

'No of course not,' he said, flustered. 'I just...'

Louise glared at him.

'I just didn't want to lose you.'

'What?'

Peter took a deep breath. 'I like you, a lot, and I don't want to see you go.'

Louise leant on the table, open-mouthed.

'I thought perhaps, in time, we might get to know one another better...' he said, tailing off at the end.

Louise shook her head. She felt a mixture of emotions; pity, ire, guilt. He normally seemed to be so confident, attractive, and yet he struggled here talking to her. She felt a sudden warmth and something took hold; in a moment her emotions seemed to have turned to lust. She reached to him, pulling him close. They kissed passionately and Louise lowered herself back onto his desk, pulling him in with her legs. He didn't resist, bending to continue kissing. She unbuttoned his shirt and ran her hands over his shoulders, pushing his shirt off. She felt hot and started to unbutton her blouse. Peter followed the journey down, kissing her neck, chest, tummy, teasing her as he moved further down. Not wanting to impede his journey she quickly pulled her skirt up and her knickers down, momentarily pushing him away as she lifted her knees. He was taken a little by surprise but returned to her tummy, kissing down to her waistband, and then below.

He moved past her skirt to the top of her thighs, kissing one and then the other. Louise was getting agitated and eagerly pushed his head between her legs. He kissed her clitoris, licking it. She groaned; it seemed she had waited so long for this moment, filled with anticipation, she could bear it no longer and lifted her hips, pressing harder against his face. He pushed his tongue inside her, flicking in and out while his hands caressed her thighs. Louise began to shake.

'More, please!' she uttered breathlessly, then looked up as he moved away. She propped herself up on her elbows as she watched him walk over to his jacket and take out his wallet. He removed a condom and hurriedly fumbled with it. Louise slipped off the desk and grabbed it. She unzipped his fly, unbuckling his belt, dropped his trousers to the floor and pulled his trunks down to his ankles. She grabbed his cock and it reacted to her touch. She smiled, enveloping it in her mouth, staying there for a moment, taking a deep breath, savouring the slightly salty taste of him. She licked up and down a few times before taking him in her mouth again, sucking deep. She could tell he wasn't going to last long, and she desperately needed him inside her.

She grabbed the condom, opened the packet and placed it on his helmet. She worked it along his length with her mouth, trying not to push him closer to the edge. She stood, lay back on the desk and guided him into her. They both gasped as he entered her. They stayed still for a few moments before he began to slowly draw out, and then in again. She trembled; she needed him to fuck her.

'Harder!' she demanded.

Peter responded by quickening his speed, thrusting deeper with each stroke. Louise moaned and tried to angle her hips, to get him even deeper. Peter began to grunt with each thrust. Louise was nearly there. She began to shudder. He fell onto his hands, supporting himself above her as he thrust in and out, intensity gripping his face.

Moments later she was rewarded by her much anticipated orgasm. She tried to hold herself in position, shuddering as she was, trying to maintain the pleasure while Peter continued to push in and out of her. Ripples of pleasure passed through her body. She knew he wouldn't be long either. As she shook it seemed to bring him closer, and closer until he exploded, his twitching within her intensifying her bliss, triggering the intense tide of a second orgasm.

As Louise's orgasms subsided she relaxed, slowly lowering herself back onto the table. She grabbed his head, pulling him down for a long, sensuous kiss. She felt as though she were glowing with pleasure, melting at the closeness she felt with him.

They heard a sound coming from outside the office. The blinds and door were closed, so no one could have seen them, but after a brief pause they hurriedly dressed, straightening their clothes.

'I'll speak with Jefferson in the morning,' he said apologetically.

Louise took a few moments to regain her train of thought; she was still a little breathless. 'OK, thanks,' she replied, almost absently.

Peter touched her arm and she looked up at him. 'C-c-could we go for dinner?' he asked, meekly.

Louise was taken by surprise. 'I've got plans for tonight,' she replied, a little too quickly.

'At the weekend, perhaps?' He was almost pleading in his tone.

Louise wanted time to think. 'I'll let you know tomorrow,' she said. She opened the door to leave, but stopped. She turned to look at him, and then gave him a peck on the cheek before leaving his office.

She found Sally in reception. 'Sorry about that,' she said. 'We'll have to catch Jefferson in the morning.'

Sally smiled at her; a knowing smile, but said nothing. They visited one of the nearby pizzerias for something to eat and drink, and parted a couple of hours later, having arranged to be in early in the morning.

Lucian was leaving her apartment when she arrived home.

'Working late?' he asked.

'Yes, I have a deadline tomorrow,' she said.

'Then I'll let you go and rest.'

She walked in and found Helen making a drink in the kitchen.

'Green tea?'

'Please.'

Helen looked at her. 'What happened?'

Over tea Louise related her evening encounter with Peter, while Helen's grin just got wider and wider.

'Are you going to have dinner with him?'

'I honestly don't know,' Louise admitted. Her emotions and thoughts were all over the place.

The next morning she was up before Helen. She washed, dressed, and went off to work. Sally was already at her desk when she arrived.

'Mr Haringay wants to see you,' she said.

'Shit!' Louise grabbed the report and made her way to Jefferson's office. The door was closed and Peter sat outside. He started to stand, but Louise waved him down.

'Have you spoken to him yet?' she asked.

'No. He was in before I was, and I was in early.'

Louise checked the clock; it wasn't even eight yet.

She sat, leant forward with her head in her hands. Peter touched her shoulder.

'About last night...'

'I'm more concerned with getting this sorted,' she snapped, emphasising the report in her hand. Peter edged away a little. She looked at him. 'I'm sorry. I'm not feeling great today.'

'It's my fault.'

'We'll talk later.'

Tina emerged from the office. 'Jefferson will see you now,' she said, holding the door open.

Louise had a flashback to her schooldays, going into the head's office for some misdemeanour. Jefferson had a report in his hand. He started to speak before they'd sat down.

'I must say I had high hopes, but I've been left quite disappointed,' he began.

'It's my fault,' Peter interjected.

'We're all adults. If Miss Coleman can't put her views across—'

'That's not my report,' Louise snapped.

The men looked at her.

She dropped her report on the desk in front of Jefferson. 'That's my report.' She felt herself almost shaking.

Jefferson put the report in his hand down, picked hers up, and began to read.

He tilted his head momentarily. 'Then where did this come from?'

'I wrote that one, using Louise's data,' said Peter.

Jefferson snorted. 'Well I could tell it was your handiwork. But I took on Miss Coleman for her expertise and analysis. And now that I have it I will evaluate her role within the organisation as I read her report. I will call you both back later.'

He waved them away, and they both left.

'About last night,' Peter started.

'Later,' she replied, walking off.

'Well?' Sally asked as Louise returned to her office.

Louise sighed. 'We'll have to wait and see.'

To pass the time they continued looking at their research, reviewing again the report detail, but the pair of them were subdued. It was almost lunchtime when Tina knocked on the door.

'Jefferson would like to see you,' she said.

Louise looked at Sally, who shrugged, and left for Jefferson's office. She saw Peter heading the same way. 'Have you heard anything?' she asked quietly.

He shook his head. 'No. And it's difficult to guess what Jefferson's thinking, so there's no point trying.'

They entered the office and Tina closed the door behind them. Jefferson motioned for them to sit. They sat in silence for a few moments, before he picked up the open report from his desk.

'Miss Coleman, I've read through your analysis and you've done a very thorough job.'

'Thank you,' she replied instinctively. Her mind began to race, trying to anticipate what he was about to say next. "A very thorough job, but not what we're looking for", maybe.

'Would you be able to oversee the strategy you've proposed?'

Startled she looked at Peter, who had a blank look on his face, and back to Jefferson. 'Yes, of course.'

'Good. I'll need a fully budgeted proposal for any additional staffing and facilities required, both here and wherever you believe would be best placed to serve our operations.'

She was taken aback. This was somewhat above and beyond what she'd dealt with before, but she was confident she could deliver. It was also a lot of responsibility for someone new to the company.

Jefferson rose and walked to her, his arm extended for a handshake. Louise automatically shook his.

'I'm so glad I brought you in; you'll be an asset to the company.'

Louise was flattered, but also realised he was leading her out of the office, leaving Peter. Once outside he moved closer to speak quietly.

'Has Peter seen your latest analysis?'

'No,' she answered quietly.

'Good. Keep it that way for the time being. Just between you, your assistant and me.'

Louise nodded and Jefferson returned to his office, closing the door. As Louise turned to go Tina stood and approached her.

'Mr Haringay has asked me to go through the internal charging system of the company with you.'

'OK,' replied Louise. Things seemed to be working out like a dream.

They returned to Louise's office to find Sally talking to Helen. Helen stood to greet Louise. Tina, on seeing Helen, offered to return later, and returned to Jefferson's office. Sally left too, leaving them alone.

'So, what's happened?'

Louise was still a little dumbfounded. 'I've got a serious project to work on!'

'That's brilliant. Is his name Peter?'

Louise went blank for a moment. 'No, I mean work.'

Helen laughed. 'So what's happening with your guy?'

There was a knock on the door. Louise opened it expecting Sally, and instead found Peter standing there.

'I just thought I'd congratulate you,' he said. 'Jefferson isn't easily impressed.'

'Thank you.'

He noticed Helen. 'Sorry, I didn't realise you were busy.'

'No, Peter, this is Helen, my friend. Helen, Peter.'

Helen stood, wearing her salacious grin. '*Hello*, Peter. I've heard all about you.'

He shifted a little uncomfortably, while Louise glared at her.

'Lucian and I are going out for a meal tomorrow evening. Why don't the two of you join us?'

Louise and Peter looked at each other, a little panic in their eyes. Flustered, they tried to refuse but Helen was insistent, and once she had agreement from both she bade them farewell.

'I'm sorry about my friend,' Louise said.

'She seems like a good friend.'

'She is.' Louise paused. 'So I supposed we'll be working on the next stage together.'

'Jefferson has asked me to take on a different role now, so you'll be on your own. But you'll be fine.'

'Thank you, but I'm still new to the company. So what will you be doing?'

Peter was hesitant. 'He wants me to look at the corporate risk in the business. It's something I've been suggesting to him for a while, and now he feels we need something done.'

'Is it what you wanted?'

'Not my first choice, but I know how the business should work so that should help. Anyway, I only popped in to congratulate you, and to say I'm glad you're here.'

Saturday morning and Helen was again off with Lucian for the day, leaving Louise to her own devices. She went over the events at work for the past few days, making a rough plan of what to do the following week. She also realised Sally was still having problems with the IT guy, though she was caught up in her own problems to think anything of it.

Her phone buzzed. It was the YMV app. It was from Anna, to make arrangements for a meet up on Monday evening. She wondered briefly why she didn't just call to ask. She looked up the address of the pub and realised it was the same place where Helen had humiliated her ex. The only stipulation was to wear clothes suitable for a girls' night out. It seemed odd that Anna would request such a thing, unless of course it was Court business, which may explain why she'd used YMV.

She went shopping in the afternoon, returning to her empty apartment. After putting the groceries away she had a drink before going to get ready for their night out; dinner with Helen and Lucian and Peter. She'd still not had a chance to talk things through with him, but then again, she didn't really know what to say. She wasn't sure she wanted a committed relationship, or maybe she wanted a relationship with the one man she didn't really know.

It was a warm evening so she wore a sleeveless dress. She didn't know where they'd be dining, but they were meeting in a wine bar close to some very elite establishments. She realised she was running late. She hailed a taxi and made her way to the wine bar.

Helen and Lucian were already there when she arrived, even though Helen was usually the late one. And then she saw Peter, who stood as she walked over. She gave him a peck on the cheek before sitting down. Their glasses were almost empty.

'Have I got time for a drink?' she asked.

'I'm sure you have,' said Helen, though Lucian gave her a look; he'd obviously booked somewhere and the time was close.

Peter stood. 'I'll get it,' he insisted. 'What would you like?'

A double date with Helen. And Peter. It would have to be something strong. And quick. 'Double brandy, if you don't mind.'

Helen raised an eyebrow.

'Anyone else?' asked Peter.

Helen and Lucian shook their heads, and Peter went off to the bar.

'Annabelle's asked me to go out Monday evening,' Helen said, as soon as Peter was out of earshot. 'Shall we go?'

'Did Annabelle ask you and a friend, or just you?' asked Lucian.

Helen turned to look at him. 'I'm sure it'd be fine if I ask her. I'm not sure I'd want to go alone.'

'If she said you, she meant *you*,' Lucian replied. 'She is usually very specific.'

'Oh. Then I'll not go unless you go,' she said to Louise.

'I have something on Monday evening,' Louise replied.

'Oh.' Helen seemed surprised for a moment. 'Are you seeing Peter again?' she said with a smile.

'No,' said Louise, not wanting to be drawn further. Peter would be returning with her drink anytime.

'Why don't you go with Annabelle alone,' suggested Lucian. 'I'm sure the two of you will have an interesting time.'

Peter returned, Helen looking at Lucian, puzzled. Louise wondered if he knew he was due to meet Anna.

She downed her drink, the others finished theirs, and they went off to the restaurant, in Chinatown.

To Louise dinner seemed to consist of mainly Peter trying to work out what Lucian did, and Lucian evading the subject. She ended up wondering too. And then they were interrupted by a fellow diner.

'Peter! I didn't think this was your sort of place!' The man was slightly older, rotund, and more than a little inebriated.

Peter stood and greeted him. 'Nice to see you Maxwell. How are you?'

'I'm good. Record profits this year, so we're out celebrating.' Maxwell looked around, smiling at Louise and Helen. His eyes stopped on Lucian. Then he turned back to Peter. 'Is Jefferson having problems?' he said.

'No...' Peter began, before being interrupted.

'Well I can't think of anyone better than this man,' he laid a hand on Lucian's shoulder, 'to weed out your problems.' He turned to Lucian, offering his hand. 'Good to see you again, especially not in your professional capacity.'

He slurred his last word, which Louise found amusing. Lucian stood and shook his hand.

'I'm pleased I could be of satisfactory service to you,' he said. 'Now if you don't mind I'm dining with my friends.'

Louise didn't think Maxwell had taken Lucian's hint, but he turned to Peter, tapped his nose and winked. 'Dining with friends, eh? Don't worry. Your secret's safe with me.'

He returned to his party, to the relief of Louise. Other diner's nearby had turned to look, as Maxwell wasn't the quietest drunk in the world.

'So what do you do?' Peter asked directly.

Louise thought Lucian was going to wriggle out of answering again, but Helen chipped in.

'Yes, what do you do?' She had one of those looks a man would dare not defy.

He sighed. 'Security,' he said.

'There must be more to it than that,' she countered.

Lucian paused before answering quietly. 'Security systems. Secure data storage and protection. Consultancy. Counter-espionage.'

Helen gasped. 'As in spies and stuff?'

'Industrial and commercial spies.'

Peter stared at him, and Louise was curious when he spoke again. 'Could I have your business card?'

Both Lucian and Peter seemed to be in somewhat odd moods at the end of dinner, so Helen and Louise returned home on their own. Sunday they caught up on washing, cleaning, and went to the gym for a swim. Lucian didn't call Helen, but Helen didn't seem much bothered. Louise wondered if something else had gone on that she was unaware of.

Back at work Monday, Louise and Sally continued with their work. They had a few days to create resource and budget plans. Peter popped into her office, asking if she was available for dinner that evening. Louise apologised and suggested lunch the following day. Unfortunately Peter was going out of the country for a few days, so they agreed to meet up when he returned.

The other notable thing that happened during the day was Sally chastising the IT guy, Phil. Louise overheard raised voices. He said something like it'd be best for her to meet him, and she told him firmly where to go. Then he said something that surprised her; he said he'd get his uncle Jefferson to have her fired. Louise stood to leave her office and have words, but stopped when she heard Jefferson's voice.

'Phileas! You're only here because my sister, your grandmother, asked me as a favour. If you wish to remain you need to treat the rest of my staff with respect.'

'Is that understood?'

After a few moments Louise heard Jefferson reassuring Sally. Phileas had been quite troublesome and his sister had hoped a job at Jefferson's firm would help put him back on track. If Sally had any more problems she should let Jefferson himself know. Louise didn't think she would have any more, judging by the way Sally had handled him earlier. Anna's assertiveness training was paying off.

CHAPTER SIXTEEN

AUXILIUM

Monday evening came, and Louise had dressed tastefully for a night out with Anna. Anna was sat in one of the cubicles, watching a couple of guys at the bar. Both men looked familiar to Louise; one had been one of the ianitors at the Court meeting, but the other she couldn't quite place.

Anna got the drinks in, and they sat and chatted about how their days had gone, Anna keeping an eye on the two guys. Eventually curiosity got the better of Louise.

'What are we doing here?'

'Shhh! Watch.'

Louise looked over, and there was a woman, dressed in a red mini-dress which she allowed to ride up her thighs, chatting to both men, sensuously touching both of them, stroking their arms, necks and cheeks. Louise thought she was a little brazen. After ten minutes the woman moved off and headed to the toilet.

Anna stood and nodded over to the guys; Louise followed. They sat on stools and Anna began to talk to them. Louise stared at the man whose face seemed familiar, but she couldn't quite recall.

'I'm sorry, but have we met?' she asked him.

He smiled. 'You chatted up me and one of my friends a few weeks ago.'

'Oh.' It took a minute for the penny to drop. Oh! She'd chatted two guys up, just as this other woman was doing, at her Master's bidding. And after going off to the toilet she'd made her exit, while two ladies were chatting to the guys. She realised the others were watching her reaction. 'It's a set-up, isn't it?'

Anna laughed. 'Of course. We wouldn't want to put anyone at risk.'

One of the guys made a signal with his hand and began talking about sport. Louise looked around, and realised the woman was returning; surely she should have left. She pushed her way between Anna and Louise, standing between the two guys, stroking both on the cheek with each hand.

'Well boys,' she purred, 'are you going to show this girl a good time?'

The ianitors looked over at the barman, who nodded. 'We can go out back, if you like, where it's nice and private.'

The woman nodded and he led the way into the same backroom where Helen had cuckolded her ex. Anna and Louise waited for a moment, before following.

'Is this supposed to happen?' she whispered to Anna.

'No,' she replied. 'But we're going to deal with this.'

They walked through the door, which Anna made sure was firmly closed after them. The woman looked around.

'Oh, boys, we have an audience. Let's show them how it's done.'

A phone bleeped.

'Shouldn't you get that?' Anna said.

'It's nothing important,' the woman replied blithely, as she started to unbutton one of the guy's shirts.

'Do you like to be tied up?' the younger man asked.

The woman smiled. 'I like the way you're thinking.'

He bent her over a table within a cubicle, fastened her ankles to the table legs, and then fastened her wrists together.

'Mmmmm, you know how to treat a woman,' she said salaciously. She was then taken by surprise as he withdrew her phone.

'I think you should read your message,' he said, handing it to her.

Though her wrists were tied together she could still read the message.

'Read it out loud,' Anna demanded forcefully.

The woman sighed. 'You have disobeyed your Master's command, for which you should be punished. Are you prepared to accept your punishment?'

The two guys had retreated, and Anna now stood beside her. 'Are you willing to accept your punishment? Or do you no longer wish to be attached to your Master?'

She looked up. Almost despondently, she replied, 'I accept my punishment.'

One of the guys passed a sports bag over to Anna, which she opened on the table beside the woman. She withdrew a paddle. 'I think we'll warm up with a spanking,' she said.

'Do I get to fuck them later?'

'You will do as the Master wishes,' Anna replied sternly, then placed the paddle down. She searched in the bag and pulled out a gag, which she placed over the woman's mouth. 'I think it best we don't hear from you. You'll only get yourself in more trouble.'

The woman looked at her, her eyes filled with insolence.

Anna picked up the paddle again. She raised the dress and pulled her panties down, baring her buttocks, and then began to spank her. One, two, three...

Louise heard the door open. She didn't look round, but heard a familiar voice.

'I'm sorry, are we interrupting something?'

It was Annabelle, with Helen in tow. Annabelle wore a leather dress with buckled calf-length boots. Louise had to look twice at Helen, as she was dressed in a leather miniskirt, white blouse unbuttoned to reveal her bra, and stiletto ankle boots. Louise was pretty sure she'd never seen anything like that in Helen's wardrobe.

'We're just dealing with a private matter,' said Anna, pretending not to know the intruders.

Annabelle walked over to the table and the woman bent over it. 'Really?' she said. 'Has she done something wrong?'

'She's disobeyed the command of her Master.'

Annabelle bent and looked the woman in the eye. 'What did she do that was so bad?'

'She wants to fuck these two guys.'

Helen had walked over to the two guys, and was stroking one of their groins. 'I can see why,' she said. 'But I don't think she could have handled them. They are *big* boys.'

'Is that so, Vee?' said Annabelle.

'I think so, Bea,' replied Helen. 'But I can always check, to be sure.' She took the guys by the hand and led them to the cubicle next to where the woman was bound to the table, out of her sight. There was a couple of zipping sounds and then Helen proclaimed, 'Oh! They *are* big boys, Bea!'

Annabelle was looking in Anna's bag, and found a large flexible dildo. 'Are they as big as this?' She walked around to the other cubicle, holding the dildo.

'Hmmm, about the same size,' said Helen.

Annabelle returned, admiring the dildo. She showed it to the woman. 'So, did you fancy a spit-roasting from these guys?'

The woman just looked at her.

Anna spanked her bottom hard. 'Answer the Lady!' she demanded.

The woman nodded slowly. Annabelle turned the dildo in her hand, and Louise noticed there was a sucker on the base of it.

'I don't think you could take this size, but maybe I'm wrong. Let's see you swallow this bad boy.'

She stuck the dildo to the table by her chin, and removed the gag. The woman just looked at her.

Anna spanked her again. 'Do as the Lady says!'

There were sucking and slurping sounds coming from the next cubicle. Annabelle walked around to look. 'Are you a hungry girl today, Vee?'

'Mmmmmmm!'

Annabelle returned.

'You have a lot to compete with,' she said. 'Vee's already started on them. Let's see if you're up to the job.'

The woman stared at Annabelle briefly, lifted herself up above the dildo, opened her mouth, and took it in about halfway.

Annabelle crouched down, taking a closer look. 'That's not very far. How can you hope to satisfy a man if that's all you can manage?'

The woman took it a little deeper, and began to gag before moving off the dildo, a little breathlessly.

'Is that it? You hoped to fuck two of them and that's all you can manage? Vee, you should come and see her pathetic attempt.'

'Sorry Bea,' replied Helen breathlessly, 'I'm a bit busy.'

Annabelle walked around to see what Helen was up to. She looked back at the woman. 'Well Vee, you're flexible.'

'I know, Bea. Comes in handy sometimes.'

Annabelle walked back and the sound of squeaking seats came from the next cubicle.

'I think you'd be lucky to get much from them when Vee's finished, so let's see if you can do better this time.'

The woman took it in her mouth again, pushing down further, and further. She managed to get a little more in her mouth before she started to gag.

'Perhaps you need a little help,' offered Anna, holding her head in place. The woman gagged again, and Anna released her.

The sound of pounding came from the next cubicle. The men began to groan and make encouraging noises. Helen moaned loudly.

Louise was a little shocked; she'd seen Helen take on two guys, in this very place to get revenge on her ex, but this was different, and she was in a relationship, unless something had changed that she hadn't mentioned.

'Come on, you can do better,' Annabelle encouraged the woman. 'Why don't you try again?'

The woman gave Annabelle a dirty look before sucking the dildo into her mouth again. She took her time, slowly sliding down, further and further. The noises from the next cubicle were getting more frequent, the threesome getting more vocal.

Annabelle walked back around and stood watching. 'You really ought to see this,' she said. 'A real treat.'

Anna asked Louise to keep an eye on the woman while she looked. She laughed before returning. She encouraged Louise to go look, which Louise did, but she was not prepared for what she saw.

The three of them were sitting fully dressed. One of the guys was slapping his thigh, and Helen had her thumb in her mouth, making slurping and moaning noises, while the guys made random breathless comments. From the next cubicle it sounded so real, and yet it was all put on. Helen smiled and winked at Louise, who smiled back and returned to her place by Anna's side.

'What did you make of that?' Anna asked her.

Louise was speechless for a moment, before answering, 'Impressive.'

Indeed it was impressive, the staging of the whole thing. Their Master was a master manipulator, and it struck Louise as ironic that just as they were in service to him, he was more so in their service, allowing them to explore, guiding them safely through what could be a minefield of dangerous behaviour. And Annabelle's skill at humiliation was again demonstrated.

The woman was gagging again, but holding herself in place with no assistance from Anna.

'I think she might be getting there,' said Annabelle. 'But will you manage it before Vee gets the guys there? Although I think you may be too late already,' she added.

After a few grunts from the men Helen appeared, dishevelled, her mouth firmly closed, apparently filled with something.

'Would you like to taste them at least?' Annabelle asked the woman, but before she had a chance to answer Helen grabbed Louise and kissed her, passing over some wine. Playing along, Louise made a show of swallowing.

Annabelle shook her head. 'Oh dear, it's too late. It's all gone.'

The two guys made a point of staggering out of the room.

'And they're all spent by the looks of them. You won't be having your way with them tonight. You'll just have to practise your technique until you can accommodate them.'

The woman's phone bleeped.

'Do you need to get that?' Annabelle asked, passing it to her.

She read the text message.

'What does it say?' Anna demanded.

'Do not defy the command of your Master,' the woman said.

Annabelle stroked her face. 'Your Master rewards his minions well for good behaviour. But he punishes those who disobey him most severely. If you wish to continue under his guidance you must learn to do precisely as you are told.' Annabelle began to walk away.

'Is he your Master too?'

Annabelle turned back and smiled. 'No one is my master. I just owed him a favour. Now your sisters,' she indicated Anna and Louise, 'will complete your chastisement.'

Annabelle and Helen linked arms and left the room.

'Have you learned your lesson?' Anna demanded.

'Yes... sister.'

'You should address me as mistress.'

'Sorry, mistress.'

'I will now reinforce your lesson.'

Anna took a riding crop out of the bag and thrashed her buttocks three times, before returning the crop, paddle and gag to the bag, and zipping it up.

'Thank you, mistress.'

Anna paused. 'I believe you have learned your lesson today. But rest assured that should I be required to attend to you again I will look upon it most severely.'

'Yes, mistress.'

Anna and Louise untied her wrists and legs and they went back into the bar.

'Could I buy you both a drink?' the woman asked.

'I'm afraid we have other business to attend to,' Anna replied, still in her dominant tone.

'OK. Thanks.' She left the bar.

Louise turned to Anna. 'Other business?' she asked.

'Do you remember how I got into trouble for sending you a drink over?

'Yes.'

'That can't happen again.'

Louise and Anna were picked up outside the bar. One of the ianitors from earlier were driving.

'Where do you want dropping off, ladies?'

'I'm in court tomorrow and have a lot of prep to do, so it'll just be home for me,' said Anna.

'Home for me too,' said Louise.

Louise was lost in thought when Anna spoke again. 'It seems it'll be a big party at the weekend.'

Louise took a few moments to think about responding, but the driver got in first.

'All the ianitors have been rostered, which is unusual. And it's booked for longer too. Any ideas as to what's going on?'

'I've not heard anything,' replied Anna. 'Except that there will be a break before the next one.'

'I heard the same thing,' he said.

Anna was dropped of first. Louise wasn't sure whether it was because she was the more senior in the Court hierarchy, or whether it was more convenient for the driver. Louise thought he was surprisingly chatty.

'Wasn't that your friend with Mistress Annabelle?' he asked.

'Yes. How do you know she's my friend?'

'I remember her from the do we had; she was a cat to your mouse.'

Louise thought there was something underlying his chat.

'Will she be joining Mistress Annabelle's Court then?'

'I don't know. I thought she was reluctant to do anything like that, but she surprised me tonight.'

'Is she...' he paused for a moment before continuing, '...seeing anyone?'

Louise thought of Lucian, but didn't know what was happening there. Helen hadn't seen him since Saturday, and things seemed a little off when they'd parted.

'I don't know,' she said. 'Why do you ask?' She knew the answer.

'I thought I might ask her out, if she joins, of course.'

'Why don't you ask anyway?'

He paused before answering. 'It's easier if it's one of our own, if you get me. Gets complicated with anyone outside the Order.'

'Oh, I see. So I could date the Master then?'

He chuckled. 'That could prove difficult.'

'Why?'

'It's a tradition of the Purple Court. Only the erae know the identity of your Master. Should anyone else discover it he'll lose his position and the Court will be dissolved, until the erae can replace him. So the only people in Court he can have any relationship with are the erae themselves.'

'So Madame...' It took a moment for her to recall Marta's Court name, '...Intenta, and Madame Aurora are the erae?'

'Two of them. He has six altogether.'

Louise's mind went back to her initiation, and the six women sat around the Master.

'Doesn't Lucian know who he is?'

He laughed. 'He seems to know everything.'

They pulled up outside Louise's home.

'That's odd,' he said.

'What?'

'Lucian's car's over there.' He shrugged. 'Perhaps he's visiting someone. He's good at keeping himself to himself.'

Louise paused for moment before opening the door. 'Thanks for the lift,' she said.

'No problem, Miss. Have a good evening.'

As she entered her apartment she had an idea who'd be in. Helen, now dressed in her more usual clothes, was giggling, with Lucian sitting beside her.

'Oh, hi!' she said, before standing and going into the kitchen. 'Drink?'

'Tea, please,' said Louise. 'Hello Lucian. How are you?'

He smiled. 'I'm good, thanks. Enjoyable evening?'

Louise laughed to herself. 'Yes. It was an interesting night.'

'How's work?' he asked.

'It's going well, though I've got a lot to do now.'

'And your colleague, Peter. What's he doing?'

'He's out of the country for a few days.'

'Business?'

'I think so. Did he get in touch with you?'

Lucian gave her a suspicious look. 'Why would he?'

'Because he asked for your card.'

Lucian nodded. 'Yes. He did.'

Louise waited, but he didn't continue.

Helen returned and handed her a drink. 'That was fun tonight, wasn't it?' She was beaming.

Louise smiled. 'Will you be seeing more of Annabelle?'

Helen sat down across Lucian's lap. 'Maybe. I wonder if I'll always feel horny afterwards...'

She started kissing him, before pushing his legs apart and getting between them, unzipping his fly.

Louise decided to leave them to it, and sought her own company in her bedroom.

CHAPTER SEVENTEEN

VESPERI

Louise immersed herself in her work for the rest of the week. They finished late Friday, and it was only when Louise arrived home she remembered there was a Court event the following day. She'd have to pick out a suit and find out where she'd need to go.

As it turned out she didn't have to find out. YMV buzzed next morning, with a message that a car would be picking her up around 4.30pm. An early start, she thought, so she decided to pack herself something to eat.

Helen disappeared after lunchtime, and Louise spent the afternoon getting ready. She packed her suit in her gym bag, plus some spare clothes and underwear, and went downstairs when the YMV app let her know the car was waiting.

The driver got out and put her bag and laid her suit in the boot. Louise noticed there were already some items in there, and wondered what he was taking to the party. When she got into the car there were already two people inside.

'We just have to pick up Anna before going to the venue,' said Aurora.

'Yes, mistress,' replied Louise, as she nodded to Aurora and the Master, before sitting, her back to the driver.

'Please, there's no need for Court formality here. Call me Rebecca. And you are... Louise?'

'Yes, Rebecca.' Louise's tone was still deferential.

Rebecca sat next to the Master, her arm linked in his, casually stroking his thigh. He was dressed in a three piece suit with purple piping, dark shirt and cravat, and in one gloved hand he held an ornate cane. Rebecca wore a black and purple corset and black fishnet tights, which seemed to emphasise the length and shapeliness of her legs. Her high-heeled ankle boots only added to the affect.

'Have you seen any of my films?'

Louise looked up at her; it was an unusual topic for small talk. 'Um, not really. Somebody had mentioned—'

'Yes.' She sounded a little exasperated. 'Word does get around. Georgia was my working name, if that's what you heard.'

Louise nodded.

Rebecca asked about her work. Louise was generic in her answers, not wanting to give too much away as to what she did, or who she worked for. Rebecca just nodded, in a knowing way, though Louise expected that some of what she'd said would have meant nothing to her. She asked Rebecca what she did, and Rebecca was equally vague, saying she was involved in property.

They arrived at Anna's, and the driver got out again to put some things in the boot before Anna got in. She looked as surprised as Louise had been when she saw Rebecca and the Master in the car.

'Madame Aurora.' Anna nodded to her and to him.

'Madame Vulpes,' returned Rebecca.

Anna also sat facing backwards, facing the Master. Louise thought she'd felt the tension in the car rise a little, but she was relieved to see Anna was also dressed casually. She noticed Rebecca didn't introduce herself to Anna with her real name.

'Now you're both here,' Rebecca began, 'there's been a bit of a change to our schedule.'

'Oh?' shot Anna, obviously not impressed.

'Ancilla Beatitas will be first helping with one of our wet scenarios. The office scene will be done later in the evening.'

Anna looked at Louise, and Louise just shrugged.

'Does she have appropriate clothing with her?' asked Anna.

'Suitable apparel will be provided.'

'Will I be supervising?'

'No. It is being organised by one of our sister Courts, who will provide suitable supervision. You will be on door duty for that time.'

Anna was obviously not happy about this change in events, and the remainder of the journey was in uncomfortable silence, with Anna avoiding eye contact with anyone.

When they arrived at their destination the Master nudged Rebecca, passing her a presentation box.

'The Master wanted you to have this,' Rebecca said, opening the box, revealing a purple choker.

Louise moved to take it out, but Rebecca closed the lid.

'Put it on inside, once you're dressed.'

Louise nodded, and took the box.

The driver opened the door. Louise made to get out but Anna held her in her seat, looking at the Master. He nodded, and indicated for Rebecca to get out first. He followed, and Louise, now getting the idea, allowed Anna to get out, and then followed.

Rebecca and the Master, arm in arm, walked towards the building, and a door with a couple of big guys standing outside. Anna started to follow, but Louise waited by the car.

'Coming in?' asked Anna.

'I've just got some things to get out of the car,' she replied.

'I'll bring them in, Miss,' the driver offered.

Louise smiled at him. 'Thank you.' She caught up with Anna, and the two of them entered. She thought it all looked a little familiar, eventually realising it was the same place she and Helen had visited. She hadn't recognised the outside in daylight.

Anna led her through to a big room with a stage and bar, and a large buffet. She turned to Louise. 'Let's eat!'

Louise followed her lead, picking up a plate and loading it with some of the food. The buffet was impressive, laid out beautifully, with exquisite food. Salmon, caviar, stuffed quails' eggs; no expense had been spared in the catering. Anna moved off and sat at an empty table, and Louise followed. She looked around and saw some vaguely familiar faces, but Rebecca and the Master couldn't be seen.

'Nervous?'

'A little,' she admitted. 'But I'm not sure what's expected of me.'

Anna smiled. 'You'll be fine.'

The food was just as delicious as it looked.

'So, what did she mean by wet scenarios?'

Anna finished chewing before answering. 'We have a few areas for the more messy fetishes.'

'Such as?'

'Water sports, mud wrestling, food play.'

'What will I be doing?'

Anna shrugged. 'I've no idea what the scene is, so I couldn't say.'

Louise looked around the room. Some people were dressed casually, some in fetish wear, some in more formal attire. She noticed a grand piano being moved onto the stage, and a drum kit was being assembled. She wondered what kind of entertainment would be happening, on the stage at least.

They finished eating, and drank their drinks.

'What now?' Louise asked.

'Await further instructions,' replied Anna. 'Whoever's running your scene will have to give you your clothes, tell you where to go, and what you'll need to do.'

'And what will you being doing?'

'I've some preparation to sort out before the scene I'm managing, but that'll be a while off yet. I suspect I'll be given arbitra duties.'

Louise noticed Marta walking over.

'Helloooo,' she said, taking a seat. 'Are you ready?'

'For what?' asked Louise.

Marta smiled. 'For your first scene.'

Louise shrugged. 'If I knew anything about it...'

Marta waved a hand. 'It was a request at short notice.'

'That's a little unusual, isn't it?' Anna said. 'The Master normally puts them off until the next party.'

Marta shifted a little on her seat. 'We're not sure when the next party will be, and he wanted to do someone a favour.'

'There seems to be a lot of favours being called in of late,' Anna mused, distractedly drumming her fingers on the table, her face thoughtful.

Marta stood. 'I'll take you to the changing rooms, and then take you off to your first room.' She turned to Anna. 'You need to change into your arbitra clothing.'

Anna nodded in acknowledgement, but didn't get up. Marta looked at Louise, who stood and followed her to the changing area. On the way she briefed her on etiquette, most of which Louise had heard before. She pulled out a hanger from a clothing rack with a PVC suit on it, handed it to Louise and indicated a changing room. Louise took the clothes and went in, surprised when Marta followed her with a basket and a container of talcum powder.

'You might need this,' Marta said, indicating the talc.

Louise undressed to her underwear and Marta, armed with talc, helped her on with the suit. They put the leggings on, and then the fetish French maid dress, which rather than being low cut, went up to her throat. Marta tied Louise's hair back and helped her on with her boots, before folding Louise's clothes up and placing them into the basket. Louise smoothed on the gloves and looked at herself in the mirror. Not her first choice of clothing, but there was something about it.

She turned to face Marta, who led her out to the lockers. After placing the basket in one of them she led Louise through the building to a room with plastic sheeting on the floor and walls.

'One of our wet rooms,' she said.

'Are you organising this scene?'

'No, but Lizzy should be along shortly.'

Two tall ladies entered, dressed in PVC top, trousers and high-heeled boots. They nodded to Marta but continued their own conversation.

Louise looked at Marta. 'Lizzy?' she enquired quietly.

Marta shook her head. Then a blonde woman entered, wearing a PVC corset and fishnet stockings, her large breasts hanging out over the top of the corset.

'Hi,' she said to them. 'Are you helping me out?'

Marta introduced Louise as Beatitas, and left them to it. Lizzy described her scene; it was her own fantasy. She talked through her signals, so if she wasn't happy and couldn't speak she could still let Louise know. After the briefing she spoke to the two tall ladies, who then left.

Lizzy knelt in the middle of the room, and Louise fastened her wrists behind her back and checked she was OK.

The two ladies returned with five men in tow. They ushered them into a corner and ordered them to strip, which they did. They began to put on a lesbian show in front of them, and Louise watched as they stroked each other, fondling each other's breasts and kissing. The men were obviously getting aroused and stroked their cocks, watching the action.

After a few minutes one of the ladies went to one of the men, and with a gloved hand stroked his cock. The other crouched in front of Lizzy and began to play with her breasts, fondling and cupping them, squeezing her nipples.

One of the men was led by his cock to stand in front of her. He was made to crouch enough to put his cock between her breasts, while one of the ladies pushed them together around it. He thrust up and down before Lizzy lowered her face to take it in her mouth, enthusiastically bobbing her head, taking him all the way in and out. The other guys watched and wanked.

They were allowed to take it in turns to be blown by Lizzy, and she seemed to relish the taste of each one, occasionally venturing down a shaft to tongue the balls. One of the ladies held the guy being sucked off still, while the other whispered in Louise's ear to hold Lizzy's head and push her down the shaft. Louise was a little unsure, but went ahead, knowing Lizzy's *safe* signal. Nearing the end Lizzy started to gag, but it was only once she'd held the cock fully in her mouth for a few seconds did Louise receive her signal. She loosened her hold and Lizzy pushed her head back, gasping for breath, but after a few seconds' recovery Lizzy was back to greedily licking and sucking the cock again.

This routine continued a few more times with different men. Louse thought Lizzy was leaving it longer each time before signalling for release, but the way she continued eased Louise's mind; this was Lizzy's fantasy and she was in control, despite being tied and held still.

Some of the men seemed to be getting close, so the ladies manoeuvred them before Lizzy. Louise got the sign to hold Lizzy's mouth open. She used both hands, gloved fingers opening and holding Lizzy's mouth wide, ready to receive the men's seed. One began to groan loudly and seemed to trigger a chain reaction; first one shot his load over Lizzy's face, squeezing the drops onto her tongue, and then another and another. For some it seemed the sight of Lizzy being spunked on was the point that pushed them over. Lizzy ended up with her lips, nose, throat and breasts covered in sperm.

She signalled Louise to release her mouth, which she did before unfastening the ties around her wrists. She helped her to her feet, stood back, and watched as Lizzy wiped her face with her hands, sucking and licking the mess off her fingers, before pushing her boobs up to lick them too.

Marta arrived shortly afterwards and took Louise back out to get showered and changed, ready for her next scene.

Louise changed into the suit she'd brought, remembering to add the choker the Master had given her, and then Marta took her to the bar, where Lucian and Helen were.

'Anna will get you when she's ready,' she said before leaving Louise with them.

Helen stood and hugged her. 'Been up to anything interesting?'

Louise paused. 'You could say that.'

'Drink?' offered Lucian.

Louise thought for a moment. She'd got another scene, and though a drink was tempting she thought better of it. 'Orange juice, please.'

Lucian signalled a barman; a half-naked Adonis in leather shorts.

'How'd it go?'

Louise turned to see Anna, dressed in her black and purple corset, with the obligatory arbitra whip hanging by her side.

'It was... interesting.'

Anna laughed. 'Was it very messy?'

Louise screwed her face before answering. 'It wasn't too bad.'

'What was it?' Helen asked.

'Thinking of joining in?' Anna asked, a glint in her eye.

Helen floundered and Louise laughed.

'I'd better go get ready. I'll come grab you when we're ready.'

'OK,' Louise said as Anna walked off.

Helen began to speak but Lucian stopped her, indicating the stage. Helen and Louise turned to look.

The band had been playing jazz versions of various songs from the 80s and 90s, but the tempo changed, with a blonde woman singing. She was dressed in a leather miniskirt, thigh length boots and a leather waistcoat, hanging open, to flash glimpses of her ample breasts as she swayed.

They watched, enthralled as the singer danced as she sung, swinging her long blonde locks between lines. She made her way over to the piano player, and when the instrumental started she slipped between his arms and began to grind against his lap, pushing his head between her breasts.

'Amazing,' Lucian uttered. 'He's not put a note wrong,' he added, by way of explanation.

The singer started again, grinding in time. From somewhere she produced a spray can of cream, squirted her chest, and thrust herself against his face. Louise was impressed he still continued to play, with no faults that she could discern.

The music began to build to a climax. Her singing and grinding became more intense until the song finally ended and she flopped down on the pianist, over his shoulder.

The applause rose from all around. It had been quite a performance. The singer licked the pianist's face clean of cream before kissing him long and hard on the lips.

Anna reappeared wearing a suit. 'It's time,' was all she said.

Louise downed her drink and followed behind to her next adventure.

They walked down a corridor, and stopped outside a door that looked familiar to Louise; it was here, she was sure, she was carried to during her last visit.

'Ready?' said Anna. 'Just follow my lead. You're now my secretary.'

Louise nodded. Anna opened the door and walked in, Louise following, closing the door behind her. There were two of the ianitores sitting with another woman. Anna took a seat behind the familiar desk, and indicated for Louise to sit on another chair next to her.

'Miss Rogers,' Anna looked at her, 'could you take the minutes?'

Louise nodded, picking up the notepad and pen on the desk.

'Present at today's meeting we have Mr Alcock...' Anna looked at one of the men, who nodded in recognition, 'Mr Cox...' the next man nodded, 'Mrs Slut...' Louise looked up at the mention of the word, but the woman nodded, 'and myself, Miss Stress.' She enunciated each word individually, for clarity.

Louise nodded and noted the names.

Anna stood and paced slowly around the desk. 'I've been chairperson here for some time now. But it seems someone,' she stood behind Mrs Slut, looking down at her, 'believes they can do a better job.' She started to tap her foot, building the tension. Mrs Slut looked around uneasily, at which point Anna resumed pacing. 'Does anyone have an issue with my leadership?'

Mrs Slut shifted a little on her seat, but said nothing. Anna walked around and stood squarely in front of her, then suddenly lunged forward, snatching Mrs Slut's chin in her hand. 'Are you trying to screw me over?'

Mrs Slut tried to shake her head but was restricted by Anna's grip. 'I said, are you trying to screw me over?' Anna repeated.

'N-no,' Mrs Slut managed to mumble.

'Let me tell you,' Anna said, 'that if there's any screwing over to be done, it will be done by me! Is that understood?'

'Yes, Miss Stress,' she managed to get out.

'Well just to make it clear...' Anna grabbed Mrs Slut's hair at the back of her head and pulled her up off the seat and over the desk. Mrs Slut screamed in surprise. Anna roughly rolled her over, and with her head hanging over the edge of the desk Anna positioned herself with her groin pressed against Mrs Slut's face.

'I've heard you're a bit of an arse licker. How about you start by licking my cunt, Slut?'

Louise couldn't see what was happening, but going by Anna's comments the woman was complying.

'That's it, Slut. Keep doing that and I might let you stay.' She ripped Slut's blouse open and roughly fondled her boobs. 'Your tongue's slowing down, Slut! Get up to speed!'

Louise glanced at the two guys, Alcock and Thomas. They were still sitting, waiting, legs crossed.

Anna opened a draw and withdrew a strap-on dildo. She moved off Slut's face and unfastened her skirt, allowing it to fall to the floor, revealing white panties, damp where Slut had just been licking, and black stockings and suspenders. She donned the strap-on and moved Slut around on the desk, so her legs were dangling off the edge where her head had just been. Anna pushed up Slut's skirt and pulled down her knickers before roughly fondling her pussy. She licked her fingers.

'It seems you're all wet, Slut. Slut by name, slut by nature, eh?'

Anna placed the dildo between Slut's legs and pulled her thighs towards her, entering her quickly. Slut gasped.

'Miss Rogers.'

It took Louise a moment to realise this meant her. She stood. 'Yes, Miss Stress?'

'Mrs Slut is making too much noise. Could you muffle her? With your muff.'

'Of course, Miss Stress.'

Louise clambered on top of the desk, hitched up her skirt and knelt over Mrs Slut's face. She lowered herself until her pussy was smothering Mrs Slut, who began to lap at her clitoris through the cotton of her panties. The desk was sturdy, but Mrs Slut was being rocked by Anna's hard pounding, each grunt with each thrust causing Louise's clit to vibrate.

'I think you need to get the full benefit of Slut's tongue, Miss Rogers.'

Louise looked around at Anna, who indicated her knickers. She realised what she meant and pulled them to one side, allowing Slut's tongue to penetrate her. It felt good, and Louise began to writhe against her mouth. Slut thrust her tongue in and out of her pussy, and Louise tried to bear down, to get it deeper inside her.

'Let's see if she can handle Alcock,' said Anna.

Louise reluctantly lifted herself off and climbed down from the desk. Anna moved Slut around again and rolled her over. Alcock approached, his zipper down and his cock out, up and ready for action.

Slut began by licking it, and then positioned it with her hands to enter her mouth. Alcock slowly pushed in, and Slut deep-throated it all the way. She grabbed his hips and pushed and pulled him so he thrust in and out of her mouth. Anna resumed her pounding with the plastic penis, causing the occasional gagging sound to come from Slut when a thrust coincided with her pulling Alcock in deep.

Louise noticed Mr Cox was unzipped, gently encouraging his cock into life. She decided to give him a hand, stroking him with a light touch of her fingers, up the shaft, around his glans, causing it to twitch.

'Mr Alcock, I do believe it's Mr Cox's turn,' Anna said firmly.

Alcock withdrew. Slut moaned in disappointment, but her mouth was full again soon enough with Mr Cox. Anna signalled for Alcock to go to her and produced a condom, which she deftly put on him and moved out of the way to allow him entry.

He pushed himself in and Slut sighed, pausing with Mr Cox for a moment, until Alcock got into a rhythm, slowly at first, building the pace gradually.

'Well Slut,' said Anna, 'Alcock in one end, Cox in the other. I'd say you're not only screwed, but completely stuffed.'

Watching Slut being fucked on the desk reminded Louise of her dalliance with Peter.

'So, shall I get one of the guys to fuck you?'

Louise looked sharply at Anna.

'Or do you want it done properly, by a woman?' Anna raised a cheeky eyebrow at her.

Alcock began to groan, slowing his thrusts, until he gave one final shunt into Slut.

'Well I guess he'll be out for the count for a while,' whispered Anna. 'Do I let Slut finish Cox, or do you want the pleasure?'

Louise thought for a moment. 'Is this Slut's fantasy?' she asked. Anna nodded. 'Then let her have all the cream,' Louise said, with a little smile.

'Mr Cox?' He looked at Anna. 'It seems Mr Alcock has taken early retirement. Could you take his place?'

'Yes Miss Stress.'

Cox withdrew from Slut's mouth and moved around to the other side of the desk. Slut turned over to lay on her back again, and Cox positioned himself between her legs. He quickly put on a condom, and after pushing Slut's legs slightly further apart, entered her with a grunt from both of them. Slut began to moan again, playing with her breasts, pulling her nipples.

'And I will now rodger Miss Rogers,' Anna announced. She beckoned Louise and bent her over so her head was near to Slut's, who began kissing her passionately, pushing her tongue into her mouth. Louise gave way, allowing her in, their tongues dancing.

Anna entered Louise with her dildo, thrusting slowly and gently. It didn't seem long before Slut began to squeal with an orgasm, which seemed to set Louise off, becoming breathless, trembling around Anna's dildo. She felt as though her knees were about to give way, glad of the desk for support. She broke away from Slut's kiss and both panted with their respective pounding. Mr Cox began grunting with each thrust, slowing down until with one final jerk he sighed and leaned forward, breathlessly supporting himself on his arms. Anna took the cue and slowed to a stop. The four kept still for a few minutes, save for their breathing.

The dishevelled Slut dropped off the desk and embraced Anna, kissing her cheek. 'Thanks, that was just about right,' she said.

Anna beamed. 'I'm glad you enjoyed it.'

Slut turned to Louise, hugged her, finishing with a peck on the cheek. 'And thank you too,' she said. 'I really appreciate your help.'

Anna retrieved a dressing gown from a cupboard and passed it to her. Wearily she put it on and left the room.

Anna looked at the men, who after cleaning themselves up and disposing of the condoms were moving the furniture around. 'Thanks boys,' she said.

'Another scene?' asked Louise

'No, they're getting ready to pack up.'

'Oh.' Louise had hoped to go back to the bar, but it seemed they were out of time.

'Did you have a good time?' Anna asked in the car.

'Yea,' Louise said brightly. 'Can't wait for the next one.'

Anna looked out of the window. 'That may be a while off,' she said.

'Why's that?'

'We think someone is trying to infiltrate the Order.'

'That sounds a bit cloak and dagger.'

'Yes,' replied Anna sourly.

Helen was alone when Louise arrived home. 'So what did you get up to tonight?' Louise asked her.

'Not much. Had a few drinks, Lucian gave me a bit of a tour of the place, spoke to a lot of people, and then dropped me off here. Said there'd been some trouble and he wanted to get to the bottom of it.'

Louise wondered if the trouble was related to what Anna had spoken about, but she would have to find out another time; she was tired, and hot chocolate in hand, she went off to bed.

Chapter Eighteen

ABREPTA

A few weeks passed and though Louise got no calls from her Master. She wasn't overly bothered because she had much to do at work. Helen was studying hard, though she did find time to have a drink with Annabelle. Louise wondered if it was just a drink, or something more interesting.

She saw Anna a few times, but usually at work. They occasionally had lunch, but it was in the company of work colleagues so Court business was not discussed.

A few weeks later she returned home after work to find Helen was out with Lucian, so she donned her trainers and loose clothing and went for a session at the gym. After her workout she showered and stopped off in the gym cafe. She enjoyed a coffee there before setting off back home, but as she walked she had an uneasy feeling. She looked around, but she couldn't see anyone following her. She made a couple of diversions to be sure, but still there was no one there. She came to the conclusion she was being paranoid.

Ahead there was someone standing at the entrance of an alleyway. As she approached she moved out to keep some distance between her and the person, and as she passed she heard a voice behind her.

'Excuse me, Miss?'

She started to turn but didn't get a good look at him because he grabbed her from behind, dragging her into the alley. Louise struggled, kicking, biting the hand covering her mouth. A car pulled up and Louise fought even harder. A man jumped out and punched the guy who'd grabbed her. Louise was suddenly free. The back door of the car was still open and she heard a voice from within shout at her.

'Get in!'

She recognised Anna but stood for a moment, confused. Then she jumped into the car, Anna closed the door and it sped off.

'What about—?'

'He'll be fine. He can look after himself.'

Louise took a good look at Anna. She was a mess; her blouse and tights were torn, she had no shoes, and there were cuts and grazes around her face and arms. 'What happened to you?'

'He tried to take me earlier, and I lost my favourite pair of shoes - you can't have a decent fight in heels.'

'What's going on?'

'There seem to have been a few attempts to take some of our members tonight.'

'How did you know where to find me?'

'Lucian activated the YMV tracker, so his men are picking people up and making sure they're secure.'

Secure. Louise seemed to wonder what she'd gotten herself into more and more. She didn't recognise the area they were driving through. 'Where are we going?'

'Lucian's offices. He's running an operation from there.'

'What about Helen?'

Anna looked at her blankly.

'She was supposed to be going out with Lucian tonight,' Louise explained.

'Sorry, I don't know.'

Louise got her phone out. The screen was cracked but she was able to call Helen. It rang a couple of times before she answered.

'Are you OK?' Helen asked, concerned.

'Yes. Are you?'

'Yes. Someone tried to grab me earlier when I went to meet Lucian, but he managed to see them off. Apparently it's happening all over the place.'

'Where are you now?'

'At Lucian's office. Where are you?'

The car pulled up outside a tower block.

'Here we are,' said Anna.

'Outside, I'd say,' Louise said into the phone.

'See you in a minute,' replied Helen, and Louise hung up.

The driver escorted them into the elevator and pushed a couple of buttons. Up they went.

The doors opened to reveal something similar to what Louise imagined NASA control would have, though on a smaller scale. Computers manned by people in headsets talking away, and then some large screens in front, with maps, CCTV images, and one with scrolling lines of information. Before them stood Lucian and Helen.

Helen rushed over to Louise and hugged her. 'Are you all right?'

'I'm fine. How are you?'

Helen stood back. 'Thankful my man was around,' she replied.

Lucian was talking to one of the headset wearers, his face filled with concern. He looked over and gave a preoccupied smile, before finishing his conversation and walking over.

'How are things going?' asked Anna.

'Thankfully most of the members of the Order are accounted for. I'm not sure what the objective was for them.'

'Them?' asked Louise. 'Do you know who they are?'

Lucian shrugged. 'Not exactly. We know someone has been targeting members' phones and trying to hack the YMV app. Now we think they're trying to grab members to infiltrate the system.' His tone made it sound vague.

'I sense a "but",' said Anna.

He paused. 'Their choice of targets is odd, and may suggest the Order already has been infiltrated.'

'Why do you say that?'

'Why else would they go for Helen, than if they knew of my involvement.'

One of the operators interrupted and Lucian stepped away to talk with her. Louise's phone rang. 'Hi Sally. Is everything OK?'

'I'm at the hospital.'

'What's wrong?'

Helen and Anna watched Louise become concerned.

'Phileas got beaten up.'

Louise paused a moment. 'Phileas?' She thought Sally had given him the brush off.

'Yeah. It's a bit weird really, but a couple of guys tried to grab me.'

'Are you all right?'

'Just a bit shaken. But Phileas is in a bad way.'

'What happened to him?'

'He'd been following me...'

'What?'

'He's been following me. A bit stalkerish, I know. But he saw me get grabbed and tried to help, got badly beat up by them. I ended up rescuing him.'

'You rescued him? How?'

'Anna had been teaching me how to handle myself, to build up my confidence, so I was fine. Phileas wasn't so lucky though. I'm going to stay here for a while, so I don't know when I'll be in tomorrow morning.'

'Don't worry about tomorrow morning. Have you spoken to the police?'

'Yeah. They've taken my statement and are talking to Phileas now.'

'Any idea who did this?'

'I've given descriptions to the police, but I didn't recognise them. They ran off when a police car appeared at the top of the alleyway.'

Louise felt a tap on the shoulder.

'Has someone tried to take your assistant?' asked Lucien

She nodded.

'Could I speak with her?'

'Sally, I'm just going to pass you over to... a friend of mine. Give me a call in the morning.' She handed her phone to Lucien, who wondered off speaking to Sally.

She went back to Helen and Anna. 'Does he think it's related?'

'Yes,' replied Anna. 'Sue Jessop's been taken.'

'Who?'

'She works at Jefferson's as well.'

'Is she in the Order?'

'No. Lucian doesn't think this is Order related now.'

'Then what?'

'He thinks it's something to do with you.'

Louise stood with her mouth agape. Why would anyone want her?

Lucian had a comfortable flat above his offices where he, Helen, Anna and Louise stayed. Anna and Louise shared one bedroom while Helen slept in the other with him, although he was up most of the night, following the progress of his team's investigations. When Anna and Louise awoke Helen was cooking in the kitchen, and he had already left.

'Where's Lucian?' asked Anna.

'He's gone to see Jefferson, and has arranged for you two to go over shortly.'

'But I have work to do this morning,' protested Anna.

'He says he's cleared your morning, as Jefferson may well be needing your advice.'

Neither Anna nor Louise ate much; they weren't very hungry, so washed and got ready to go. Helen took a call on the intercom and said they could go down. A driver met them out of the elevator and escorted them to a car. They rode in silence.

They went up to Jefferson's office, and Peter was waiting outside. 'Do you know what's going on?' he asked.

'Not entirely,' replied Anna, before Louise had a chance to answer.

The door opened and Tina emerged. 'Jefferson would like to see you all now,' she said.

The three of them followed Tina in, who unusually closed the door behind her, staying in the room. Sitting at the table were Jefferson, Lucian, and a young woman, who appeared very distressed.

Jefferson stood. 'This is Sue Jessop,' he said. 'She was our leak.'

Peter started to speak but Jefferson waved him down. 'She's had a fairly traumatic time of it, I'm afraid. She's been repeatedly kidnapped, threatened, and forced to divulge information. So I think it's for the best if we can get her as far away from here and those people as possible for the foreseeable future.

'Louise,' he continued. 'You need people on the ground in Australia. Sue knows how we do things here, and so could be an asset over there. Could you brief her after our meeting?'

Louise nodded.

'Tina. Could you take Sue to Louise's office?'

Sue stood and Tina opened the door, allowing Sue through, before following her.

'Please sit.'

Anna, Peter and Louise did so.

'How did this come to light?' asked Peter.

'We'd been following her for a few days,' replied Lucian. 'I had my suspicions she may be the leak, but didn't realise there was more to it.'

Peter gave him a quizzical look. 'More to it?'

'Yes. The organisation behind it. They tried to take Louise, Anna, Louise's assistant, and her friend.'

For a moment Louise was unsure who Lucian meant by 'her friend', then realised he meant Helen.

'But something else came to light last night,' Lucian continued. 'They tried to grab someone who managed to identify one of her assailants.'

Tina returned and sat by Jefferson.

'Who did they try to take?' Louise asked.

'Annabelle,' Lucian answered.

'Who's Annabelle?' asked Peter.

'An acquaintance of Anna's and Louise's,' Lucian replied quickly.

'Do we know who tried to grab her?' Louise asked, wondering if she really was the connection.

'Helen's ex-fiancé.'

'So the police have him in custody?' Peter said, a little impatiently.

'No. We haven't gone to the police, and without further investigation, we won't.'

'Shouldn't we leave evidence gathering to the authorities? Tell them what we know and let them get on with it?'

Lucian sighed. 'Let me give you some background. I've been tracking a particular organisation for some time. I believe they've been behind some recent attempted breaches into various systems, sometimes to gain commercial information, and other times to track individuals.'

'I believe this same organisation was responsible for the attacks last night. We now know Miss Jessop has been taken a few times. She is pumped for company information.'

Louise was shocked, and now understood why Jefferson made the offer he did.

'Why didn't she tell anyone?' asked Peter.

'Because they'd threatened her. There are several members of the organisation, she never sees faces, and if one was caught others would come after her.'

'It sounds like one of those East European gangs. She might not be safe even in Australia.'

'As I said, we've been tracking them for a while. They're only in London. They seem to revel in torturing people, and any information they can get that's worth money only goes to fund their activities.'

'And what is this organisation called?'

'They call themselves the Order.'

Louise gasped. Peter gave her a puzzled look.

'So can't we tell the police about this *Order?* They sound like a bunch of sick people to me.'

'Which Order do we tell them?'

Peter looked at Lucian. 'There's more than one Order? I thought you said they were only in London?'

'They call themselves the Order, but there are other more respectable Orders who have nothing to do with this. The Order of Saint John, the Order of the Maltese Cross. And there is another issue with going to the police.'

'And what would that be?'

Lucian didn't reply; he just stared at Peter.

Jefferson stood, looked out of the window, and sighed. 'Back in the early seventies a group of friends and I started a group. We all enjoyed the swinging scene, but there were some pretty nasty diseases going around, so we started our society, and we would know that any other members we met would be clean. We all enjoyed sex and had regular meet ups, where we'd eat, drink, and partner up. It was all consensual. The ladies liked it because they could enjoy themselves without fear of catching anything, and they wouldn't get the reputation of someone who sleeps around, as we were very discrete. And of course, the male members enjoyed being around ladies who were uninhibited. We called ourselves the Scarlet Court, and for almost a decade we met. New members were screened, again discretely, before being introduced into our Court.

'That changed in the early eighties though, with the outbreak of AIDS. We felt we could not continue as we were, so the Scarlet Court disbanded.

'However, some of our members had other interests; fetishes, if you like. Some liked wearing rubber, leather, PVC. Some enjoyed bondage. And others enjoyed the domination scene. Because of the discrete nature of our society other Courts were founded, each based on a particular fetish or interest. Within these Courts penetrative sex wasn't necessarily the norm, and where it was, safe sex could be practised more easily than in the Scarlet Court. Of course the understanding was that it was all consensual. People joined, participated, or left of their own free will, discretion being the main requirement, allowing people to leave behind their normal lives.

'Even with their differences the Courts worked together, forming an organisation that straddled all Courts, helping them with their screening of new members, making sure everyone was safe. This organisation became known to its members as the Order.'

Peter began to speak, but Jefferson silenced him.

'This is not the same Order. Our Order was based on enjoyment of our activities with mutual consent. This other Order appears to be based on exploitation.' Jefferson almost spat out the last sentence.

'Are you still in the Order?' asked Peter.

'No.'

'Then how do you know they haven't turned?'

Jefferson regarded him for moment, before nodding at Lucian, who paused before answering.

'Because, Peter, you're the only person in this room who didn't know about the Order.'

Peter looked around; Jefferson, Lucian, Anna, Louise... Tina.

Tina. Louise looked at her, but Tina continued to watch Jefferson.

Peter managed to gather his thoughts. 'Does this other Order know about your involvement?'

Jefferson looked at Tina, who replied. 'We've not seen any threats, or attempts to access any of his systems or properties.' She sounded a little like Lucian.

Jefferson responded to the looks of confusion in the room. 'Tina isn't just my assistant. A few years ago I was receiving some, let's say, *disturbing* messages. At Lucian's suggestion I took on Tina to, ah, handle my security arrangements. What started out as a temporary arrangement quickly turned into a permanent position, and Tina is now properly employed as my assistant. A role which, I must say, she has also excelled at.'

'So you already knew Lucian?' Peter asked. Louise could see annoyance in his face.

'Yes,' replied Jefferson. 'He's been doing work for me for some time. But his trade and reputation being what it is, we don't like to broadcast the fact we need to use his services from time to time. I would have introduced you once you were settling in to your new role, but you jumped the gun on that somewhat.

'But back to the matter at hand,' Jefferson continued. 'We cannot approach the authorities as yet, until Lucian and his team have enough evidence that won't implicate people from our Order.'

'But your own nephew was attacked,' said Peter.

'The attack was on Louise's assistant, not him. And the police are treating it as a random attack for now. That's how it needs to stay.'

'For the sake of the Order,' Peter snorted.

'For the good of this company!' Jefferson exclaimed.

The meeting broke up not long afterwards. It was awkward, and it seemed to Louise that Peter was really not happy about the revelations. She returned to her office via the kitchen, grabbing a coffee en route. She'd forgotten about Sue Jessop, who sat waiting for her.

They talked through what the plan was, though Louise was careful what she disclosed, just in case, telling her enough about what they wanted. For the next couple of nights Sue would be staying in one of Lucian's safe-houses, until her passage to Australia and accommodation was sorted.

Sue left the office and Louise began to ponder, but it wasn't long before her thoughts were interrupted when Peter entered.

'So, is your *kink*,' he sneered the word distastefully, 'sex in public places? Office buildings?'

Louise stared at him. 'What?'

'In my office. Was it some sort of dare?'

She paused for a moment, putting her cup down. 'That is the only time I've ever done anything like that. I haven't had one night stands, or sex in anything like a public place. I could ask you if you're in the habit of seducing female colleagues in your office!' She stood, her hands balled into fists on her desk.

Peter looked like a rabbit caught in the headlights. 'What? No! Never!'

'Then why accuse me?'

'Then what is your kink?'

'Ooh, I've arrived at the right time I see,' said Anna, walking in.

Peter scowled at her.

'If you're nice to me,' Louise began, 'I might tell you. I might even show you.'

'And trust me, it would be worth seeing,' Anna added.

Peter looked between them.

'But now,' continued Louise, 'I would like a private conversation with my fellow pervert. Bye, Peter!'

Peter narrowed his eyes before leaving, closing the door behind him.

Anna laughed. 'Well, that was a turn up for the books,' she said.

'What, Peter?'

'No, Jefferson being a member of the original Court.'

Louise dropped into her seat. 'Yes, I've been thinking about that.'

'Really? Are you wondering if your boss still has it in him?' Anna smiled cheekily.

'No. I wonder if he knows the Master of the Purple Court.'

Anna turned serious. 'Don't!'

'What?'

'Do not try to find the Master. It would be disastrous for the Court, and the Order.'

Louise snorted.

'Seriously. I'm saying this as your arbitra, and not just a friend. You really cannot go looking for him.'

Louise stared back at her, then relented. 'OK, I won't. I just wondered what he's like.'

'Don't go there,' said Anna sternly.

Louise sighed. 'Lunch?' she offered, wanting to break the tension.

Anna brightened. 'My call,' she stated. 'I know a sweet little Thai place near the British Museum.'

'Sounds good to me,' Louise said as she stood and grabbed her coat.

CHAPTER NINETEEN

EX-DOMINE

Lunch was pleasant, with light-hearted conversation. Sally called to say that Phileas was OK but she was going to take him home. Louise suggested she take the rest of the day off. When Louise returned to the office she sat contemplating again the potential connection between Jefferson and her Master. Anna had warned her off, but she was even more curious; what harm could it do, after all?

She went up to Jefferson's office and caught him alone, with Tina not around.

'Louise, what can I do for you?' he asked.

'Can I ask you about the Master of the Purple Court?'

Jefferson regarded her for a moment. 'I used to know him.'

'Used to?' she asked, without thinking.

'Are you, by any chance, a member of the Purple Court?'

Louise nodded.

'And Anna?'

'Yes.'

He smiled. 'Interesting. I know the first Master, but there have been a few since I would imagine.'

'Of course.' Louise kicked herself for not realising it would be a different Master.

'I'm overdue a visit. Would you like to come with me?'

Louise gave him a puzzled look.

'I think I'll go see him this afternoon. I suppose there would be no harm in you coming along.'

'OK. That might be nice.'

When Tina returned from her errand she organised a car, and it was a little over an hour later when, after driving through some of the Essex countryside and finally through a golf course, the three of them arrived at a large Georgian house.

Louise was impressed. 'Is this his?' she asked, wondering if the current Master was similarly affluent.

'This is the nursing home where he resides,' replied Jefferson.

The three of them entered, signed in, and Jefferson led the way to a room. He knocked and entered; Tina and Louise followed. In a leather armchair facing out of the window was an old gentleman, Louise estimated in his eighties, dressed in a three-piece suit and cravat. The style was familiar to her, but whereas her Master was robust, this man was frail.

He looked around. 'Ah, a new face. Come in! Come in!' He waved a bony hand and Louise went over. 'And who might this pretty young thing be?' he asked.

'I'm Louise. I work for Jefferson.'

'Jefferson always had a good eye for attractive ladies,' he said.

Louise blushed. Jefferson intervened and the two gentlemen chatted over things. Louise retreated to where Tina was, sitting in a chair by a bed, nonchalantly flicking through a magazine.

One of the staff popped her head around the door and asked if everything was OK. She scowled when she caught sight of Louise and Tina, before leaving.

'So, how do you know Lucian?' Louise asked.

Tina looked up momentarily, before looking back down at the magazine. 'I used to have my own Court.'

'Oh!' The reply took Louise by surprise. 'Does it no longer exist?'

Tina sighed and put the magazine down. 'I got bored and wanted to do something else, so I promoted a replacement to be in charge of it, and I left.'

'Which was it?'

'The Court of Humility.'

Louise thought for a moment. 'Annabelle, Bella... I think she's in that Court. Do you know her?'

Tina regarded her for a moment. 'She was my replacement.'

Louise was surprised again.

'Lucian asked me to join his team of ianitors, but I wanted to be away from the Order for a while. Then this thing with Jefferson came up so I took it for a few months.'

Louise didn't know what to say. Jefferson came over and asked Tina to join him. They left the room, so Louise went over to the old Master again.

'Salve, dominus,' she said.

He looked up at her, slightly puzzled at first, and then realisation dawned across his face. 'We didn't use Latin when I was in charge,' he said.

'Oh. When did that start?'

'I'm not sure whether it was the current boy, or the boy before. I think you're currently on the fifth Master now. But I don't keep up with those matters any more. I hear things from time to time, but that's all behind me now. Just a glorious dream.' He sounded wistful.

'Do you know the current Master then?' she asked.

He looked up at her again. 'I don't even know who succeeded me. He was handpicked by my ladies, and then he picked three of his own ladies.'

'Ladies?'

'Yes. The six ladies who really run the Court. You must have seen them.'

'I'd never thought about how a new Master is...' she paused for a moment, looking for an appropriate word.

'Installed,' he said. He grabbed one of her hands, kissed it and patted it. 'Don't go looking for him,' he said. 'He might seek you out, but that will be in his own time, and when you are both ready. But don't go looking for him. It will only cause problems.'

Tina returned and said they were leaving. Louise said goodbye before following her out. 'Where's Jefferson?' she asked.

'He's talking to one of the managers, and then he'll say his farewell.'

'It was a short visit.'

'Yes,' was all Tina said in reply as she started to look at something on her phone.

They got in the car and waited for Jefferson.

He came out about ten minutes later, not looking too pleased. He got into the car, instructed the driver to return to the office and said no more on the journey back, choosing only to look out of the window at the passing scenery. Louise looked out of the window too, while Tina continued to scroll through whatever she was reading on her phone.

Back at the office Louise spent time catching up, working late. She returned home to find a note from Helen to say she was going away for a few days. She tried to call her to get more detail but her phone was switched off, or out of range.

Louise settled into bed and quickly went to sleep; the day had been tiring, and informative.

She woke on Saturday a little later than normal, to the sound of someone knocking. She sleepily dragged herself out of bed and pulled on her robe before opening the front door.

Anna pushed past her. 'You should have the chain on that,' she chastised.

'What?' Louise replied.

'Have you seen the paper this morning?'

'Wh... uh... no.'

Anna held up a copy she had; on the front page was a badly beaten up David, Helen's former fiancée. The headline read *My torture at the hands of the sick Order*.

Anna was furious. 'Where's Helen?' she demanded.

'I don't know,' replied Louise.

'What?' Anna seemed to panic.

'She left a note to say she was going away for a few days.'

Anna strode into Helen's bedroom and looked around. 'No signs of a struggle,' she murmured to herself.

'What?'

'He's mentioned Helen specifically in the article. She isn't safe. Do you know who she's gone away with?'

'I'd guess it would be Lucian,' Louise said tentatively.

'Lucian doesn't take breaks,' she said, taking out her phone and making a call.

'Lucian, is Helen with you?'

Louise saw Anna pause, take a deep breath, and then sigh in relief. Anna listened for a few minutes, which seemed an age to Louise waiting to find out what was going on. Eventually she spoke again. 'Thanks Lucian. That's a relief.' She hung up.

'Lucian had a tip off about the article and arranged for Helen to go away until it blows over.'

'Where is she? Can I talk to her?'

'He's sent her to one of his safe-houses abroad. Her phone will be off so it can't be traced, but she's quite happy where she is. She just wishes you were there to keep her company.'

Louise laughed nervously, partly out of relief. 'So Annabelle beat him up badly then!'

'He wasn't like that when Annabelle left him. She got a mention too, though he doesn't know enough about her for people to work out who she is, but I suspect some of his "friends" worked him over to make it look worse.'

Louise was stunned. 'What are we going to do about all this?'

Anna slumped into a chair. 'I don't know.'

Louise felt numb; Helen seemed to be safe, but what if someone connected her to Helen? Would she have reporters knocking on her door? Then while she made coffee there was a knock on the door, which Anna answered.

'The police,' Anna told her when she returned.

Louise stopped in her tracks. 'What did they want?'

'They wanted Helen, but I told them she'd gone away for a few days, and we didn't know where.'

'And they left it at that?'

'The Detective Sergeant recognised me, and knew better than to push his luck.'

Louise smiled.

Anna stayed with her for the rest of the day. They didn't go out, but chatted, watched television and generally kept themselves occupied, trying not to think about things. When they both got a YMV message in the evening they looked at each other before reading it.

Due to a recent turn of events the YMV application will not be used, except in emergencies. Treat all messages received as suspicious, until you can confirm the identity of the sender.

Louise didn't recognise the signature on the message.

'It's Lucian,' said Anna. 'There's no need to check the identity of that sender.'

Anna spent the night, sleeping in Helen's bed. Neither of them were in the mood for play. She left the following morning as she had things to catch up on.

Around lunchtime Louise's YMV buzzed. All it said was *You've got mail*, and had her Master's signature.

She turned on her computer and checked her regular mail; nothing out of the ordinary. She then thought to check on the site where she'd initially met him, and there was indeed a message from him.

I hear you've been looking for me.

She thought back to the visit to the old peoples' home.

I was curious to meet the first Master.

Do you know there's a penalty for trying to find your Master's identity?

Of course, Master.

She felt a little happier; a webcam session with him would pass some time and take her mind off things.

He replied with an address, telling her to be there 6pm prompt.

Louise stared at the screen. Perhaps things weren't going to be as bad as she first thought.

CHAPTER TWENTY

EXITUS

The address was out near Kew, so Louise allowed herself plenty of time to get there. Unsure of what was expected of her she'd put on a blouse, skirt, jacket and flat shoes; if she was going to be stood for ages she didn't want to do it in heels. She felt excited as she contemplated what her punishment might entail; an element of bondage? Spanking? Humiliation?

The tube train was quite busy, which was not unusual for a Sunday late afternoon. She arrived in plenty of time, and after finding the house in the Georgian terrace she spent twenty minutes walking around the area killing time. At five minutes to she walked up the steps from the street. She noticed the downstairs front room curtains were drawn, even though it was still daylight. There was a note on the door.

Louise, let yourself in. Lock the door behind you.

With her heart pounding she pushed at the door. It swung open. She walked in, gently closing it behind her, and taking the catch off to lock it. Ahead of her were some stairs, with the entrance hall continuing beside them. To the right was a door, slightly ajar. She pushed it slowly. The room was dimly lit, illuminated only by a lamp on a desk.

'Take a seat.'

It was the familiar computer voice. She looked around the room, and thought she saw a figure in one corner, but realised it was a coat, hat and wig on a stand. Out of the corner of her eye she saw movement. It was him, wearing the familiar mask, but with just a white shirt, which wasn't tucked in, and trousers.

He walked to the desk and sat behind it, indicating for her to sit on the opposite side. Louise closed the door and took the seat in front of the desk. She sat with her eyes downcast. She heard him typing.

'You've been trying to find me.'

'I was curious.'

'And now you're here.'

She paused, unsure whether an answer was called for.

'We cannot continue as we have been.'

She looked up, confused. 'How do you mean?'

'The Order is in trouble, and I see no way for our Court to continue without jeopardising its members' safety.'

She rose slowly to her feet. 'What are you saying?'

'I wanted it to be you.'

Louise walked around the desk to stand in front of him. He didn't seem quite the same presence now as when she'd seen him in Court, or at the events. 'Wanted what to be me?'

He began to unfasten his mask. Louise stopped him.

'If you take it off in front of me you can't be Master any more.'

He nodded.

Louise felt herself begin to well up a little. She didn't want to feel responsible for the Court. 'No.'

He tilted his head at her response.

'No,' she repeated, more adamantly.

He turned his head slightly, as if awaiting more from her.

'We can find a way through these troubles. Just don't give up. That isn't very...' she struggled for a moment to find the word, '...Masterful.'

He snorted.

She found his miniature computer, the source of his 'voice', and closed it, turning off its light.

'You must carry on,' she continued. She straddled his lap. 'So I can continue in my devotion to you.' She turned out his desk lamp, and then turned back to him. She bent her head forward, kissing his neck. Her hands found the buttons on his shirt and began to unfasten them, stroking him as they moved downwards, his chest toned and hairless. She stood, spreading his legs open, so she could kneel between them, and then followed the opening of his shirt down with soft kisses. She eased the shirt off his shoulders, feeling his shoulders and biceps as she did. He moved his arms back, shuffling forward slightly on the chair to accommodate, dropping the shirt off behind him.

She reached his trousers and fumbled with his belt buckle, getting it loosened, and then unbuttoned his trousers and fly, pulling them back enough to reveal his penis. She stroked, and it responded to her gentle touch. He was shaven there too, his meticulousness impressing her. She began licking along his length, starting at the base and working to the tip, kissing it gently, and then slowly taking it into her mouth, gratified when it grew even more. One of her hands slid down his shaft, finding its way to his balls, also shaved. He shifted a little to allow her full access to his cock and balls. She slid all the way down, taking him fully. She felt him twitch so she stopped for a moment, before slowly sliding back off, licking his tip again.

Before she could continue he was reaching for her arms and drew her up in front of him. She stood, allowing him to unbutton her blouse. He stood and removed her blouse, gently caressing her shoulders as he did so. He pulled her to him and kissed her; he'd removed his mask. Considering his shaven state elsewhere she was a little surprised to feel the bristles on his chin. His hands caressed her back, hitting her erogenous zones at each pass, causing her to shudder. He made to pull away but she brought her hand up to hold his head in place, so she could enjoy his kisses for longer. She ran her fingers over his clipped hair, making sure he didn't try to draw away again until she was ready.

He managed to stop kissing her lips and began a trail across her cheek, down to her neck, lingering a little longer with each kiss. Louise moved her head to one side, allowing him to kiss more of her neck, enjoying the tingling sensation it sent through her body. His hands began to wander, one caressing her back, each fingertip touch becoming a point of pleasure on her skin. The other stroked up her side, making its way to her pert breast, tracing around it, his hand just brushing across her nipple, and she involuntarily arced her back in response, snatching a sharp breath.

She couldn't identify his scent, but she liked it. She moved her hands around his back, trying to imitate his touch on her, hoping he would be feeling the same things she felt. One strayed down to his trousers, pushing them down. He assisted and allowed them to drop to the floor. She was now able to stroke and massage his firm, naked buttocks.

He moved away from her neck. He cupped one breast and began to lick around the erect nipple. He moved over to her other breast, catching her off-guard when he took her nipple between his teeth, giving a gentle bite.

He drifted lower and lower with his kisses, playing around her navel, and then lifted her skirt before removing her panties. She leant back on his desk to allow him to do so, and ended up being perched there while he began to kiss up her thighs, getting closer and closer to her. She leant back on the desk, her arms supporting her. He raised her legs over his shoulders while he progressed closer, and closer, to her pussy.

She gasped the first time his tongue darted across her clitoris, and it seemed to be an age before it passed over again. She tried to writhe around a little, to encourage him, but he simply clamped her legs still, holding her steady so he could go where *he* wanted.

His tongue spent time licking around her clitoris. He then changed to his fingers, which softly caressed around her clit, causing her to shudder. Then she felt his tongue again, this time pushing its way inside her, his fingers still massaging around her clit.

He would intermittently withdraw his tongue, only to kiss the soft insides of her thighs, before resuming his penetration, all the while his fingers working their magic on her tiny bud.

An intense feeling began welling up inside her. She tried to resist, to hold off for as long as possible, but she could only resist so much and an orgasm burst from within her. She sat up and grabbed the hand that was so skilfully manipulating her clit; it was getting too intense. He continued to lick her pussy, thrusting in and out with his straightened tongue. She rocked a little with each wave of intensity, until it subsided.

Louise closed her eyes, still rocking slightly, listening to the gentle lapping of his tongue in her pussy. She realised she'd been holding her breath, and let it out slowly. She stayed there for a few moments, before holding his head between her hands and guiding it up to her. She kissed his lips, a long, lingering kiss, tasting her own juices. She held him tight and he put his arms around her. Then she pushed him away and he fell into the chair, which was exactly where she wanted him.

She straddled his lap and kissed him again. Her hands wandered down his chest to find his penis; his hard, throbbing, cock. Holding it she manoeuvred until she felt it against her pussy, and then slowly lowered herself onto it; down, down, until final she was all the way down, and he was all the way inside her. She paused, savouring the feeling of him.

She bent over to kiss him, holding his head with one hand, the other supporting herself on his shoulder. She pushed her tongue inside his mouth and exchanged flicks with his. He moaned, and the vibrations seemed to go right through her.

She ground her pelvis around, making the most of the feeling of him inside her, and she moaned. One arm slipped around his shoulder, her other hand still holding his head as they continued to kiss. She began to rock back and forth, picking up speed, and then she began to slide up and down his length. She groaned and he groaned.

His arms reached around her, one caressing her back the other holding one of her buttocks, steadying her as she moved on him. She continued, kissing, and occasionally gasping for breath. She stopped to grind again, to enjoy feeling him inside, but that would give way to the need to fuck, so she resumed riding him, kissing him all the while.

He began to moan continuously. She hoped he was close as his deep moans were going through her, sending herself onward to another orgasm. He grabbed her arse, slowing it down as he thrust upward. She wasn't sure whether it was the sensation of his twitching inside, ejaculating, or the vibration of his moans, but it triggered her own orgasm, causing her to shudder all over.

As their orgasms subsided they relaxed, she still on his lap, head over his shoulder, both panting. When the regained their breath she carefully got up off him. She managed to find her panties and put them back on, and her blouse. She straightened her shirt, and tucked it back into her skirt.

The desk lamp went on again but she dared not look round. His arms moved around her, and she turned to see he was robed and masked. They embraced for a while, before she withdrew.

'I'd better go now,' she said.

He just nodded.

'I shall await my Master's summons,' she added.

He paused before nodding again.

She turned her back on him, straightened herself up, and left his house.

His house.

Louise could easily find out who he was, now she knew where he lived. But she didn't want to. She wanted to see more Purple Court life first.

CHAPTER TWENTY-ONE

EPILOGUS

Walking back to the station she was pulled from the street into one of the paths to the houses. At first she feared the worst, but then realised her abductor was Marta.

'What are...?' Louise began, falling silent when Marta clamped a hand over her mouth.

'What are you doing here?' she whispered, annoyed but removing her hand.

'He called me to see him,' Louise whispered in reply.

'To his house?'

'Yes. Why?'

'Did he take his mask off?'

'What?'

'Did he take his mask off?'

Louise thought for a moment. He had, but she knew what might happen if she said so. 'I haven't seen his face,' she answered.

They could hear footsteps walking down the street. Marta indicated she should remain silent.

A woman walked by; a woman Louise recognised from the care home. They waited for her to pass.

'She works at the care home,' Louise whispered, without thinking.

'She's also the senior era in Court,' Marta replied, then popped her head out to look up and down the street. 'It's clear now, but don't tell anyone you've been here. Understand?'

Louise nodded. 'Yes, Mistress.'

Marta stared at her for a moment. 'He was going to give it up, wasn't he?' she demanded.

Louise paused; could she trust Marta? 'I think so,' she replied.

'What changed his mind?'

Louise shrugged. 'I don't know if he has.'